The Earl Breaks Even

Gambling Peers, Book 3

Matilda Madison

© Copyright 2024 by Matilda Madison
Text by Matilda Madison
Cover by Dar Albert

Dragonblade Publishing, Inc. is an imprint of Kathryn Le Veque Novels, Inc.
P.O. Box 23
Moreno Valley, CA 92556
ceo@dragonbladepublishing.com

Produced in the United States of America

First Edition October 2024
Trade Paperback Edition

Reproduction of any kind except where it pertains to short quotes in relation to advertising or promotion is strictly prohibited.

All Rights Reserved.

The characters and events portrayed in this book are fictitious. Any similarity to real persons, living or dead, is purely coincidental and not intended by the author.

ARE YOU SIGNED UP FOR DRAGONBLADE'S BLOG?

You'll get the latest news and information on exclusive giveaways, exclusive excerpts, coming releases, sales, free books, cover reveals and more.

Check out our complete list of authors, too!

No spam, no junk. That's a promise!

Sign Up Here

www.dragonbladepublishing.com

♣

Dearest Reader;

Thank you for your support of a small press. At Dragonblade Publishing, we strive to bring you the highest quality Historical Romance from some of the best authors in the business. Without your support, there is no 'us', so we sincerely hope you adore these stories and find some new favorite authors along the way.

Happy Reading!

CEO, Dragonblade Publishing

Additional Dragonblade books by
Author Matilda Madison

Gambling Peers Series
A Duke Makes a Deal (Book 1)
The Baron Takes a Bet (Book 2)
The Earl Breaks Even (Book 3)

Chapter One

As Mabel Meadows, the former Comtesse de Retha, strolled along the Serpentine with her sister, Leona, one morning in London's Hyde Park, she eyed the shallow waters with suspicion. She was not fond of water, and the serene, glass-like surface of the lake gave her pause. Though she had crossed the Atlantic three times now, she had done so with significant discomfort and while the Serpentine was a man-made lake that sat in the center of a carefully cultivated park, Mabel couldn't help but wonder what sort of mysterious things lurked beneath.

"Alfred took me here just the other day," Leona said, beaming. "He's terribly fond of this park."

"Is he?"

"Yes. He seems to know everything about it."

"Is that so?" Mabel asked, her tone betraying that she wasn't particularly interested in her soon-to-be brother-in-law.

It wasn't that she didn't like him. On the contrary, Alfred Trembley was a very kind, pleasing sort of man, but his personality mattered very little to her. In Mabel's eyes, he was taking her only sister away, and for that, Mabel couldn't find it in her heart to genuinely like him.

Alfred Trembley had fallen madly in love with Leona during his tour of the East Coast of the United States. He had come to a dinner party while visiting friends in Philadelphia who just so happened to be neighbors of the Meadows family. Mabel, Leona and their father, Robert Meadows, had attended and Alfred was instantly drawn to Leona. They formed an attachment to one another rather quickly, and when the Englishman had declared his love for her a few weeks later, Leona had happily reciprocated.

"For instance, did you know that the Serpentine used to be a river itself? I believe it was called Westbourne. It was a tributary of the Thames."

"Really?" Mabel replied unenthusiastically, tucking her hand into her pocket.

She pulled out a small deck of playing cards and began bending and ruffling them back and forth against her palm in an absentminded sort of way. It was a ridiculous little habit, one she had started years prior when she had stolen a deck from her father's office. He had let her keep it and she had been known to keep cards on her at all times. The fluttering of the deck in her hands was soothing.

Leona noticed her sister's tinkering.

"I wish Papa could have made the journey," she said, smiling sadly. "I think he would have enjoyed meeting Alfred's family."

"That's optimistic of you. You know how Papa feels about the English."

"English shipbuilders," Leona corrected her. "He has nothing against the rest of them."

As the chief shipbuilder for the United States Navy, Robert Meadows was not only consistently busy but frequently unable to leave his home and work behind, limiting his opportunities to travel. He had recently undertaken a project that would not let him go for several months. Because Leona and Alfred had been so eager to marry as quickly as possible, and since Alfred's mother, the dowager countess, requested it, the wedding was set to take place in England. Mabel had stepped in to chaperone her sister overseas.

Apart from supplying his daughters with luxurious lifestyles,

Robert Meadows had left Mabel and her sister to be raised by a series of maids, governesses, and tutors. Ever since their mother died in childbirth nearly seventeen years ago, Robert Meadows had preferred to keep his children at arm's length. Mabel believed that he had grieved deeply, but as she had never actually witnessed it, she could only assume that it was simply too painful for her father to maintain relationships with his daughters. She had tried countless times to foster a connection with him, but he had always kindly rebuffed her, which had unfortunately led to Mabel seeking out attention elsewhere.

"I'm sure Papa will visit once he has a chance," Mabel said. "Likely on one of his own ships."

Leona nodded, yet she seemed unconvinced. Mabel cleared her throat, deciding to return to the previous subject.

"Come. Tell me more about what Alfred said about the rivers. Westbourne, was it?"

"Oh. Well, he said Westbourne was originally one of the rivers that London used for drinking, but that it has since become polluted."

"Is that so?"

"Yes. And you know, the Trembleys have a home in Henley-on-Thames, right along the river's edge. Boxwood Park."

"How fascinating," Mabel said, though she didn't really think so.

Try as she might to feign interest, Mabel couldn't bring herself to focus on her sister's words. Something was bothering her. A sort of unease that had continued growing since arriving in London. Every time she thought about her sister's marriage, she became melancholic and a disquiet would fall around her. Mabel would only have her sister's company for a little while longer before she would have to return to her father in Philadelphia. The idea of traveling the Atlantic again, alone, made her heart heavy.

"It's a beautiful morning, is it not?" Leona asked, as they strolled arm-in-arm along the dirt path. "I always thought London was supposed to be dreary and wet, but it's really rather charming."

Mabel glanced over her shoulder to see their young supervisor. A footman named George, dressed in blue and gold livery with his arms straight at his sides, followed the two sisters at an even pace behind them at a respectable distance. The Earl of Trembley had insisted that one of his footmen accompany them during their morning walks, and as guests of the earl, she permitted it, though it felt as if they were being spied on.

"I see very little charm about it," Mabel said under her breath as she shuffled the deck of cards.

"What was that?" Leona asked.

Mabel cleared her throat as she stopped fidgeting with the cards. Placing them back in her pocket, she turned to Leona, and plastered a false smile on her face.

"Nothing, dear."

But her sister gave her a contemplative gaze.

"You hate it here, don't you?"

Mabel tried to stifle a sigh as she observed her sister. Leona was the picture of demure innocence with her angelic face, pale blonde hair, and warm brown eyes. She was dressed in a lace-trimmed pale blush-colored gown as she glided along the banks of the Serpentine. She was gentle and kind, with an open heart for nearly every creature under the sun, and was just as beautiful on the inside as she was on the outside.

And Mabel was her opposite in every way.

With raven hair, blue eyes, and a penchant for trouble, Mabel had had a troublesome youth that had spilled into her adulthood. Today, she had dressed in a cardinal-colored Redingote-style gown, a fashion in strict contrast to her sister's.

"I do not hate it here," Mabel lied, dipping her lace parasol down as another herd of gawkers stared as they walked by. "I only find it... a bit trite."

"You're lying. I can tell. Oh Mabel, I wish you would give this city a proper chance."

"Well, I'm trying, but it's difficult," she said honestly. "And how can you tell when I'm lying?"

"You always tilt your head as your brow lifts, like this." Leona made a ridiculous, exaggerated face, causing Mabel to laugh. Leona's face melted back to its usual smile. "It's true."

"Goodness, I hope I don't actually look like that."

"Only when you lie."

"Which is rarely."

One of Leona's pale brows lifted to show her doubts, but Mabel had been sincere—after all, each sister had their own definition of lying. Leona, who had always seemingly had more in common with the saints than other children, believed anything untruthful was a lie. Mabel, on the contrary, would contest that lying was more complicated to define.

"It's just that, I've never seen so many people stare so openly before," Mabel said. "There seems to be no shame in it."

"Yes, but," Leona began. "You know why they are staring, don't you?"

Oh, it was apparent, but Mabel hadn't expected that her divorce status would cause such a stir. While it had incensed certain circles back in Philadelphia, where her notoriety had all but put her poor father into an early grave, she hadn't believed that her reputation would be viewed as such a provocation here.

Why should anyone here care about her divorce? She was no one to these people, particularly to the members of the ton. Yet since arriving at the Earl of Trembley's home two weeks earlier, there had already been two articles written about her divorce in the gossip pages. And they hadn't been particularly flattering.

"Of course, it's obvious, but I can hardly change who I am," she said nonchalantly, ignoring the ache in her heart at the thought that she was the cause of her sister's disappointment— that her sister had not received the welcome she deserved from society because of notoriety by association.

Mabel had come to terms with her demoted position in societal circles, but it bothered her that Leona had to suffer because of it. It would have been easier for Leona if she had stayed in

Philadelphia, thousands of miles away from the peerage and their judgment. Mabel had experienced enough lords and ladies to last her and her sister several lifetimes. It would have been easier if Leona had just married a nice merchant from Philadelphia and kept an ocean between her and the aristocracies of Europe.

But that hadn't happened. Leona had fallen in love with an earl's brother and ignored all of Mabel's warnings. She had tried to explain that these people were not the simple, well-to-do merchants that filled their social ranks back home. They were different. *Inherently* different. They were part of a class that didn't exist in America, and they would forever make sure that Leona knew she was incomparable to them, just as Mabel's in-laws had done. If Leona had any self-preservation, she would have rebuffed Alfred's advances, turned her back on his offer of marriage, and run as far away from him as possible.

Only she hadn't, and now they were being subjected to the scathing glares of strangers who knew little more than what the papers told them.

As if hearing Mabel's thoughts, Leona gently bumped her shoulder into her sister's.

"You will stay, won't you? I don't think I could go through with it all. Not alone."

"My dear, I would not have crossed the Atlantic again if I didn't intend to stay for some time." Mabel shivered at the memory of their passage. "You know how I feel about water."

"But you were always such a marvelous swimmer when we were children. Do you remember?"

"Yes, but you're forgetting that I nearly drowned that one time."

"Oh, I remember," Leona said with a frown. "The moment I realized you were in danger was terrible. I froze completely. It was like when we used to play outside in the winter as children and the snow would get underneath the collar of our dresses and slide down our backs."

"I hated when that used to happen," Mabel said with a shudder.

"When you went under the water, I thought you were lost, but you insisted—"

"Yes, and see what it has gotten me? A fear of water," she said.

Leona shrugged.

"You know, Alfred nearly drowned once. When he was at school. His brothers saved him, thankfully, but he does not fear the water."

"How fortunate for him," Mabel answered.

After a stilted moment, Leona leaned into her sister, lightly bumping her arm against hers again.

"You will not abandon me here, will you, Mabel?"

What she wanted to do was grab her sister's hand and force her back home with her. The dread she felt at the thought of her sister becoming part of this society was just as Leona described it, like a chunk of snow was sliding down her back. But she couldn't do anything about it. Not when Leona had made up her mind. So, instead, she gave her sister something between a smile and a grimace.

"Of course, I won't."

If her sister had paid attention to Mabel's marriage, she would have known there was no reason to wed anyone, particularly when she was so young. They were well-to-do ladies after all, and even if they weren't of the first society in Philadelphia, they were wealthy enough not to settle. They certainly didn't need to marry anyone, especially people overseas.

But Mabel had done the same thing, hadn't she? Three years earlier, she had believed herself desperately in love and had been eager to become a comtesse. How foolish she had been back then.

"I do so like Alfred's family," Leona said as she scanned ahead, lifting her head up so that the sun could shine on her face. "His brother Fredrick is an amusing fellow."

"He is. I quite like his fiancée, the lady Violet. I'm surprise they were open to the idea of a double wedding."

"Oh? Why's that?"

"Well, it just seems something that wouldn't be done here. Particularly as members of the aristocracy."

"Yes, but they don't seem nearly as frightening as you made them out to be," Leona said smartly. "Not all members of the ton are cold, miserable people."

"No, just the family I married into," Mabel said darkly.

"Come, let's not think about that," Leona said. "How do you like the countess? She is a delightful person, isn't she?"

Mabel smirked despite herself. She did genuinely like the matriarch of the Trembley family and the way she seemed to rule over her sons despite being half the size of them. But "delightful" was not the word she would use to describe the dowager Countess of Trembley. Despite her charms, including her deep affection for her sons, she was also known to be capricious, wavering back and forth between being irritated with her boys and doting on them. Mabel believed she was rather fierce, as mothers of multiple boys must be, but she was too much of a lady to let her guests see.

"I quite like the countess, though she is rather surprising," Mabel confessed. "I had imagined a sour, dour woman. One who couldn't see past her own upturned nose."

"Oh, Mabel, you've nothing but contempt for members of the ton."

"And why shouldn't I?" she asked, one brow lifting. "England, France, Germany. It doesn't matter. All these European peers are the same. They loathe Americans."

"Did the comte's family..." Leona began but shook her head. "Never mind."

Mabel knew that her sister was curious about her former marriage, and Mabel rarely spoke in detail about it. Today, however, she was feeling generous.

"You may ask me," Mabel said.

"Did the comte's family treat you poorly when you first arrived?"

The Comte de Retha, Pascal Anouilh, had been a passionate man who had come into her life like a zephyr. Mabel had quickly fallen for his charms, and when he confessed his love for her, she had been overjoyed to accept his proposal, eager to have him sweep her away to his castle in the north of France. She had believed him when he told her that they would be happy there, for why wouldn't she have? But all too soon she had realized what a mistake she had made.

"The comte's family never got the chance," she said with a slight bitterness.

"Why is that?"

Mabel sighed, gazing out over the sparkling water as they came to a halt. A pair of swans were moving gracefully over the top of the water.

"Because they refused to meet with me," she said, remembering her first days in France.

"But why?"

"I was not to their liking, I suppose."

Leona frowned.

"Why, that's ridiculous. You're one of the finest ladies I've ever known."

Mabel smirked.

"You, my dear, are too flattering."

"I'm not flattering, I'm telling the truth."

"Well, thank you."

"Was he..." Leona began, but seemed unable to finish.

Mabel didn't wish to divulge too much to Leona. There was no need to taint her innocence by telling her that Pascal had turned out to be a cruel, brutal man who took pleasure in Mabel's misery.

At first, she had tried to be accommodating. To please her husband as best she could, even once she realized that their relationship had been based on lies. But Mabel hadn't been raised to quit. She had believed that the love she genuinely had for

Pascal would be enough. Eventually, he would see that his choice of bride had been a good one, and he would come to care for her.

But it had all fallen apart within a year.

When she returned home and pursued a divorce, everyone had been shocked, and Mabel had faced her share of censure in the past two years. But in all honesty, the past two years had been some of the best of Mabel's life. She had spent nearly every day with Leona, safe under the protection of her father and their wealth.

"We needn't talk about the comte. This is your time, my dear. Let us talk about the Trembleys."

"Well, we've talked about all of them, except the earl."

Mabel misstepped at the mention of the earl before she regained her footing.

"Yes, well, the earl. He is another matter entirely."

Leona glanced at her sister, the crease between her brows deep.

"Is he? I thought he was amiable enough."

"There's something about him I don't quite like," Mabel said, frowning.

"Oh, don't say that," Leona said quickly, glancing over her shoulder to make sure they weren't overheard by their escort. "The earl is perfectly likable."

But Mabel wasn't convinced. Upon first meeting Derek, Earl of Trembley, he had misused her title and refused to call her by her proper, divorced name. It had irked her, not only because she wasn't happy being reminded of her former title, but because he had blatantly ignored her request. This discourtesy gave her a bad taste for the Earl of Trembley and made her struggle to see any good in him.

The only thing she could say in his defense was that he didn't *look* like a disagreeable man. With his dark, rust-colored hair and hooded brown eyes that had flecks of amber in them, the earl was a man of smooth features. He was not eye-catchingly handsome, yet the longer one observed him, the more beguiling he became.

His mouth, for instance, had seemed as simple as any at first glance. But when he spoke, haughtily as was his nature, Mabel longed to hold her fingers to his lips and silence him. The sharp shape of his jaw, meanwhile, was such a defined line that his cheeks appeared indented. It unnerved Mabel to have such a ridiculous desire to run her fingertips against his skin.

She shivered. What a silly thing to want to do, especially to a man she found so conceited. No, it was not wise to think about the earl like that. Not at all.

"There's something unlikable about him."

"Unlikable? I think that's an unfair description. The earl is quite agreeable. He's so, well, dignified and distinguished," Leona said as she lifted her chin and set her shoulders back, mimicking the earl's rigid posture in an almost comical way. Mabel smirked. "You must admit, he's rather impressive."

Mabel would admit no such thing as she harrumphed. From the first moment they were introduced, Mabel could name a dozen things that she found lacking in him. But while she did not like him, she could not help but be intrigued by certain cracks she had noticed in his polished demeanor. The earl wasn't as perfectly flawless as he would have everyone believe. Most notably, there seemed to be a slight, almost undetectable shake to his hands at times. They seemed to quiver whenever he grew agitated, which was usually whenever Mabel was nearby. Upon realizing that she had noticed, he placed them behind his back immediately, but she found her eyes drawn to them all the same every time they were in a room together.

"There's an arrogance about him," she said a little too loudly, almost as if she were trying to convince herself. Leona gave her a confused look and Mabel regulated her voice. "I mean to say he's vain. And the way he breathes, I find distasteful."

"The way he breathes?" Leona repeated, somewhat amused. "I didn't notice anything about his breathing."

"Come, tell me more about Alfred," she said purposefully. "He's occupied so much of your time since we arrived. I rarely see you during the day, except for during our morning walks."

Leona smiled shyly as a pretty pink touched her cheeks.

"He is kind, and considerate, isn't he?" She beamed as they continued to walk. "Just yesterday, he asked what my favorite dishes were, to list them from one to twenty."

"Twenty? Can someone have so many favorites?"

"I do not know, but he said he should want only my favorite things made every day for the rest of our lives, so that I never have to suffer any displeasure."

Mabel tried desperately not to roll her eyes.

"My, it does sound as though you two are quite taken with one another."

"We are more than taken with each other, Mabel. We are in love."

Love. What a juvenile pursuit. Indeed, love happened only in fables and stories. It did not exist in the real world. Mabel had made her own attempt at it and had found that only heartbreak and pain as her reward for trusting someone so completely. Really, the only thing she could ever hope for now was someone to rely on, but even that seemed too far outside her grasp.

Mabel didn't wish to break Leona's heart with the truth however, and so she only nodded.

"Well, it sounds like it," she said reassuringly, rotating around to see the footman. "I wonder if we should return to our carriage? I'd hate to keep poor George out all morning."

The footman was close behind Mabel and Leona. He appeared as serious as any man could, which made Mabel want to laugh. Her maid, Juliette, had been at odds with the footman since their arrival.

"I'm sure he doesn't mind. Besides, the earl was most considerate to afford us an escort."

Mabel didn't think the earl had been considerate at all. She knew the footman was only there to ensure they didn't embarrass the Trembley name, and she found it most irritating to be followed.

"Yes, most considerate," she mused quietly.

"See? And the housekeeper, Mrs. Bramble, has grown accustomed to our daily walks," Leona said pragmatically as she glanced over her shoulder. "Besides, I would hate to stop simply because we are thousands of miles from home. I do enjoy them so."

Mabel grinned at her sister.

"So do I. And believe me dear, regardless of where we end up, we shall always make an effort to attend to our morning walks together."

Chapter Two

"Where the devil are they?" Derek, the Earl of Trembley, asked his brother in the family parlor of Trembley Terrace. "It's not done, you know. Ladies don't just waltz about London on their own first thing in the morning."

He reached into his coat pocket and tugged out the silver pocket watch his father had given him nearly a decade ago. He opened it, made a sort of gruff noise, and glared at his youngest brother. It was half past ten in the morning, and their two female guests had been gone from the Trembley home for nearly two hours.

"There's no need to worry, Derek. They've just gone for their daily walk," his brother Alfred replied with a shrug. "It's something of a routine for them. They did it every day while in Philadelphia."

Derek snapped the watch shut and shoved it back into his pocket.

"Well, we're not in Philadelphia, Alfred. London is a far cry from what those two are used to and I should have thought that you would at least have managed to go with them at this point," he said, walking about the room. His eye caught the large portrait of their family hanging over the fireplace, and he paused as he peered at it.

It was a piece Derek had disliked when it had been completed nearly ten years ago. He had felt too old to be in a portrait with his parents and brothers, as that was mostly done with young families. His father had insisted, however, and no one had ever dared to question the late earl. He had been a man of unwavering conviction, propriety, and honor, and he had tried his hardest to instill his beliefs into his sons.

It had worked, for the most part. While Derek and his brothers wouldn't ever be categorized as ne'er-do-wells or cads, they all had their fair share of amusements, as any wealthy, entitled, and attractive young men could expect. Derek had even hosted a secret card game from time to time for the upper echelons of society, an event his father had never been pleased about.

"I've tried, but Leona has made it clear that she likes some uninterrupted time with her sister," Alfred said, pulling Derek out of his thoughts. "I wouldn't want to intrude."

"So, you just let your fiancée dictate the rules?"

Alfred frowned.

"Well now you're making me feel as if I've done something wrong," his brother said, shifting his weight from one foot to the other. "They fared just fine in the States. And George went with them."

"We are not in the States," Derek said with the same disdain his father had often used when referring to the colonies. "And George is not a chaperone, although I might have to increase his pay for the added responsibility of watching after our guests. But regardless of what protection he may offer, the fact remains that they are ladies and should be managed as such."

"You'll have a fine time telling the former comtesse that," Alfred mumbled.

The silver-blue eyes of Mabel Meadows flashed unwantedly in Derek's mind. Alfred's affection for his new fiancée, Leona Meadows, was understandable—despite being American, the girl's polite manner and sweet nature easily won admiration from everyone. But her gentle comportment was not shared by her sister.

The former Comtesse de Retha, or as she insisted on being called, *Miss Meadows*, was a blistering western wind of a woman. With raven hair and a knowing smirk that always seemed on display, Derek found her most annoying, like a pebble in one's boot. She and her sister had only been in London for two weeks now, and she had done her utmost to appall him with the way she would constantly interject herself in private conversations, dress like a courtesan, and flirt with every male in his home, from footman to duke.

Every man except him, of course, which Derek was more than grateful for. She was the sort of woman who seemed as if she would be more comfortable in a tavern than a parlor room, and Derek had disliked her the moment she stepped into his home.

"She is a blistering woman," he said with a frown.

"Oh, I wouldn't say that," Alfred began, then laughed at seeing Derek's face. "Really. I will admit that at first she can be somewhat, well…"

"Loud? Abrasive? Intrusive?"

"Excitable," Alfred said diplomatically. "But she really is a kind woman. Her only desire is to see Leona happy and as I share her desire, we've come to understand that we have several things in common."

"Besides her sister?"

"Yes. For instance, she had two siblings—"

"Good lord, save us from another Meadows."

"But their youngest sister died as a baby. Their mother did not make it through the childbirth."

Derek's mouth snapped shut as a wave of embarrassed heat spread through him over his thoughtless words. Damn it.

"I didn't know that," he said gruffly.

"Neither Miss Meadows nor Leona speaks of it much. I did not know about it at all until Miss Meadows told me while we were sailing across the Atlantic."

"Why would she share such a thing with you? And why

wouldn't your own fiancée?"

Alfred shrugged.

"Evidently it was a very painful experience for Leona and she doesn't like to discuss it, but Miss Meadows believed it was imperative that I know. She is very protective of her sister and doesn't wish her to know a moment of unhappiness."

Derek could understand being protective of one's siblings.

"Very well. So, she has the redeemable quality of caring for her own sister. One could argue that it's not so much of a virtue as what's to be expected."

"I was not aware that I was charged with listing her virtues—I was merely stating what things we have in common," Alfred stated smartly.

Derek sighed and rotated his hand in the air.

"Very well. What else do you have in common?"

"Well, Miss Meadows is a fan of card tricks. And cards in general actually. She always carries a set of playing cards on her and is a rather talented faro player."

"Is that so?" Derek asked. He had seen her dallying with a deck of playing cards once or twice. "Is that why she's always fiddling with those cards?"

"Actually, yes. She's a collector."

"Of playing cards?"

"Yes. She was rather excited about coming to England because she believes there's a better chance at finding a particularly elusive set of cards. The Flemish Hunting Deck."

Derek glanced at his brother.

"The what?"

Alfred waved his hand in the air.

"It's an antique set of cards, from the sixteenth century. She's talked about it several times since arriving. I'm surprise you haven't heard her go on about it."

"I try to leave the room whenever she speaks," Derek replied.

"A fine way to get to know someone," Alfred said under his breath, yet not quietly enough.

Derek gritted his teeth, annoyed to be chided by his younger brother. Clearing his throat, he tried to sound contrite.

"Is she any good? At playing cards, that is."

"I believe so. I've not played against her."

"No doubt she learned it from her previous husband."

"I don't think so."

"Why not?"

Alfred cocked his head.

"Miss Meadows has a knack for insulting people in a very flattering way. It's almost charming. But there is little warmth or humor in her voice when she speaks of the comte. From what she has said, it seems as though he was a man with little nuance or knowledge."

Derek struggled not to roll his eyes.

"Well, what do you think a wife would say about her former husband?"

"I suppose that's true. But Miss Meadows is an unusual woman, even by American standards."

"I've never much supported the idea of divorce," Derek said, lifting his chin. "Marriage is simply a matter of math."

Alfred blinked.

"A matter of what?"

"Math."

"So, I heard you correctly," he said, disbelieving. "What on earth possessed you to come up with the idea that marriage was a matter of math?"

"It's quite obvious," Derek said simply. "Marriage should be an equation that totals up the value of person, station, and beliefs. If those three standards should match up with another person, then divorce would not be needed. It's people's lack of self-control that leads them to marry those who are unmatched to them, mathematically, resulting in divorce. Of course, some people don't consider these things." He shrugged. "But really, even when a couple is not well matched, they should still honor the commitment that they've made to one another. For what purpose should they get divorced? If they've chosen badly once, they seem all too likely to just marry the wrong person again should they try a second time. They should just stay married and keep away from the rest of society."

Alfred tilted his head.

"I see. And have you told Silas about your beliefs on marriage and divorce then?"

The smugness Derek possessed for a brief moment disappeared as his shoulders dropped. His oldest friend, Silas, the Duke of Combe, had himself divorced his first wife nearly three years ago. In that case, well and truly, it had been the only logical thing to do. He had been miserable and in such a way that his marriage had wrecked his mind. Thankfully, Silas met his second wife, Clara, shortly after he returned to society and had been blessedly happy ever since.

"That was different," he said in defense of his friend and himself. "The only other option Silas had was to lose his mind if he stayed married to that devil of a woman."

"Well, how do you know Miss Meadows didn't have an equally good reason for ending her marriage?"

Derek opened his mouth to argue but then snapped it shut. He didn't much care if she had a good reason or not. All he knew was what he had read in the papers. That she was a social climber who had abandoned her husband. That and everything else about Mabel Meadows made him uncomfortably agitated. He highly doubted her motives for divorce were anywhere near as justifiable as Silas's.

His brother eyed him, a hint of humor on his lips.

"My, how you've changed, Derek. Wasn't it just two Octobers ago that you were supposedly having an affair with—"

"Come, Alfred, that was different."

"How so?"

"I wasn't the one married."

Alfred let out a barking laugh.

"Ah, I see. When did you become such a stickler for the

rules?"

Derek regarded his brother, wanting to argue, but knowing that he could not, for Alfred's words were nothing but the truth. There had been a time when he had simply ignored the rules, but his gambling and carousing days were decidedly behind him now. He revolved back to face the family portrait, his eyes steadily on his father.

The former earl's death—while not unexpected, given how his health had suffered his last year of life—still felt, at times, unbelievable. Derek had always believed that his father would overcome anything, including sickness. The former earl had always been the sort to command everyone's utter devotion. To be reminded that someone so forceful could be humbled by death had shaken Derek. For the first months after his ascent into the title, he had been numb, barely even registering what was happening around him as he was tasked with managing three estates, two terraces, a hunting lodge in Cumbria, a position in the House of Lords, several businesses from merchant ship investments to banks and more.

It had been a tremendous amount to learn, particularly since he had always tried to avoid his father's pointed, yet tedious lessons while growing up. Derek had always been more concerned with his own entertainment or that of his brothers. He also believed he would have ages to learn how to run the family's business affairs. And while his father had always been a strict man, he had not pressed the point too heavily. He had also likely thought that no illness could ground him and that there was time aplenty for Derek to grow into his responsibilities.

But that had not been the case.

"He can't see us, you know," Alfred said quietly, standing beside his brother, glancing up at the painting.

"Can't he?" Derek asked, more to himself than to his brother, as the tremor in his hands began. Instantly, he brought his arms behind his back and interlocked his fingers to stave them off—or at least to hide them. It was ridiculous, this new habit that had seemed to form following his father's death. Every once in a while, his hands would shake without reason, and recently, it seemed to be getting worse.

He cleared his throat before speaking again.

"It seems he's always watching us. Judging us from beyond."

"You act as if you believe he would be disappointed in what he saw."

"Of course, he would be," Derek said, facing Alfred. "I've managed to keep afloat all that he put into place, barely, but it's all so damn exhausting. And I'm aware that I shouldn't be complaining, and I'm not, but he always seemed to handle everything easily, while I seem to be drowning."

Derek stared at the portrait and wished that he saw more of his father in himself. But alas, the resemblance was not there—not in his character and not even in his features. While all the Trembley men had inherited their father's height and broad shoulders, only Derek had been given his mother's dark, reddish brown hair, and dark eyes. His brothers much more strongly resembled the late earl, with dark blond hair and green eyes, leaving Derek to come off as less aristocratic and far more severe than his brothers.

But such were the cards he was dealt.

"He always said he couldn't manage half his business without mother's help," Alfred said.

That was true. Their parents' marriage had been arranged, but they had come to deeply love and respect one another over the years. Their marriage was a true partnership, and it had been clear to their sons that they relied on each other in a way that was anything but common among the other families of their acquaintance. That's not to say they didn't argue. In fact, they often disagreed on things, but their ever-present devotion to each other and to their sons had meant that they were always able to find common ground in the end, which had in turn given Derek and his brothers a base idea of what was most important in life.

"I wouldn't bother mother with this," Derek said. "They're

my own responsibilities." Alfred chuckled then, causing Derek to glance at him. "What's so amusing?"

"I didn't mean for you to pester Mother. I meant that, perhaps, you should find your own helpmate. Find a wife."

Derek rolled his eyes at his brother's obliviousness.

"As if it were that easy."

"It is."

"Not when you consider all the qualities that I require in a wife. Whomever I marry will be the next countess. She will have to be intelligent, diligent, and graceful. She will likely have to possess a strong sense of self, not to mention a commanding presence—"

"Good lord, she's meant to be a wife, not a general. I can't imagine having to seek out such a woman to wed."

"But the weight of this earldom is not on your shoulders, is it?" Derek said. "You may have the pleasure of falling in love and marrying whomever you like. My wife will require more than just my fancy."

"Careful, Derek. You're coming dangerously close to insulting me and my chosen bride."

He crooked back to his brother.

"You know I don't mean it like that. Your fiancée is a charming girl. It's just, as the head of this household, my choices are more scrutinized than yours. Although, as lovely as she is, I can't help but wonder…"

"If you're going to try and talk me out of this again, I'd really rather you jump out the window."

Derek sighed. He had tried three times to convince Alfred that he was making a poor choice in marrying Leona, but his brother wouldn't listen. He was set on marrying the American, which gave Derek a great deal of worry. His brother was so blinded by love that he couldn't see how ill-suited he was for Leona and she for him. He could only fear it would lead to unhappiness for them both in the end. But his brother had shown less and less patience with every attempt that Derek had made to get him to see reason. Continuing to press the point would likely lead to nothing more productive than an argument between them.

"Are you sure you wish to go through with this?" Derek asked before he could stop himself. "Marrying someone so vastly different?"

The good humor displayed on Alfred's face morphed into frustration.

"For the umpteenth time, yes."

"But they're both so different from us. The comtesse in particular, but your Leona is almost too innocent a girl to understand what a life in the ton would be like. She will not fare half as well as you expect." He shook his head. "It's a shame Agatha Brinsley married Lord Appleton."

If Derek had hoped that mentioning Alfred's former sweetheart might stir up some emotions of regret, it had the opposite effect. Alfred let out a laugh.

"Thank the Lord she did! Otherwise, I'd be saddled with her."

"But you liked her at one point, did you not? I believe you planned your trip to America to ease your heartache after she chose Lord Appleton."

"I did, but honestly, I will be forever grateful to Agatha for choosing Appleton over me."

Derek frowned.

"But why? She was a perfectly appropriate choice for you. Well spoken, demure, clever, but not so much so, and she was from a well-bred family."

"Yes, she had all the makings of a lovely English bride."

"Well then?"

Alfred's shoulders lifted and then dropped.

"I don't know how to explain it to you, Derek. Perhaps it's not something that can be explained, but as fond as I was of Agatha, I realize now that the infatuation I felt for her is not the same as love."

Derek stared at him.

"Isn't it?"

His brother rolled his eyes.

"I'm quite happy with my choice in wife, Derek and as to your worries about how we'll go about in life, particularly our social lives, I wish you would cease fretting. Leona and I will find our way. I doubt there is anything we cannot overcome together."

Derek couldn't stop himself from rolling his eyes this time, so he twisted away from his brother and peered out the window that overlooked the street.

"Very well," he said after a moment. "And who knows? Maybe Leona will adjust well to life in England. Her sister, however—"

The sudden, sharp pat on the back knocked Derek from his thoughts and cut his words off abruptly. Frowning, he turned, only to see his brother's fiancée and Miss Meadows standing in the doorway. Leona was smiling, her attention solely on Alfred, but her sister was doing that half-glare half-smirk she did whenever she overheard something she wasn't supposed to.

Which happened often as she had a habit of appearing out of nowhere.

"There you are," Alfred said, crossing the room in several strides. He reached for Leona's outstretched hands and drew her close, although not too close, as he led her over to a seat. "How was your walk this morning?"

"It was lovely, thank you," Leona said. "I'm afraid we took a bit longer than usual, however. I hope George didn't mind. Mabel was curious how far Hyde Park stretched and so we walked the entire perimeter."

"Is that so?" Alfred said, glancing over his betrothed's shoulder. "And how did you find it, Miss Meadows?"

"It is very well kept. Not a hill or valley in sight," she said, her silver-blue eyes flashing at Derek, as a sudden discomfort lodged in his throat. "It must be quite a vigorous exercise for members of the ton."

Derek glared at her, aware of the insult.

"Mabel, please," Leona said softly.

"It is quite sufficient as an exercise," Derek said. "For proper ladies."

"Derek," came Alfred's warning voice.

"Oh, well then that explains it," Mabel said, her gaze shining with challenge. "Unfortunately, my sister and I are made of sturdier substance than blown glass."

"And I suppose the roughed landscape of Philadelphia allows for exercise of a more vigorous disposition?"

"The *most* vigorous, your earlship."

"Mabel, dear," Leona said, her tone somewhat high. It was apparent that Mabel had used the word *earlship* only to antagonize Derek, but before he could adequately set her down a peg, her sister stood up. "Let's go ready ourselves for the day. We shan't want to be dressed in these dusty clothes all morning."

For a moment, Mabel didn't move. Instead, she only glowered at Derek, who had the sudden outrageous desire to take hold of her and teach her some manners.

Derek blinked, then coughed and turned his attention away from her. There was absolutely no room in his busy mind for those sorts of thoughts. With all the weighty business matters to see to, he could not afford to be distracted, particularly not by the most aggravating woman he had ever met—one who was completely lacking in propriety and humility, and who was far too confidant for a divorcée.

No, Mabel Meadows was not the sort of woman he should have any feelings for other than disdain. Nor was she anywhere near the ideal sort of woman who would make him a proper wife. She was far too shrewd and beautiful, with an overly robust nature. The exact opposite of everything that should be found in a countess.

The sisters left the parlor almost as quickly as they had entered, much to Derek's pleasure, but the expression of reproach from his brother gave him pause.

"What?"

"Must you antagonize that woman?"

"Antagonize her? She was the one who implied that members of the aristocracy could barely manage to walk three steps along a flat piece of ground."

"And with most of the families living in Mayfair, she would be correct."

Derek scoffed. "Turning your back on your own kind then?"

"No, but I'm not above calling a spade a spade. Listen," Alfred said, standing up from the settee. "I know you don't like them—"

"That's not true."

"It is, though. And I can understand it, at least from your point of view. But Leona and I are to be wed and it would make me very happy indeed if you would at least pretend to be pleased about it."

Well, that was an unfair shot. Of course, Derek wanted to be happy for his brother, but it didn't negate the fact that Alfred had chosen the wrong girl to marry. As kind and sweet as Leona was, she would be eaten alive by the ton. She needed a stronger spine to enter this world, and Derek doubted she would last very long, which would only cause his brother grief.

But how could he protect his brother if he insisted on being allowed to make his own choices, as bad as they were?

Derek gave his brother a false sort of smile and nodded.

"Very well," he said unconvincingly. "I'll try to curb my behavior and limit my interactions with Miss Meadows, if only to make your life easier."

Alfred gave him a skeptical look.

"Right, thank you," he answered before shaking his head. "I should find Mother. She was concerned about something or other last night to do with the welcome ball we're throwing for the Meadows sisters tomorrow night. Evidently, it's not tulip season, and yet she's frantic to fill the whole house with tulips."

"Why?"

"You know mother once she has her mind on something. She is determined to send a message to the ladies of London that her son has made a love match. Or at least that's what she said when I asked." He paused. "Honestly, I think everyone is making too much of this."

"Well, as annoying as it is for me to agree with mother, I must. It is our duty to celebrate our own and to let all of London know that the family supports these marriages."

"Be that as it may," he said, shaking his head. "At least Fredrick agrees with me."

"Of course he does," Derek said. "He'd sooner run off to Gretna Green and avoid the pomp and circumstance of a lavish wedding—particularly if it meant that he could avoid being hounded by mother's aggressive planning. But it is to be expected when one marries, isn't it? I still don't know how she convinced you both to have a double wedding."

Alfred shrugged.

"It's easier this way, I suppose," he said. "Excuse me."

With a nod, Derek watched his brother exit the parlor just as he let out a sigh. It was not that Derek wanted his brother's relationship to fail, but really how could it not?

These American ladies, though monied, didn't have any idea of the responsibilities of the position the Trembley family held. It wasn't the Meadows' fault, but their country had simply removed hundreds of years' worth of history, leaving them with no foundation to understand the way things were done on this side of the pond. Should his brother marry a woman from such a background, it would surely end in misery. It would be best to avoid the entire thing.

As Derek exhaled, a stillness settled over the room as that last thought repeated.

It would be best to avoid the entire thing.

Yes. Yes, that would be best, yet how could he manage something like that? His brother would refuse to listen to reason. Could he recruit a friend or two to help him? Yes, either Silas, or Gavin, the Baron of Bairnsdale would surely be more than willing to help him.

Just then, the clock on the mantel struck ten, and before the chime ended, Derek was convinced of his plan. He would break up the young couple for their own good, and eventually, they would both see that he was right.

Chapter Three

THE SHEER NUMBER of flowers that continued to be brought into the Trembleys' home throughout the next day was causing a bit of a commotion. Several carriages from all around the city had happened upon the Mayfair mansion all at once, and Mabel had peered out of her window in amazement as hundreds, if not thousands, of red tulips wrapped in brown paper, were brought into the house that morning and continued to be delivered well into early afternoon. The dowager countess had undoubtedly wanted to display her family to their best advantage for the Meadows' welcome ball, and she had put all her efforts into presenting Leona to London with the utmost hospitality.

Mabel couldn't quite understand it either. The earl's disdain for Leona and her was apparent to anyone who cared to see it when they were in the same room, and she was sure he would have expressed as much to his mother, since he was the head of the family. But it seemed that the dowager countess was either ill-informed of her oldest son's opinion or didn't care. If it was the latter, Mabel would be sure to express how much she adored red tulips.

If it was the former, however, she would have to tell the countess herself. It might be somewhat reckless, but perhaps the earl's mother would see how ill-suited her youngest son and Leona were together. Indeed, if someone pointed it out to her, she would realize how incompatible their families were, and this engagement could be stopped before it was too late.

Mabel's maid, Juliette, stood behind her as she placed an ornate, gold hair comb near the back top of Mabel's raven hair. Pleased with herself, she nodded as Mabel watched her through the looking glass.

Juliette had been with her since her marriage to Pascal and had been the only kind soul she had met in France. Juliette had supposedly been mistreated by Pascal's family for quite some time prior to Mabel's arrival, although she was always hesitant to explain what exactly she had experienced while under their employment. All she would say was that Mabel was different from the others, and Mabel assumed from that statement that the rest of Pascal's family hadn't been particularly kind to Juliette—which came as no surprise to her.

When Mabel had planned her escape from France, Juliette was the only person she told, and to her surprise, the maid had begged to accompany her back to America, likely fearing what might happen to her in terms of punishment when it was discovered her mistress had fled. Still, ever since, Juliette had become a loyal companion and the mastermind of Mabel's signature, sultry appearance.

"Bien," she said, more to herself then to Mabel. "Ne vous bougez pas sauvagment."

"I never move about wildly," Mabel answered.

Though Juliette understood English, she refused to speak it. She didn't like the way the language sounded. Mabel didn't mind as she understood French perfectly, but also refused to use it, as her former husband's family had berated her for the supposed lack of refinement her accent held.

"Alors pourquoi êtes-vous toujours en désordre quand vous venez au lit?"

"When have I ever come to bed a mess?" Mabel asked as she stood up. She smoothed out her skirts. "Surely, you're exaggerating."

Juliette rolled her eyes, an insubordinate act, but one that Mabel had come to find amusing.

"Allez. Je ne peux rien faire d'autre."

"You've outdone yourself. Thank you, Juliette," Mabel said as she exited the room.

Deciding to check on Leona to see if she was ready, she walked down the hallway a few paces to her sister's room. Knocking gently, she pushed open the door only to find her sister, dressed in a robe, staring at three separate gowns that were hanging from the painted paneled dressing screen that stood in the corner of the room.

"Leona, what are you doing?" Mabel asked, closing the door behind her. "It's nearly time to go down."

"I can't decide what to wear," she said without glancing at her sister. "I thought the peach gown would be best as it's the most demure, but then the icy blue one does compliment my hair. Yet, the yellow one is my favorite."

Mabel stared at her sister as she noticed her toes tapping rapidly against the floor. She was a bundle of nerves.

"My dear," Mabel said, coming forward. She reached for her sister's hands, distracting Leona's concentration away from the dresses. "If you'd rather not go through with this, there's no reason to force yourself."

Leona pulled her hands away.

"It's not that," she said, shaking her head. "It's just that… I don't want to disappoint Alfred."

Mabel inhaled deeply, stifling a sigh. It was commendable, caring so much about Alfred's feelings, but really. There was no reason to worry so over the man, and Mabel would have said as much if her sister didn't appear so tense.

"The peach one," she said after a moment.

"Really?"

"Yes, and don't give it another thought. Now I'll go down and try to distract the others from the fact that you're taking so long."

"Thank you, Mabel."

"Yes, well. It should give me plenty of time to cause a scene," she teased, only to laugh apologetically at Leona's strained gaze. "Oh, my dear, I'm sorry. I was only jesting. I've no intention of causing a scene, I assure you. Come," Mabel said to the maid who was attending Leona. "Help her finish getting ready, would you?"

"Yes ma'am," the young maid said with a quick curtsy before hurrying Leona back behind the screen.

Mabel left the room and made her way to the grand staircase. With hands resting on the gold-painted, wrought iron railing topped with a smooth, polished wood, she descended the stone steps slowly, entering the large foyer, where parquet wooden floors were scrubbed and waxed to a mirrored shine.

Mabel couldn't help but appreciate the house's beauty. It had been outfitted with every luxury, but always in the best of taste. It was beautifully maintained, and also beautifully decorated. Even this simple foyer featured cream-colored walls adorned with paintings of Grecian mythologies. They were conversation pieces, and Mabel admired them, loving the Greek mythos herself.

Walking across the foyer, Mabel paused before a hallway table with a mirror hanging above it. A towering crystal vase stuffed with red tulips blocked most of her reflection from view. Still, she could see that her hair was stylish, and her gown, a yellow satin piece with a sheer black overlay with tiny rosettes scattered across, gave her a very appealing presence.

With her smaller chest, long torso and wide hips, Mabel always thought her body resembled one of the Three Graces by Raphael. It might have been a conceited thing to think if it weren't true. It might also have been considered an indelicate comparison for her to make, but Mabel was not prudish when it came to her form and was aware of its effect on men. She smirked at herself, appreciative of Juliette's clever sense in fashion. With her maid's taste for colors, Mabel always managed to make an entrance that could not be ignored.

Just then, Mabel saw the dowager countess begin her descent

down the staircase in the mirror's reflection. Dressed in a deep crimson gown with white satin sash at the waist and trimmed across the bodice, the dowager countess emerged from the stairs looking as regal as a queen. Her reddish-brown hair had been curled and set in a tasteful style that framed her face.

"Oh, my dear Miss Meadows," she said as she reached the landing. Mabel twisted to face her. "How lovely you are."

"Thank you, my lady. Might I say you are stunning in that gown."

The countess's slim cheeks turned pink with pleasure at the compliment as the corner of her eyes crinkled.

"That is kind of you to say. I've actually not worn this color in several years," she said, her hand going to her stomach, almost in a bracing way.

"It suits you."

"Well, I wanted to match my gown to the tulips. I can't allow the smallest flaw in my appearance today. Lord Nesby is coming, and he's a terrible gossip," she said, holding out her arm. "Come. You shall accompany me to the drawing room. I believe our guests will arrive shortly."

"Yes my lady," Mabel said, taking the woman's arm as they walked. "May I ask who Lord Nesby is?"

"He's one of those sorts who likes to critique everything he sees and tells everyone his opinion. This would not matter if everyone had the sense to ignore him, but unfortunately, when he speaks, everyone listens. I'm not quite sure how he's managed it, but his opinion has become a standard for what is fashionable."

"Is that so?"

"Yes. Luckily, our families have been neighbors for many years and so he always casts a kind word to us. However, it is always earned, I assure you."

"Neighbors?" Mabel asked with a frown. "I'm surprised he hasn't been introduced to us then."

"Oh, not here, dear. In Henley-on-Thames. The Trembley country home, Boxwood Park, sits on the edge of the river and the Nesby home is across from it," the countess explained, pausing before a glass vase. She shifted it slightly, presumably so that the best of the blooms showed. To Mabel the quality of the flowers appeared interchangeable. "Even still, I'm sure he will try and agitate me about Alfred and Leona's engagement."

"Why is that?"

"Because it's a bit surprising, I suppose. A Trembley marrying an American is, well, a bit odd. I hope you won't take offence, but the fact is that some won't understand the reasoning for it. While several peers have married women from across the pond, they've done so because their coffers were dry and they could no longer afford their lifestyles without an influx of funds from a well-heeled heiress. But the Trembleys have always managed quite well. Since there's no financial need for the match, there will be people who will see Alfred's choice of bride as a slight to his own social class. Of course, it's ridiculous, but then there are ridiculous people in the world. And Nesby is one of those people who lives for drama. Unfortunately for him, I will not be baited. Which is why I've paid particular detail to everything this evening."

"Well, I believe your efforts have been successful. I've never seen such a well-manicured home."

"My dear, I would tell you to stop flattering me, but I'm afraid my nerves need all the praise I can get for tonight. To be honest, I don't know why I'm so nervous," she said with a slight chuckle. Mabel wondered if perhaps the countess was doubting the compatibility of Leona and Alfred as well. "And it's most aggravating to attempt to make everything perfect and yet, I can't help but want to prove that the Trembley home is the definition of grace. It's a rather ridiculous cycle, I suppose."

"Not if you enjoy it, my lady."

"I do, but it can get tiresome. Come."

With vaulted embossed ceiling tiles and four large pillars separated, the Trembley ballroom was one of exaggerated wealth and refinement. Mabel had done her best to be unimpressed with the home, but every room in the Trembley home truly was a thing of beauty.

Pale yellow painted wall panels, outlined by tangerine wall columns and white crown molding, gave the room a warm, inviting aura. The ceiling above showed a detailed mural of celestial beings.

It was another scene from Greek mythology. A bearded god in dark robes held a lute and had his hand outstretched to a stunning woman set before an enchanting starry sky. Mabel was lost in her thoughts, mesmerized by the visual, when she heard the announcement of the Duke and Duchess of Combe.

Mabel glanced across the room, noting the finely dressed couple. She knew she would likely avoid them for the entire evening, as well as the Baron and Baroness of Bairnsdale. Having met them upon her initial arrival, Mabel quickly learned that the duke and baron were close friends of Derek, and she did not wish to cross paths with any of the earl's confidants if it could be at all avoided. No doubt they would treat her with the same thinly veiled scorn as the earl. Though their wives had been approachable, Mabel was too cautious to make any overtures of friendship toward them. From all her dealings with members of the ton, she believed it would be better not to trust anyone too much and to keep her distance.

Dozens of people gathered in the ballroom as the musicians began to pluck at the strings of their instruments. Several guests were peering at Mabel, obviously interested in seeing if the divorcée was as scandalous as the papers had made her out to be. Taking a deep breath, Mabel held her chin up high and greeted the first gentleman that the countess introduced to her.

"Miss Mabel Meadows, may I introduce, Lord Nesby?" the dowager countess said.

Mabel curtsied deeply to the short, white-haired gentleman with deep set pale eyes and a small, pointed nose. Given the way he was dressed in a finely made black evening suit, with gold threaded buttonholes, Nesby certainly looked like he was an avid participant in the dandy style. His dress was impeccable, his hair cut a la Brutus and with a knowing smirk on his face, he seemed to convey that he knew everyone's most carefully buried secrets.

"Ah, Miss Meadows. The lady of the hour," he said, taking her hand to bow over it with a flourish. "What an honor it is."

"You are too kind, my lord," she replied. "But my sister, Miss Leona Meadows, is the one who's getting married."

Nesby bent back up, one white brow arched.

"Oh, I do know that. It's only that I'm equally as interested in meeting you. It's not every day we're graced with French aristocracy."

Mabel's smile shrank a little, not entirely comfortable with the way his licentious gaze scanned down her front side, lingering over the bodice of her gown.

"I could only claim that title for a short time, my lord. Today I am as I have always been, wholly American. Nothing more." Deciding to try her charm on him, she leaned a fraction of an inch forward. "And really, I prefer the English to the French."

He tilted his head.

"Is that so?"

"Yes."

The man smirked.

"I suppose I cannot fault you for wanting to distance yourself from your former country. France is, after all, filled with French people."

Chuckling politely at his weak jest, Mabel smiled and pulled her hand back, yet not so quickly as to cause offence.

"Come, Nesby. My future daughter-in-law has finally arrived," the countess said, steering him elsewhere.

The ball commenced with couples coming together on the ballroom floor as a waltz began. Mabel graciously accepted a dance from Fredrick, who introduced her to a number of other gentlemen, all of whom asked to be added to her dance card.

Mabel had to admit that it was rather flattering to be so sought after. It was undoubtedly a boost to her ego, and she would be remiss if she didn't acknowledge that she enjoyed how annoyed the earl appeared when their eyes caught one another's. He had no right to appear so peevish when she knew that her behavior had been entirely appropriate, but then his dark, honey flecked, brown eyes almost always glowered at her, no matter what she was doing. With the ballroom awash in golden light, cascading down from the chandeliers, the earl's carefully styled coiffure seemed both effortless and exact and an unanticipated thrill ran through her at seeing his brown hair shimmer with red beneath the glow of the lights.

Mabel shook her head and tried to refocus her attention elsewhere. She did not care what shade the earl's hair was when the light touched it. Upon being introduced to her dance partner, she pushed Derek out of her mind. This was a night to be enjoyed after all, and enjoy it she would.

For the next hour or so, Mabel danced with a number of gentlemen, each the son of a different so and so, who was very important—or at least that seemed to be what they implied. Not once, but three times she was given a lesson on the hierarchy of the ton. She was already well versed in it however, and she hadn't asked for any further explanation. But it seemed nearly every man she spoke to wanted her to know what an absolute *treat* it was for her to be dancing with someone as important and eligible as him.

It was draining.

After the eighth consecutive dance, Mabel needed a rest. Moving toward the refreshment table, she held her chin high, noting the curious stares she was receiving from older and younger ladies alike.

Eight dances in a row were simply not done, given the delicate nature of women, and they all seemed somewhat appalled by her indelicate stamina. Mabel knew she had shocked them, but then, who did she have to impress? Her sister was already betrothed, and the ton already had their opinions. She certainly wasn't going to curb herself in the pursuit of her pleasures for no better reason than to satisfy a few strangers.

Reaching the refreshments table, Mabel was handed a long-stemmed crystal glass filled with sweet, chilled lemonade. She drank it swiftly, just as a pair of ladies, who didn't seem particularly pleased to be so close to her, turned away to continue their conversation. Mabel placed her glass on the table, and nearly left when she heard one of the ladies mention the earl.

"—and Trembley hasn't hosted a game in ages."

"Well, I think he's reformed his gambling habit since inheriting the title, hasn't he?"

"Vices cannot be so easily forgotten. Earl or not, I would set my sight on a more financially stable gentleman."

"But Trembley is vastly wealthy."

"Or so he would have one believe." The other lady paused to sip her drink.

"What do you mean?"

"Why else would he force his youngest brother to marry an American heiress, unless there was some sort of financial trouble within the family? He likely lost their fortune in a gambling hell."

"Hush, Annabelle. You can't possibly know that for certain."

"I would bet my finest dress on it. The earl isn't worth troubling yourself over. But do you know who would be a fine match for you? Mr. Cleary."

"Cleary?" the other said aghast. "He's almost sixty."

"My, how picky you are."

"You're just trying to deter me from Lord Trembley because you fancy him for yourself."

"Why, Bridget Schuster, how dare you?"

Mabel rolled her eyes and walked away from the table toward the edge of the dance floor. It seemed the countess had been correct in her assumption of the ton's gossip about Alfred and Leona's marriage. And was the earl really all that sought after that friends would openly squabble over him? Surely not. There were at least two dozen men in attendance tonight who were classically more attractive than Derek, though if she had to name one off the top of her head, she couldn't exactly think of one to pick.

That gave her a moment's pause. Undoubtedly, one of the

gentlemen she had danced with was more striking than Trembley. Yet, for her life, none of their smiles seemed to interest her as much as his scowl did.

Peering around the room, she spotted the earl on the dance floor, moving effortlessly as he chatted with a demure young lady dressed in white. Mabel studied his face briefly as it flashed her way whenever he turned.

His brows were straight and robust over his dark eyes, not arched in the least. He was almost too large for his partner. Indeed, Mabel might argue that he was too big to be an aristocrat. The broadness of his shoulders may be a family trait, but overall, Derek was a man of physical strength such as one might expect from a man who had to labor for his living. She wondered what activities kept his arms so large, but she couldn't fathom it.

Mabel bit her lip, annoyed with herself. So, he was attractive. What did it matter? There were at least half a dozen other problems with him that would detract from his handsomeness and it was this list that she found herself repeating as she strolled out of the ballroom.

Groups of people lined the long hallway that led to a courtyard at the back of the manse. A large stone terrace overlooked a very well-kept garden filled with topiary. Torches had been lit to line the crushed stone path, most likely to prevent lovers from liaising. Mabel walked down the curved marble steps that wrapped around an impressive swan atop a large ball.

It was unfair that the gardens were as equally lovely as the house. Perfectly sculpted yew shrubs had been cut into various shapes. Cones, spheres, spirals, and more cast long shadows across the garden. Mabel inhaled slowly, noticing the scent of roses in the air, likely from the pale pink blooms that climbed the back wall of the Trembley home. A sliver of a waning moon hung high in the sky and Mabel found herself watching it as she reached the bottom of the steps.

Her hand softly touched a yew bush as a familiar, feminine voice spoke above her on the balcony.

"It's a fine party, don't you think?"

Glancing up, Mabel saw Lady Combe on the arm of her husband. The tall, dark duke seemed intimidating in contrast to the fair, ethereal aura of his wife.

Mabel pressed herself against the rock wall as she listened.

"Very fine," he replied, his tone deep.

"You're doing remarkably well," she said softly.

"These things are always easier when you are near." Mabel frowned, unsure what they were speaking about. "Although, I'm afraid I'll have to leave you for a bit."

"Oh? Why is that?"

"Derek's requested my and Gavin's presence."

"For a round of cards?" the duchess asked, her tone teasing.

Mabel's brow ticked up. Was the earl hosting one of his infamous card games?

"No, my love, but I'll be sure to inform you of whatever he is up to soon enough."

"You needn't, you know."

"Ah, but I like telling you secrets."

Mabel couldn't help but smile at the sweetness between the couple. For a pair of peers, they were far more tender with each other than she would have expected.

As the couple walked away, Mabel moved from behind a large, rectangular yew hedge. Deciding that she had had enough of a break from dancing, she gathered the yellow skirts of her dress and climbed the marble staircase to return to the ballroom.

Just as she reached the top of the balcony, she saw the baroness and her husband heading toward the duke and duchess. Curiosity simmered within Mabel's chest as the two men exchanged words, their wives grinning at one another as if some great secret was being shared.

Was the earl hosting a card game? If he was, Mabel would very much like to be a part of it, though it was likely they would refuse to allow her to participate. Still, as the duke and baron left their wives behind on the dance floor, Mabel skirted along the ballroom walls, doing her best not to be seen as she followed after them.

She did not go unnoticed, unfortunately. Thanks to her brightly colored dress, she was easy to spot, and several ladies watched her with a great deal of suspicion. Particularly the wives of men whose fidelity could be questioned. No doubt, they feared she was off to an assignation with one of their husbands. Of course, they didn't know that Mabel had little desire to dally with married men. If anything, she would be keeping herself far away from the sort of man who would pursue an affair behind his wife's back.

That's not to say she intended to be alone forever. While she had no plans of ever marrying again, Mabel knew that eventually, she would likely find some enterprising gentleman who would agree to a discreet arrangement back home in Philadelphia.

Whirling down the corridor, Mabel saw no one—the duke and baron had vanished from view. Undeterred, she hurried down the hallway, glancing over her shoulder to ensure no one pursued her. Taking a left, she saw a series of doorways, each with the doors open, except the first. The first door on her left was firmly closed.

Pressing her ear to the door, she heard nothing. Confused, Mabel was about to turn around when she heard male voices coming around the corner. Panicked, she gripped the brass handle, pushed the door open, and closed it quietly behind her.

She found herself in a massive library, with two stories worth of books lining the walnut bookshelves. Two large leather sofas sat before a marble fireplace, where a roaring fire had been lit despite it being a summer night. A gigantic wooden desk sat in the corner of the room, near a circular, carved staircase that led up to the second floor.

Mabel was impressed and nearly gave in to the urge to spin about the room in wonder—but then she froze in place when the door handle turned. Remembering herself, she dashed across the room to the heavy, canary-colored velvet curtains. She stepped behind them to hide herself, and the fabric settled around her just as she heard the door close.

"Sherry?" a familiar masculine voice asked as two others murmured their acceptance.

Mabel peered out from behind the curtain and saw not one but three men moving about the library as if they had been here hundreds of times before.

"Theirs will be a union in opposites," Derek said, taking a swig of the drink that the baron handed him. "It will be a disaster."

"'Disaster' might be a bit of an exaggeration."

"Is it? Do not deny hearing at least a dozen times tonight alone about pedigree and propriety, both of which are lacking in our current guests," Trembley said, causing Mabel to frown. "Well, perhaps propriety is not so much lacking in the younger sister, but the comtesse is certainly an entirely different breed of woman."

Mabel tilted her head, trying to catch a glimpse of the earl. Instead, she saw a pair of kind, bright eyes glancing up in response to the ruffling of the curtain. The baron saw her—their eyes locked.

Heart pounding, she clenched her teeth as the earl and duke continued to speak to one another, unaware of what their friend had spotted. To her wild surprise, the baron tipped his head, as if to say that he understood, and turned his back on her, not making a single move to alert his friends to her eavesdropping.

"Perhaps we should continue this discussion elsewhere?" he interrupted the other two as Mabel made a mental note to be forever grateful to the baron.

"Why?" the duke asked, seemingly confused as he sat.

"She's impossible," Derek continued, ignoring the baron. "The comtesse has no propriety. No care for her reputation or her sister's, nor how her scandalous behavior affects those who house her."

"That's rather harsh, isn't it?" Gavin asked. "I haven't witnessed anything so outrageous."

"Haven't you? She danced eight times in a row. Twice with repeating gentlemen."

"You were counting?" Gavin asked.

"It was repeated to me several times by a dozen or so guests," Derek countered, his tone defensive.

"Yes, well, it is inappropriate," the duke said, his voice dry with sarcasm. "To think, a lady, dancing at a ball."

Mabel bit the inside of her cheek to stop herself from smirking. She liked the duke.

"Go on then. Have a laugh at my situation."

"You're being reactionary, Derek," the baron continued. "She's done nothing untoward. If anything, those gossip pages have been most unfair to her—not because she has done anything to merit it but because they wish to sell more papers."

Mabel bobbed her head, agreeing wholeheartedly.

"I wish I was being reactionary," the earl said. "I wish my brother would have discussed this whole matter with me before proposing abroad. What the devil was he thinking?"

"That he was in love?"

"The hell with love and the men who preach it," Derek said firmly. "I'm forever surrounded by people falling in love and disregarding their best interests. It's become tiresome, to say the least."

Mabel gave a firm nod again despite herself. She didn't like to agree with the earl, but he made a fair and reasonable point. His friends, however, seemed less impressed with his comment.

"As entertaining as this has been, I'll ask you to excuse me," the duke said, sounding tired. "I really must be finding Clara."

"I should return to my wife too," the baron said, following the duke toward the door. He sighed before adding, "Sorry for not being very helpful. But I'm sure Alfred will fare well enough in this marriage."

"Hmm..." the earl began before shaking his head once more.

The clicking of the door shutting once the duke and baron left relaxed Mabel's shoulders slightly. Peering from around the curtain again, she saw the earl staring into the fire with his arms folded across his chest. He looked more than contemplative. There was a weight that seemed to hover around him.

Mabel frowned, curious as to why he was so tense. In spite of herself, she began to step away from the shelter of the curtain. If she had any sense, she'd wait until this man had finished with his moment of peace and returned to the party to act as host. Then she'd be able to slip out with no one the wiser that she'd ever been there at all. But logic could not hold her back. Her feet were moving before she could help herself.

"Good evening," Mabel said loudly, stepping out from behind the curtain.

To her surprise, the earl did not jump or even appear startled. He crooked his head and crudely inspected her up and down before his gaze met hers, causing an unwelcome lump to form at the back of her throat.

"How is it," he began, rotating fully to face her, "that I've become desensitized to your sneaking about already?"

"I wasn't sneaking about."

"And yet you were purposely hidden, eavesdropping on a private conversation."

"I was enjoying a moment's reprieve from the ball when your unannounced company barged in," she countered, her fingers trailing against the back of a chair before her. "A woman alone, in a room with three men? Is it any wonder I chose to secure my safety by staying out of view? As for the charge of eavesdropping, I feel that's more your fault than mine. Really, I would think a man of your position would make sure the room was clear before speaking so freely."

"I never had an issue with privacy before," he said shortly. "What do you want, comtesse?"

Mabel did her best now to glower, annoyed that he seemed determined to use her title. A title she no longer had and that she had *repeatedly* asked him to leave aside.

"It's not what I want, but possibly," she said slowly as her courage came to the forefront, "what *we* want."

The earl did not flinch, but he looked highly skeptical.

"What are you talking about?"

"Despite our differences, we do share a common preference."

"Is that so?"

"Yes."

"And what would that be?"

"We prefer that I return to Philadelphia as soon as possible," she said pointedly. "And that my sister return with me."

"Well, I regret to inform you that my brother has no plans to sail back across the Atlantic any time soon."

"I didn't say I wished for your *brother* to be in Philadelphia."

The meaning of her words settled between them as the earl's dark eyes glinted with confusion, then understanding, and then interest. He nodded slowly.

"I see."

"Do you?" she asked, her head tilting. "Because if you do, I think we might be able to help each other."

"Are you suggesting…"

"I'm not suggesting anything, Trembley," she said, forgoing the 'my lord' nonsense. She would be his equal in this. "I'm simply saying that it might be fortuitous for both our siblings and extended families if our incompatibilities were somehow demonstrated for all to see."

His head turned to the side, and Mabel had to beat down the sudden awareness of his neck. Why she should be so interested in it, she did not know, but it was curiously thick.

"What you're not suggesting is interesting," he said carefully. "How would we go about it?"

"Oh, I don't know. Making a scene or two should extinguish whatever silly feelings are between my sister and your brother."

"A scene or two?" he repeated with abhorrence. "Are you mad?"

"You know, you're not the first to ask," she said smartly. "But why drag this out? My sister and I could be on a ship home in a week if you let me attend to this."

"That is precisely my point. You will be departing—so the consequences of your actions will not fall on you. But *I* will still be here, which means I will be forced to clean up after the trail of destruction you are proposing to leave behind you. No," he said, finishing his drink. "I'll handle it myself."

"Alone?"

"Yes."

"But it was my idea."

"And I thank you for it."

Mabel glared at him. The arrogance of this man was unmatched, but he was a fool if he thought she would give in so easily. Smirking, she decided to shock him.

Taking several steps toward him, Mabel lifted her hand and slowly peeled the crystal vessel from his fingers. He watched her, willingly letting go of his glass as she took it and, pressing it to her lips, swallowed the contents without a grimace. Then she returned it to him, licking her lips as she did so. His gaze flickered to her mouth, and for the first time since meeting the earl, Mabel sensed the stirrings of something she had long since resolved to ignore.

Desire.

Steeling herself to keep from showing any reaction, she tilted her head.

"Very well. If you're so arrogant as to believe that you can do this without help, I wish you luck."

"Arrogance has nothing to do with it."

"But when you fail—and you will"—she continued, ignoring him as she walked by him, taking the deck of cards off the table—"I'll gladly help you, once you give a heartfelt apology."

To her surprise, the earl actually grinned. She split the deck with her hands and began to shimmy the cards back and forth between them, just like she did when she became fidgety. How odd that this simple conversation would spur that behavior.

"You're wildly out of your depths, comtesse." His tone was low, just above a whisper. "And if anyone's going to apologize, it's going to be you, for that smart mouth of yours."

A vibration went through Mabel, like someone had just plucked the strings of a violin. Something was tempting about the earl—that much was true. But Mabel had to remind herself that she had no use for titles. And she certainly had no use for him.

"I highly doubt that," she said, dropping the cards to the table.

She brushed past him, but the earl's large hand wrapped around her wrist, stilling her. Mabel felt time slip away as the warmth from his grasp seeped into her skin. She studied his dark gaze.

Neither spoke, though it seemed a world of information passed between them. Mabel's pulse beat furiously against his palm, and the minor movement of his bottom lip made her uncomfortably warm. For a moment, she was sure he would lean in and claim a kiss, but just as she readied herself for such an experience, he drew back and let go of her wrist.

Momentarily unstable, Mabel let out a shaky breath she hadn't even realized she was holding and shook her head before moving past him.

"Excuse me," she whispered as she rushed from the room.

As fast as she could, she left the library without a backwards glance. The last thing she wanted to see was curiosity on the earl's face. Soon enough, the earl would come to her, begging for help in his efforts to separate their siblings, and when he eventually did, she would oblige but only after she had made him pay for his dismissive behavior tonight.

Chapter Four

THE MARRIAGE BANNS for Fredrick and Alfred and their respective brides were printed that week in the Sunday paper, as well as a detailed account of the Trembley ball. The countess's Tulip Ball, as it was being called, had been a smashing success, even considering that there had still been a mention of Mabel's unfashionably prolific dancing.

With the wedding now only a few short weeks away, Derek and the rest of the family were subjected to a series of events their mother had planned that they would attend together. Firstly, they would appear at the Gold Cup at the Ascot races, followed by the opera the next evening. After which, they would retire to Boxwood Park for a few days to watch the annual rowing race that was held in Henley-on-Thames. At that time, the Trembleys would be hosting their yearly regatta party.

Then, after that, they would return to London to spend the week in residence before the wedding, which was scheduled to take place at St. George Church. Leona and Mabel would stay at the Combe House that week with Fredrick's fiancée, Violet, and they would use the time to prepare for the bridal procession.

This meant Derek only had about three weeks to get his brother to see that he was making a mistake. Thankfully, he had concocted a flawless plan to get Alfred to see that Leona just wasn't right for him.

The morning of the ladies' day at Ascot races caused a bit of buzz in the Trembley home. Derek and his brothers were well known in the racing world, having bet on them quite regularly long before they surpassed their mother in height. As ladies' day was the most fashionable day to attend, the journey to Ascot was arduous, with carriages and crowds blocking the main drive to the races and slowing their movement to a crawl.

As the head of the family, Derek escorted his mother in his carriage, where they were joined by Alfred and Leona. Thankfully, Mabel was with Fredrick and Violet in a second vehicle, giving Derek some much-sought-after space from her.

Mabel had continued to make quiet comments whenever she passed him, stating that he would have better success with his plan should he involve her in forming his strategy. He had to admire her arrogance, even though it was preposterous to think that he would need any help from her to break up his brother and his fiancée. The two of them were so ill-suited that it would hardly involve an ounce of effort. And once he made Alfred see that the entire thing was a mistake, he would happily escort both Meadows sisters to the coast and wish them bon voyage on their journey.

Although, as he glanced across the coach to where the engaged couple sat, oblivious to everything except each other, a small, near miniscule part of him regretted that he had to tear them apart. It was obvious that there was a genuine connection between Alfred and Leona. But Derek was certain that their feelings for each other were not strong enough to weather the challenges they would face if they were to wed. There was simply no recourse for it. The Meadows had demonstrated their lack of ability to hold themselves to the highest standards so as to blend in with the Trembleys' echelon. Mabel, in particular, had an obvious disdain for not only everything to do with the peerage but everything to do with England itself. Just that morning, she had made an emphatic speech about the inferiority of British breakfast cuisines. His brothers and mother had found the whole thing amusing, but Derek could see she wasn't jesting. She loathed London, and he would be more than happy to help evict her from the city.

And he had just the plan to do it.

Suddenly, a slim elbow pressed into his ribs. Turning his head, he saw his mother giving him a peculiar look.

"Yes?" he said while Leona giggled at something Alfred said.

"There's something mischievous about your face this morning, Derek," his mother said quietly. "I don't like it."

"Ah, Mother, he can't help it," Alfred said. "He was born that way."

"Alfred," Leona admonished with a slight swat of her hand against his chest.

"Have no fear, my lady. I've withstood far worse than that from this one," Derek said.

"I don't know why all my boys must constantly insult each other. It's exhausting."

"It's how we show we care for one another, of course," Alfred said, glancing at Derek. "Isn't it?"

Unable to keep a smirk from crossing his face, Derek nodded.

"Yes. It developed after Mother insisted that we quit attempting to shake the house down with our wrestling matches, as I recall."

"Did you wrestle one another often?" Leona asked with genuine interest.

"Oh, constantly. And with unceasing vigor. It was dreadful," his mother said, rolling her eyes upward. "The walls would quake whenever the three of them were alone for longer than two minutes. They would come, tumbling down the stairs, a pile of arms and legs, yelling and quarreling, without any regard for who was around."

"We were an energetic bunch," Alfred said with a wink.

"It tested my nerves, I'll tell you. And their father never helped, except to coach one or the others to land a punch the proper way." She shook her head. "It was unbearable."

Derek's smirk shifted into a genuine smile.

"He really was good at that," Derek said. "He taught all of us the finer points of pugilism."

"You were the best at it though," Alfred pointed out. "Father always said so."

"A ridiculous thing to be proud of," his mother said, but then she never really understood it. Not like Father had.

Derek and his brothers were overly energetic in their youth, and when their father had finally decided to help harness it instead of trying to squash it, he had picked activities for each of his sons to give a focus to their energies. While Fredrick had excelled in riding and Alfred in fencing, Derek had proven to have a singular boxing talent. So much so that his father had often commented that if his son hadn't been born a gentleman, he might have made a fine living in the ring.

The late earl had been instrumental in each of his sons' extracurricular activities, and Derek and his brothers had been pushed and praised by their father until they became more than proficient. It had been a bonding experience, with each of them cheering the other on to the point where it brought them closer. And their father had made a point of being there to support all three of them. To do well in the sport their father had chosen for them had brought each of the Trembley brothers a great deal of pride.

"Hopefully, you two will be blessed with girls," his mother continued.

Leona's cheeks became pink as the carriage shifted to a standstill. Derek was brought back to the situation as the door swung open.

A sea of people swept out over the lawns of the racetrack as Derek escorted his mother out of the carriage. Hundreds of finely dressed ladies and gentlemen walked about the area surrounding the track. The sun was shining and the smell of upturned earth hung in the air, as the track had been run the previous day for practice races.

Spinning around, Derek waited until Fredrick, Violet, and Mabel exited their carriage and came toward them, then led the way through the crowded lawn toward a door at the back of the grandstand. The wooden staircase there lead up through the back of the pavilion, and an usher was waiting at the top to take the family to their family box, situated under a large wooden canopy.

The Trembley box was one of the most coveted at these particular downs, as it was directly front and center. It was second only to the royal box, which stood in a separate building.

Everyone who was anyone was expected to be in attendance, which was precisely what Derek had hoped for. He was slightly dismayed to see that the box diagonally behind them to the right was unoccupied. Still, it was early, and he hoped the Appletons would arrive shortly.

Agatha Brinsley, the newly minted Viscountess Appleton, had been courted by Alfred quite avidly some months before. They had seemed to be very much in love, but when she had the chance to marry someone with a title, she abandoned Alfred. It was this heartache that had actually led Alfred to take his transatlantic trip.

Derek did not relish the idea of causing his brother heartache by exposing him to the woman who had broken his heart, but it had to be done. There was a rumor that Agatha now regretted marrying Lord Appleton. While there was no helping her situation, Derek hoped that seeing the woman he used to love might shake Alfred from his current infatuation.

And if Leona could witness the apparent connection between Alfred and Agatha, perhaps she would grow disenchanted with her fiancé.

"A lovely day for the races, isn't it, my lord?" Mabel said, her resonant voice cutting through the noise of the crowds around them.

Derek curved to see her bright blue gaze sparkling with mischievous intent.

"Indeed," he answered shortly.

But his ire only seemed to amuse Mabel. She grinned at him, and god above, Derek's muscles tightened from his neck, down his abdomen, to his legs. He knew his body was reacting to her, and as much as he loathed it, he couldn't ignore the physical reaction, nor could he deny that she aroused something in him. Mabel was beautiful, and he was only a man, but that was as far as it went. Except that, in the next moment, she leaned toward him, and her eyelashes fluttered down to her cheeks as she spoke, stirring something else he wasn't quite able to name.

"Tell me, are you still planning to go ahead with your campaign alone?"

Derek purposely breathed through his mouth, ignoring the gentle scent of roses that seemed to emanate off her skin.

"As a matter of fact, I am."

"I could help, you know."

"As I've told you, at least a dozen times now, there is no need for that," he said. "I can manage it myself."

"Can you?"

"Yes."

"Then I hope you have everything well in hand," she said, lifting her gaze again as she held her hand out to him.

Fighting back the urge to be charmed by her quip, he took her fingers and helped her to her seat. He had meant to let go of her hand once she was settled, but something in him pushed, and he couldn't bring himself to do so without squeezing first. Mabel's face lit up with curiosity as his hand fell away.

"I do," he stated firmly.

Just then, a caller announced that the first race was to begin in a matter of minutes. Derek leaned forward, nodding at Alfred, who had just returned to the box after placing their bets.

The horses were brought up to the starting line in a row, single file. Leona, who was seated next to her sister, leaned forward for a closer look.

"This is so different from the Hempstead Plains," Leona said. "So many fashionable people are here."

"I believe it's a rich man's sport over here, my dear," Mabel said.

"As opposed to a poor man's sport?" Fredrick asked.

"All betting is a poor man's sport at the end of the day," Mabel countered. "The only people who can afford to gamble are people who have money to throw away—because it *will* be thrown away."

"And what if they win?"

"A happy coincidence, but not one they should expect to last long," Mabel said as the horses were lined up.

"Oh! There's the one I picked. Bizarre," Violet said.

"A very smart choice, my love," Fredrick said to his fiancée. "I believe I have Touchstone."

"And you, Miss Meadows?" Derek asked before he could help himself. "Have you chosen a horse?"

Mabel glanced at him. She seemed hesitant at first, as though she thought he had only asked with the intention to mock her and was waiting for the chance to sting her with a sharp quip. But when he didn't say anything further, she squinted as if she didn't quite believe he was asking her a sincere question.

After another moment, she spoke.

"Anticipation."

All of Derek's attention remained on her.

"I beg your pardon?"

"My horse, its name is Anticipation. But I put in a trifecta with Bizarre and…what was your horse, dear?" she asked, turning to face Leona.

"Splendid Pool."

"Yes, Splendid Pool."

"You put in a trifecta?"

"Of course," she said, gazing back to the greens. "I'm rich, after all."

To his own surprise, Derek laughed, genuinely amused by her audacity. Just then, the crack of a pistol echoed across the crowd, and Mabel jumped slightly in her seat next to him. The horses sped as fast as they could around the track, galloping as the dust beat up in a cloud around them.

The beating of the hooves on the earth sent vibrations through the ground, up to the wooden floorboards of the grandstand as people on the lawn began to shout and root for their picks. It was the best part of any race: the speed, the hope, the desperation. And yet, Derek could barely focus on any of it because the length of Mabel's thigh was pressed against his.

His gaze dropped to where their legs met. Even though he wore crème-colored trousers and she was layered beneath what was likely half a dozen layers of silk, a hot, pulsing sensation seemed to beat at the spot where they were in contact. Derek could hardly make sense of it. Neither was behaving inappropriately. Hell, he was surrounded by family, friends, and hundreds of people, yet the whole focus of his world had suddenly come down to this one point.

He gazed out of the corner of his eye to see if she was reacting in the same way, but she seemed utterly focused on the race. The only hint of recognition was the slight heightening of color on the crests of her cheek. Of course, that could have just been from the excitement of the race or the warmth of sitting in such close proximity with others during a summer day. Most likely, the color was from one of those causes, for Mabel wasn't the type of woman to blush over something as insignificant as being crowded in a tight place with a man.

Just then, Mabel and everyone else in the box jumped up in shouts and cheers, leaving Derek somewhat confused. He had missed the finish.

"There!" she said, laughing as she turned back to glance down at him. "A more beautiful ending I could not have asked for."

"Aw, blast," Violet said, surprising her mother-in-law. "Er, I mean, fiddlesticks."

Fredrick and Alfred burst into laughter as Derek stood.

"We won, Mabel!" Leona said happily. "We did it."

"Brilliant choice, my dear. Hopefully, your luck will spill over into the other races."

"Oh, but it was you who picked them."

Derek's brow ticked up.

"Yes, but because you liked the name so," Mabel said quickly.

Derek leaned toward her.

"If I were a betting man, I'd say that you've played this 'poor man's sport' before," he teased.

Mabel turned, her mouth poised to say something cutting. He could tell when her focus suddenly shifted. She tilted her head at something she seemed to have spotted over his shoulder.

"I believe someone is trying to get your attention," she said.

Disappointed that he hadn't heard her would-be rebuttal, Derek twisted and saw Lord Appleton lifting his hat at the Trembley box as he descended the steps. The man had long, reddish sideburns and a short nose. On this day, he was dressed in a purple coat. A pretty brunette held onto his arm, her eyes round with shock as she surveyed beyond Derek—her eyes, no doubt, falling on Alfred.

"Lord Appleton," Derek said with a nod of his head. "Lady Appleton. A pleasure to see you both."

"Trembley," Lord Appleton thundered, then bowed to the countess. "Lady Trembley. My, it seems the entire family is out today, right? And a few more, it would seem?"

"Forgive me," Derek said, his body rotating to present Mabel and her sister. "May I introduce the Comtesse de Retha and Miss Leona Meadows."

"Former comtesse," Mabel corrected him as she pushed past to offer her hand. "A pleasure to meet you."

The viscount appeared amused by Mabel's correction but took her hand and lifted it to his lips. To Derek's confusion, a sudden urge to swat her hand away from the man's mouth coursed through him.

He frowned, unsure what to make of his sudden reaction.

"And Lady Appleton," Mabel continued when the viscount released her hand. "What a stunning dress."

"Thank you," the viscountess said, her tone uneven. "Hello, Lord Trembley, Lady Trembley, Lord Fredrick. Lord Alfred." Her voice seemed to shake a bit on the last name.

Alfred came up to join them, pushing his way in between Mabel and Derek. Pleased with himself, as this would undoubtedly cause an argument between his brother and his fiancée, Derek shifted down the box to give Alfred more room to get close to the viscountess. But then he found himself standing next to Mabel again, who had been displaced by Leona. Confused, he glanced back to where he had just been standing.

"Lady Appleton, my I introduce you to my fiancée, Miss Leona Meadows?" Alfred asked.

"F-fiancée?"

"Yes."

"It's a pleasure to meet you, Lady Appleton," Leona said with a chin dip. "Alfred has told me so much about you."

"Has he?"

"Yes. He said we would undoubtedly be great friends should we ever meet. He's always spoken so highly of you."

"Oh, well… I look forward to getting to know you. Congratulations on your betrothal."

Lady Appleton's face conveyed a whole series of emotions. Still, as the conversation continued, it became evident that not even the presence of his former love would shake Alfred from his devotion to Leona.

Bollocks.

Gripping the tickets in his hand, Derek glanced out over the track.

"Oh no," Mabel's voice came, low and inconspicuously. "Tell me that wasn't it."

Derek clenched his teeth.

"I haven't the faintest idea what you're speaking of."

"Goodness, don't you speak with your brothers?" she whispered into her shoulder so no one but Derek could hear her. "Alfred has talked at length about Lady Appleton to Leona. He's been completely honest with her about his former attachment—and fully transparent about the fact that his feelings for her are entirely in the past."

"How do you know?"

"Because my sister tells me everything." She shook her head. "Tell me you've something else planned?"

An usher came down the stairs with a tray of refreshments, interrupting the conversation with Mabel. Irritated, Derek moved to the back of the box, standing while the usher passed out lemonade as the next race was lined up.

While he had spoken with Alfred about his feelings for Agatha, he hadn't truly believed his brother was over his former relationship. Not until now. As he watched a pale Lady Appleton say her goodbyes before returning to her box with her husband, Derek wondered why he hadn't listened to his brother.

He supposed it had been an understandable miscalculation. After all, Alfred had been quite devastated before his trip to America. Yet it was obvious that the only one affected by the meeting today had been the viscountess, and that hadn't been Derek's goal.

It wasn't going to be as easy to separate Alfred and Leona as he had anticipated. While his mind churned to discover something that would effectively end their attachment, a Mr. Bentley suddenly appeared, exchanging pleasantries with Fredrick. They had attended school together and been part of their social circle since childhood. Though the gentleman spoke directly with Fredrick, who was introducing him to Violet, Bentley's view kept bouncing back to Mabel.

It seemed no matter where she went, men couldn't help but stare at her. And while Derek hated himself for being counted among them, he wouldn't allow her to distract him. No, he needed to focus.

"How grand," Violet was saying to Mr. Bentley when she turned. "Mabel? This is Mr. Bentley, a friend of Fredrick's and of the family."

"Ah, we actually already met," he said, taking her hand. "At the ball the other night? We danced. Twice."

"We did," Mabel said, and Derek noted her tone was somewhat higher than usual. "Of course, yes, Mr. Bentley. How do you do?"

"Very well indeed," he said eagerly.

"I didn't know you were such good friends with the Trembleys."

"Oh, yes, for many years. I used to spend a good portion of my summers just across the river in Henley-on-Thames. My uncle lives across the water."

"Oh, your uncle is Lord Nesby? I met him the other evening."

"He's just invited us to join him at the British Museum to view the new King's Library exhibit," Violet said before adding. "King George just donated his father's collection to the museum. Over sixty thousand volumes."

"What a voracious reader," Mabel quipped, causing the young man to laugh while Derek's agitation flared. "We would love to come, as long as my sister and her fiancé could accompany us as well?"

"Oh, absolutely, Miss Meadows. The more the merrier, I always say."

"Is that so?" she asked the tone of her voice dropping into something seductive.

Derek clenched his jaw. It was one thing to behave brazenly with him, but Mr. Bentley was what he and his brothers considered a good lad. He was not prone to drink or gamble, and while that left little in common as far as hobbies go, Derek and his brothers were always somewhat protective of the young man, who was obviously in over his head when it came to a worldly woman like Mabel.

It simply would not do to let the poor man get trampled on by a woman of Mabel's life experiences.

"Yes, that sounds like a fine idea," he heard himself say.

Bentley bowed to him with a friendly expression on his face.

"Really?"

"Er," Mabel began, squinting with suspicion. "I wasn't aware that you had a liking for museums, my lord."

"On the contrary," he said. "I find that I'm quite interested."

"Is that so?" Alfred asked.

"Yes," Derek said, only now noticing everyone was watching him. His brothers, in particular, were observing him as if he had just swallowed a fish whole. "What?"

"Well, it's just that you've never wished to go to the museum before," Fredrick said. "Whenever we've asked you to join us, you've always called it a great bore."

"Yes," Alfred added. "I believe you even said once that you'd rather have hot pokers jab at your feet then visit a building filled with…what did he say?"

"Old rubbish," Fredrick answered, a teasing look on his face.

Derek glared at the two of them, both of whom seemed to be having great fun teasing him.

"Very good then. I shall see you all tomorrow. Goodbye, Miss Meadows," Bentley said, his observation lingering on Mabel for a moment longer before turning away.

While Violet and Fredrick took their seats for the next race, Mabel came to stand next to Derek, who was trying very hard to not be so aware of the close proximity of their bodies.

"I don't know what you're up to," she said beneath her breath as the race began. The shouts from the crowds drowned out her words to all but Derek, who leaned toward her to hear. "But if you think to repeat another lackluster attempt to separate our siblings, you may wish to rethink your strategy before failing again."

"I will not fail again."

"You wouldn't have the first time if you'd accepted my help."

He glanced down at her. For some reason, having these small, private conversations in full view of everyone made Derek feel daring and adventurous. He wouldn't admit to liking having a secret with her, but it was interesting just how electrified he was whenever she would whisper to him under her breath.

"And what, pray tell, would you suggest?"

"Oh no," she said with a slight shake of her head. "I offered my help, and you rejected it. No, I'll require an apology and a concession before I help you now."

"What sort," he began slowly, "of concession?"

But Mabel only winked before brushing past him. Taking a seat next to his mother, Derek had the sudden uneasy sensation that he wasn't as in control of things as he had initially believed.

Chapter Five

"I'M SURPRISED BY you, Mabel," Leona said the following day as Juliette fixed her hair. She sat before the vanity in Mabel's room as they prepared themselves for their trip to the museum. "Accepting an invitation from Mr. Bentley. That's not like you."

"What's so surprising about it? You know I love books," Mabel said as she fixed a woven gold bracelet that had once belonged to their mother to her wrist.

Although it wasn't fashionable for unwed ladies to go about town with excessive jewelry, since Mabel was a divorcée, she was permitted a few privileges that wouldn't garner her side glances. Besides that, people were staring regardless, so why not let them admire a fine piece of jewelry?

"Yes, but I spoke with Mr. Bentley during the ball and he's, well, rather... nice, isn't he?"

Mabel smirked.

"You mean, too nice for me, is that it?"

Leona turned, her eyes wide.

"Oh no, it's not that!" she hastened to say, nearly tripping over her words.

"It's all right dear," Mabel said reassuringly. "He *is* too nice to suit my tastes, but I couldn't refuse his invitation."

"Why not?"

Mabel bent over her shoulder and held up a pair of earbobs next to her ears as she viewed them in the mirror.

"Because the look on the earl's face was too tempting."

"Oh, Mabel," Leona said, her tone disheartened. "I wish you wouldn't tease Lord Trembley. Not to mention it's wrong to accept such an invitation from a man, who appeared genuinely interested in you, for no reason other than to bother another."

"Leona, you're too sensitive to this world," Mabel said, straightening up. "Accepting an invitation to a museum—within a larger group of people, mind you—isn't tantamount to accepting a marriage proposal."

"Still, it isn't nice to do so solely to bother Lord Trembley."

"He's a grown man. I'm sure he'll survive it."

Leona made a face as if to say she disagreed but she let the conversation end. Mabel did not suffer the idea that men of position and power would wilt from teasing. If anything, she felt it would do the earl some good to have his pride punctured a bit. These British gentlemen were so unlike the gentlemen from Philadelphia. There was a sense of entitlement among them, an inherited knowledge that their words, their likes and dislikes, could and would shape the world they lived in. They all seemed stunned when met with the slightest bit of resistance, and it entertained Mabel beyond words just how indignant Derek Trembley became whenever she spoke out of turn or disagreed with him.

"Perhaps if you were kinder to him, he would not be so prickly with you," Leona suggested.

Mabel wanted to retort that the earl was not capable of being anything *but* prickly…and yet she couldn't bring herself to say it, since she knew it wasn't true. She had seen that there were other moments where he would be sympathetic, particularly to family members. Just last night, for example, when the family had settled down to dinner, Derek had apologized for having a previous engagement and not being able to attend the meal. His mother had appeared somewhat crestfallen, and the earl had taken her hand, reassuring her that he would be home for breakfast.

As the memory replayed in her head, Mabel thought back to the other thing she had noticed—namely, that the countess seemed to be somewhat troubled. It didn't happen often, but Mabel did notice that every once in a while, the dowager countess would become nervous, but not in a usual way. When something did not go as expected, the woman's left hand would begin to shake, seemingly without control, just like her eldest son. Mabel wondered if it was a family trait. All the Trembley men seemed aware of their mother's condition and would swiftly come to her aid. Whenever she seemed particularly agitated, the one physically closest to her would spring into action. Last night, it had been Derek.

He had gripped his mother's shaking hand and held it, rubbing her forearm until the shudder dispersed, which only took a moment or two. Really, it wouldn't have registered to anyone if they were in a larger group. Still, Mabel had been unfortunately so aware of Derek that she had witnessed the tender moment. And to her surprise, a warmth had passed through her at the earl's sensitivity.

Warmth? For the earl? *That* was an emotion that needed eliminating promptly.

So, in a moment of rebellion, Mabel had made a comment, quietly enough so only Derek heard, that it would be to the benefit of the table to have a peaceful meal for once. The annoyance at her audacity that shone on his face made her both ashamed and giddy all at once. But he hadn't retaliated. She had expected some sort of blistering comment or biting quip, and when he hadn't unleashed any, she found that it had bothered her all night.

Once Leona's hair was finished, the two made their way downstairs. Mabel wondered if perhaps she had been too cutting to the earl the night before and internally debated whether or not she should simply behave herself around him today.

Upon reaching the foyer, Leona went directly to Alfred, who was between Derek and Mr. Bentley, who had decided to travel with them that morning instead of meeting them at the museum. The earl had taken out his silver pocket watch and glanced at it with a frown, as if they were late.

"Miss Meadows," Mr. Bentley said, coming forward to offer her his arm. "May I help you to your carriage?"

"Goodness me," Mabel said, charmed by the man's manners. "You really mustn't make such a fuss over me."

Mr. Bentley's face dropped.

"But, of course I should. You are a lady."

"Being monied does not make someone a lady," the earl said beneath his breath, causing Mabel to glare.

Maybe she wouldn't behave today after all.

"Well thank you, Mr. Bentley. And yes, you may escort me. It's a comfort knowing that gentlemen such as yourself exist in this city," she replied, giving Trembley a pointed gaze.

"Let's not tarry," Alfred said quickly.

"Indeed," Leona agreed as she and her fiancé hurried behind Mabel as if to put a buffer between her and the earl.

It was really rather silly, Mabel thought as they entered the carriage. She and the earl didn't need to be separated from one another as if they were combative children. But as maddening as they found each other, they did want the same thing, and she had to concede that they were technically on the same side.

The morning air was exceedingly warm, to the point that by the time they reached the museum, Mabel was grateful to find relief in the cavernous stone building. It was a fashionable thing to do, visit the museums, and Mabel was soon aware that the trip would be about being seen instead of actually giving much attention to the artifacts that lined the halls of the great building.

Mr. Bentley was a mild, if somewhat cautious, companion who was far too gentle for Mabel's liking. He took every precaution to not overwhelm her as he answered her and Leona's questions. He had a vast knowledge of the Roman occupation of

Britain, and while the subject matter might have been tedious, he made it all sound rather intriguing. At one point, Leona must have smiled too brightly at him, for Mabel noticed Alfred's chest puff out somewhat as he shepherded her away to view another exhibit, leaving Mabel alone with Mr. Bentley. The earl had disappeared nearly twenty minutes prior, and Mabel did her best to purposely not care where he had gone.

"I hope I didn't offend Alfred," Mr. Bentley said as he and Mabel were left alone to gaze at a display of partially broken statues found in Greece.

"Oh no," Mabel reassured him. "I just think Leona found what you were talking about rather interesting and… well, I suppose it pricked Alfred's possessiveness a bit to have her so attentive to someone else. Ah, to be young and in love."

"I wouldn't know, unfortunately," he said. "I've never had the pleasure of falling in love."

"Well, there are people who would say that it is a wonderful thing to experience. But if I'm being honest, I don't think there's much to get excited about."

"Really?"

"Yes."

"Is that because…" He began before shaking his head as if he had just remembered something. "Never mind."

Mabel peered at him.

"You needn't stand on silly protocols with me, Mr. Bentley. I would rather you speak with me honestly than be polite."

The young man's cheeks became bright red.

"Well, I was just going to ask if you didn't think love was worth it because you had never experienced it before."

Mabel smirked, though she didn't feel delighted by the question. She had, actually, believed herself to be entirely in love when she married. The feelings had been quite real…but they had been founded on a false premise. Her husband was not the man he had pretended to be, leaving her to gradually recognize that she had fallen in love with someone who didn't actually exist.

"On the contrary. I have experienced love and I decided that it was not made for people like me."

"People like you? Why, how can anyone not be made for love? That seems a rather desolate idea, doesn't it?"

"I don't believe so," she said, shaking her head. "Romance is lovely for those who require it. But some people don't."

Mr. Bentley appeared like he wanted to argue the point, but his face changed to surprise when he glanced over her shoulder.

"Oh, Miss Meadows, if you would please excuse me," he said quickly as he moved past her. "I'll only be a moment."

"Of course," Mabel said, watching after him as he left, headed straight across the large room to an elderly man with a square face, salt and pepper hair, and bushy white eyebrows.

His expression was not pleasant.

Oh well. She faced the scarred statues once more. Perhaps if she were more interested in Mr. Bentley, his companion might tickle her curiosity, but Mabel was finding the half-winged statue of Psyche to be far more compelling.

Tilting her head as she stared at the stone sculpture, she vaguely remembered the story of Psyche and Eros. He had stolen her away from her family, refusing to let her see his face and asking her to trust him without any reason. Psyche had obeyed him, for a bit, before her sisters—jealous of her situation—had convinced her that she was living with a monster to trick her into sneaking a look at him anyway, in defiance of his rules. She had suffered for that choice, but she'd found redemption in the end, and Eros and his beloved lived happily ever after.

Mabel let out a puff of breath. Of course, they had because someone had written their story to succeed. It was unfortunate life couldn't turn out that way.

"You might want to take some pity on Mr. Bentley," the dark, masculine voice of Derek suddenly said behind her, closer to her ear than she would have expected. "He's not nearly as jaded as you are."

"A mistake made by most," she said without turning around.

She ignored the heat that flooded her extremities as she saw Derek, leaning against a pillar. "Were you spying on us?"

"Hardly," he said. "I've been here for a quarter of an hour, at least. You two walked into my vicinity."

"Well, for someone so particular about eavesdroppers, you might have made your presence known," she quipped. "And as for being jaded, I simply believe that young people should be made aware not to trust so easily. Particularly people they find attractive."

"Does Mr. Bentley find you attractive?"

"Yes."

"Rather sure of yourself, aren't you?"

"It isn't vanity on my part. You can tell," she said, leaning forward slightly. The earl's pupils widened, and much to Mabel's ire, her heart beat faster than it had a moment ago. "It's in the eyes."

"You mean the way he looks at you?"

"No. I mean the intricacies of his face. How his mouth curves up and quivers just so. How his pupils widen and his breath becomes shallow from excitement." Derek stared at her with something akin to fascination, and she felt her self-control falter. She swallowed and tried to regain control of herself, ignoring the swift uptick of her pulse. "Every person is the same when they see something they desire. Whether it be a lady or a horse or a meal."

Derek's eye squinted.

"Is that so?"

"Of course," she said, spinning around. "But, Mr. Bentley should be made aware of the fallacy of love. It might save him from some future disaster."

"And you're planning to teach him this lesson?"

Mabel laughed.

"Heavens, no. Although I'm sure it would prove entertaining," she said as she gazed across the room to where Mr. Bentley stood, speaking to the sour-faced elderly man. "But I've other business to attend to."

Derek stared at her.

"I'm glad to hear it," he spoke after a moment.

"Why is that?"

"Because the young chap fancies you and if you were just trailing him along, well, I would find that rather dastardly."

"Oh, would you?" she quipped. "Well, take comfort in this, my lord," she said, leaning toward him as her voice dropped. "You needn't worry. I've no intention of playing with people's hearts. Particularly Mr. Bentley."

"That's good of you."

"I'll only kiss him once and be done with it."

Derek's eyes snapped to hers. Mabel only said that because she saw Mr. Bentley returning over the earl's shoulder.

"I'm sorry I was taken away," Mr. Bentley said just as Derek opened his mouth to say something. "I hope you'll forgive me."

"Of course," Mabel said, taking his arm to steer him away from Derek. "Now, tell me more about the Romans. How long ago were they in Britian?"

"Over three centuries, actually."

As Mr. Bentley continued to enlighten Mabel about all things Roman, she glanced over her shoulder to see a flustered earl. She had shocked him and left him speechless, which was precisely what she'd wanted to do. To her surprise, however, once their trip to the museum was finished, Alfred informed them that his brother had left the museum before the rest of the party.

"Did he not say where he was going?" Leona asked.

"He did not, unfortunately."

"Well then, shall we go to Gunter's Tea Shop?" Mr. Bentley asked. "They have dozens of flavored ices that I believe would prove refreshing on a day like today."

"I believe we can manage that," Alfred said. "Would you like to, Leona?"

"Yes, absolutely."

"Will it not be busy?" Mabel asked, suddenly weary as her hands slipped into the pocket of her gown.

She thumbed the edges of her card deck, but refused to bring them out.

"It may be."

"If it's all the same, I think I'd prefer to return home." A wave of lethargy had come over her. "The museum was most stimulating, but I'm afraid I've had enough of crowds for the day."

"Oh, yes, of course," Mr. Bentley said as if nothing could possibly make more sense. "I'll see you home at once then."

Leona would not drop her scrutinizing gaze, and for the entire ride back to the Trembleys' Mayfair home, she seemed on the verge of speaking. Thankfully, she waited until after they returned, and Mr. Bentley bid them farewell.

"What was that about?" she asked as she followed Mabel up the stairs in the foyer.

"I'm tired."

"But you're never tired."

"Which is probably why I am so exhausted now."

"Are you ill then? Do you have a fever? Or maybe you're nauseous—"

"Leona, I'm fine," she said upon reaching her room. She quickly shifted her body so that her sister could not enter. "I'm just a little weary is all."

Leona frowned.

"If you were ill, you would tell me, wouldn't you?"

"Yes, of course. I only want a little rest, that's all."

It was obvious she wasn't pleased with Mabel's answer, but she relented.

"Very well. Perhaps I will rest too, before dinner."

"A fine idea. I'll come to your room in a few hours then."

Leona nodded, though it was apparent from the frown on her angelic face that she didn't quite believe her sister. Mabel smiled before entering her room and closing the door. Leaning against the wooden door, she sighed.

It wasn't like her to be despondent. Believing that she was

tired, she undressed and laid in bed but found no rest. Tossing and turning, she wasn't sure when she fell asleep, but was surprised that when she opened her eyes, it was dark.

Confused, she sat up and scanned her room. A rectangular tray with a silver cloche sat on the small table between the two wingback chairs before the fireplace. Apparently, she had fallen into a deep enough sleep that she had missed dinner, and a tray had been brought up for her.

Stretching her legs over the edge of the bed, she went to the hearth to see the polished walnut mantel clock. Eleven o'clock.

Goodness. She had slept for quite some time. Having no appetite, she tried to lay back down, hoping that sleep would come over her again, only to find that she was tossing and turning. Her mind could not hold onto a single thought, and after several minutes, she sat back up.

"Bother," she murmured as she walked to the wardrobe and plucked out an aubergine silk dressing gown.

She had gone to sleep too early and was now wide awake. Wrapping herself in the robe, she crossed the bedroom and opened the door, deciding to go to the library. Hopefully, she could find a book that would settle her mind.

The entire house was fast asleep, and as she walked through the hallways, she found an almost calming sense come over her. It was really rather peculiar that she felt so at ease in this place, even if she saw its owner as bothersome, but then she didn't think too deeply about it as she made her way down the staircase.

As quietly as she could, Mabel reached the landing and hurried down the hallway, remembering the last time she had been in the library. It had been the night of the ball, when she had eavesdropped on the earl and his friends.

She found herself wondering about the earl and why he had left the museum without telling his brother where he was going. A nagging little voice in her mind told her that she would probably do well to steer clear of the earl for a day or two. Her little quip about kissing Mr. Bentley had likely aggravated him, and as much as she had enjoyed his reaction in the moment, she found now that she regretted it.

When she reached the library, she stepped inside and closed the door behind her. To her surprise, the oil lamps were still brightly lit, despite it being so late in the evening. Crossing the elongated room to reach the bookshelves, Mabel sighed loudly, wondering what book she could possibly find that would entertain her or at least might bore her enough to put her to sleep.

But before she reached the wooden bookcases, she paused, suddenly feeling like she was being watched. Mabel swallowed and cocked her head slowly, looked across the room. There, seated at the card table that sat before the fireplace with a split deck of cards in each of his hands, was the earl, watching her.

Chapter Six

D EREK STARED AT Mabel, who herself appeared momentarily frozen. The warm light from the oil lamps cast her in an unearthly golden glow, and for the life of him, he couldn't remember what problem he had just been trying to solve.

"I..." she started after a moment before trailing off, seemingly unsure what to say. "I just came down for a book," she said at last.

Derek nodded as his hand shuffled the deck of cards. He finished and placed it on the table before standing up.

"I didn't mean to interrupt," she said, sounding almost apologetic.

"You're not," he said. "I was just taking a moment to work out an issue."

"What issue?"

He had been reading a letter from his steward, Mr. Franklin, who was overseeing the renovation of the fish folly that sat on a small island in the middle of the river Thames at his country home in Henley-on-Thames. It had sustained an extensive amount of damage the year before due to excessive spring flooding, and Derek had been trying to decide whether to write Mr. Franklin back with instructions on how to handle the issue or to travel to the country to tend to the matter himself.

It was one of a dozen things that needed to be addressed at

Boxwood Park, and he was glad that Parliament would let out in a few weeks so that he could return and deal with everything on site. While Derek enjoyed the hustle and bustle of London life, it was good to have a reprieve every few months. With this summer being scorching, Derek longed for the sanctuary of his country estate.

"Nothing to concern yourself with," he said as she came forward.

"Do you play?"

He glanced back at the table.

"I do."

"I do as well," she said, studying him. "Faro, in particular." When he didn't speak, she smirked. "Care for a game?"

"There's only two of us."

"I think we can manage."

"Wouldn't your Mr. Bentley take issue with your playing a card game in the middle of the night? Alone with a man, dressed in your nightgown?"

When he said it, he thought he sounded like a sullen child, but to his surprise, a blush rose to Mabel's cheeks. She bit her bottom lip, almost as if she were ashamed of something. Derek couldn't concentrate on whatever that might be as he was transfixed on her mouth.

"I deserve that," she said, lifting her chin. "I didn't mean what I said, you know. I only meant to aggravate you."

"And why would your kissing Mr. Bentley aggravate me?"

"I was wondering the same thing."

Derek shook his head and laughed despite himself. He *had* been aggravated—infuriated, actually, if he was being honest, but he wouldn't admit it to her.

"Shall we?" she asked, motioning at the table.

"I don't think so."

"Oh," she said, mischief in her dark eyes. "Are you not very good?"

The idea that a Trembley wasn't very good at cards was

laughable, but there was a teasing in her tone that gently pulled at him, making him want to tease her back.

"I'm exceptional," he said, his tenor deep.

"So am I," she said, and every inch of him agreed. "Shall we?"

Derek wasn't sure why, but he suddenly wished to play, and not simply because he enjoyed cards. The small details emerging from a game like Faro were suddenly impossible to give up.

He dipped his head, and she pushed past him, the delicate scent of rose blooms hovering in the air around her. It was intoxicating, and he nearly closed his eyes as he inhaled, but he steeled himself and turned back to sit in the chair he had just abandoned.

"You carry a deck of cards with you often, do you not?"

"Yes, I do."

"Why is that?"

Her slender shoulder came up and dropped.

"I find shuffling a soothing habit. I learned to play cards as a girl, after my mother's death. My father had been teaching me how to play, but he stopped after she died. I always found something about the fluttering of the cards engaging, so I took his playing cards. I suppose I developed a bit of an attachment to them." She picked up the deck of cards and began shuffling them. He watched her intently. "It's silly, I suppose."

"I don't think so," he said. "Having cards on you seems a rather healthy habit. At least you've not taken to drinking to deal with your nerves. I know several gentlemen who have done just that."

"I've found that I'm not quite compatible with alcohol, though how I found that out, you'll never know," she said, seeming equal parts amused and mortified as she sat down. "You know, I didn't think anyone would be awake when I came down here." She placed the deck on the table and he cut it in two before she picked it back up. "I was hoping to find a book to read. I'm afraid I fell asleep too early."

"Yes, I heard."

"Did you?" she asked.

"I was informed by George that you retired early."

"Ah yes. Your spy," she teased. "Tell me, do you supply all your guests with handlers?"

"No," he answered as he began dealing the cards.

"I see."

"Do you?"

"I believe I do. You don't trust that I can manage myself, even though I'm a fully grown woman who's managed herself for several years."

"In your own country and hometown. London is worlds away from Philadelphia."

"I handled myself just as well when I was in France," she said as she placed the deck on the table, turning the first card face up.

"Is that so?" he asked, forcing himself to sound nonchalant. The truth was, he was actually very interested to learn about her life before coming to London. "Your husband didn't care how you came or went?"

"No. He didn't."

Derek glanced up from his cards and noted the studied neutrality of her face, as if she was repressing every expression by sheer force of will. What did she mean "no"? Why would her husband not worry about her coming and going? Something about the finality of her answer irked him, and he wondered what sort of man the comte had been.

"Tell me what you were thinking about, before I interrupted you."

He wasn't sure what he should say, not wanting to confide in her, and yet, something urged him to do so.

"To be honest, I was thinking about how strange it was that I used to dread going to Boxwood Park when I was younger and now I can't help but want to be there. Even a few years ago, I did not look forward to having to leave the city to attend all the dreary house parties and hunts in the country."

"You prefer the city?"

"Well, that's just it. I thought I did. I always used to. But now I find that I'm quite ready to be done with the city and spend the next several months in the country by the time Parliament concludes its session."

"I can understand that," she said as she laid down her cards. "I win."

"So you did. Again?" he asked as he gathered the cards.

She nodded, then continued her previous thought.

"I always thought the city was far more entertaining. And there is always something to do, no matter the time of year. Being surrounded by people, even when you're quite alone, always seemed to boost my moods when they turned melancholy."

The cards nearly slipped from his hand, but he regained them in a flash. Yes. He had had a similar experience, particularly after his father died. The country had seemed to be far too quiet, and he had hated the way he was constantly alone with his thoughts. At least in the city, he could distract himself with plays or visits to his club.

"But every once in a while, the crowds, and the endless chatter, well… it drains a person, I believe."

He nodded in agreement. Yes, the shine of London's nightlife had dimmed for him in recent years. His friends were all married, and soon his brothers would be as well, and without them, the city seemed a little larger and colder, not quite as full and engaging as it once had been.

He knew he was lonely. What he *didn't* know was what he was going to do about it. The time was not far off when he would have to find a bride, but besides several attractive ladies who always tried to step in his way, he hadn't found anyone to stir anything except physical reactions. Which were fine and good, even required in a wife, but every lady he spoke to seemed too blank. Not to say that they didn't have clever minds, but none had ever challenged him.

Except, of course, Mabel.

"You know, it's rather lucky for me to have run into you," she continued as she scanned her cards.

To his eternal embarrassment, Derek's hand began to shake slightly. It was maddening, to say the least. Why his hands would shake for apparently no reason infuriated him. No doubt it made him appear weak or nervous.

Dropping his cards, he tucked his hands into his pockets and glared at her.

"And why is that?"

To her credit, she kept her eyes on her cards and pretended nothing had happened. Which made him grateful, yet also irked him.

"We need to discuss our situation."

Her calm blue eyes seemed to shine in the firelight. She was a forward woman, seemingly afraid of nothing. Even being alone with a man in the middle of the night. But then she had nothing to fear from Derek. Or at least that's what he told himself.

"That being?"

"Separating our siblings from this ludicrous union."

Surprise, and then disappointment, flooded his senses, but he remained still. She was correct, of course. They needed to figure out how to separate Leona and Alfred once and for all.

"And I suppose you have a plan?"

"A better one then parading a former paramour out around Alfred. Really, he's far too smitten with Leona to pay attention to anyone else. Haven't you noticed?"

"All men are smitten with their fiancées."

"Would that that were the truth," she said, a bitter note in her tone, but she continued. "Regardless, Alfred is. Dangling another woman in front of him is not going to change that. What we need is to think of something that will show both of them that neither are truly aware of how detrimental this marriage would be. Maybe plant a seed of doubt between them."

"We don't exactly have months to discourage them," Derek said as they laid down their cards. Damn it. She'd won again.

"The banns have already been posted. We leave for Boxwood Park in a week's time, and the two will be married by the end of the month."

Mabel's brows arched.

"Which is why you need my help."

Derek stared at her momentarily and then pushed his chair back and stood. He walked toward the small, cylinder-shaped cupboard where several glasses and a bottle of amber liquid sat on the marble top. Pouring two glasses, one for himself and one for Mabel, he brought them back to the table and placed one in front of her. He hadn't asked if she wanted one, but he believed she might and wasn't surprised when she took a sip.

He *did* need Mabel's help, but he recalled what she said to him at the races. She wanted an apology and a concession from him after the way he'd refused her aid before.

Taking a large sip of the burning liquid, he sat down, mildly amused at how her face scrunched up at the taste. She coughed slightly but waved her hand before he could ask if she was all right.

"I suppose you have an idea as to how we should break these two apart?"

"Well, it's not so much a plan but rather a series of little events," she said, waving her hand as if to explain. "If there were little things, small fractures that could be caused here and there, then the weight of their own concerns could create a larger fissure. For example, my sister has a pet peeve when it comes to waiting on others. She likes to be prompt."

"A fair point."

"She also doesn't respond well to being ignored."

"No one does."

"She also dislikes sweet pea flowers, impractical footwear and arrogance."

Derek gave her a speculative glance.

"Impractical footwear and arrogance I can understand, but why doesn't she like sweet pea blooms?"

"They were our mother's favorite flowers."

Derek frowned.

"Then wouldn't she be partial to them?"

"Not when the entire house was filled with them for weeks after she passed. The scent always reminded Leona of that sad time. She cannot stand them now. I do not blame her, as it was rather dreadful."

The mention of her deceased mother seemed not to bother Mabel, though Derek was sure it was a sore subject, no matter how well she masked her feelings.

"That's understandable, I suppose. My brother informed me how your mother died. I'm sorry for your loss."

Mabel shook her head.

"It was many years ago."

"Yes, but—"

"I'd rather not talk about it actually," she said quickly. "Now, tell me what your brother dislikes."

To Derek's surprise, he couldn't think of anything his brother didn't like. Alfred was always the most easygoing Trembley brother and rarely complained about anything.

The longer the silence grew between them, the more confused Mabel's face became.

"Surely you can think of something," she said. "He's your brother."

"Well, he doesn't like cheating—at card games, that is. And he's not too fond of poorly written poetry, I suppose."

"Is that it?" she asked, sounding a little frustrated.

"He doesn't like being frivolous with his money. He's rather practical in dress. More so than Fredrick and I."

Mabel's face lit up.

"Well now, that's something I can work with."

"Is it?"

"Yes. I'll simply take Leona out for an extravagant shopping spree and then have her show him everything she's bought and tell him all the prices for each item."

He had to hand it to her. She seemed to know how to do this. The fact that she was so skilled in creating discord concerned him somewhat, but he batted that thought away.

"Very well," he said slowly. "I suppose we should work together then."

"Ha," she said, that maddening, dazzling smirk appearing on her face.

"You don't wish to?"

"Of course I do, but I already offered my services and you denied them." She stared at him for a moment. "I require a heartfelt apology after being so carelessly rejected—as well as a concession."

Irritable humor fell over him at her self-importance. She was bothersome, that was certain, but then his annoyance was mixed with a wild sense of yearning. Who did she think she was, demanding such things from him?

"Why make me apologize?"

"Because I want it."

"And you always get what you want?"

"Only when I've decided to."

That made Derek laugh. At the very least, she was an entertaining opponent. He took another mouthful of whiskey, this one burning far less than the first few sips.

"Very well. Miss Meadows, I am sincerely sorry for having ignored your generous offer to aid me in this quest of separating our siblings before their wedding. Will you forgive me, and help me prevent them from making the gravest mistake of their lives?"

"I accept your apology and I will help you," she said as she took yet another sip. "For the price of a kiss."

Derek stilled, unsure if he had heard her right. He looked up and saw her no longer smiling but gazing at him intently.

It didn't matter that he had wanted to kiss her since the moment she first entered the family parlor, the day she and her sister arrived in London. Back then, propriety had stopped him. She was a divorcée, no innocent miss when it came to the bedroom, so he couldn't be accused of corrupting her or tainting a purity that she no longer had. But she was still something of a walking scandal, and kissing her would only invite more trouble.

Yes. He had to repeat that to himself several times before he spoke because it would be far too easy to give her what she wanted.

"You are aware that such a request might reflect poorly on yourself."

Mabel laughed again, only this time Derek thought he caught a nervousness to it. *Was* she nervous, being so bold?

"I was married, before, if you remember. A kiss is hardly anything."

"I suppose not."

"Unless you've never been kissed?"

She was teasing him, and Derek couldn't help but chuckle.

"Why do you want it, though?" he asked, after a moment. "We've hardly been civil to one another."

"Yes, I know."

"Then why?"

"Well, you've made it perfectly clear that poor Mr. Bentley wouldn't survive a kiss and I still am curious."

He cocked his head.

"Curious about what exactly?"

"If Englishmen kiss better than Frenchmen," she said softly.

Derek rolled his shoulders back instinctively.

"We absolutely do."

"Well, rumor would have most people believe the opposite, I'm afraid."

"I guarantee it."

"Then prove it, please."

He was amazed that such a request should make him feel so many different things at once, but if he was anything, he was duty-bound. For England, he told himself as he turned to her.

Derek's arm reached out as he grabbed the leg of her chair and pulled her abruptly close. She clearly hadn't expected that, but before she could choke out a sound, Derek reached his other hand out to touch her face as he drew her close enough to kiss her.

He had meant to shock her, to deliver what she asked for with purpose, but the moment their lips met, a strange alertness seemed to heighten within him. He slowed his kiss as his eyes closed, taking in all the senses of her. The taste of her mouth, the scent of her skin, the feel of her cheek. He held her face and leaned closer as he deepened his kiss, searching her mouth with his tongue, only to be met with the velvety touch of her own.

Mabel's hand came up, her fingers trailing along the side of his neck before she suddenly drew back, turning away so that he couldn't see her face. He instantly felt as if he had been pushed off a cliff, but as their erratic breaths settled, she peeked back at him, and the wonder he saw in her expression made his insides knot.

It had been ages since a woman had caused such a reaction in him. While he had known his fair share of female companions, none had held this illicit hold over him. Mabel was forward and delicious, and while a part of him was very eager to continue to toy with her as much as she wanted, a deep knowing told him that he was entering dangerous waters.

"I didn't mean to—"

"Oh no," she said quickly, shaking her head. "You've proved a very interesting fact."

"Have I?" She nodded. "May I ask which you prefer then? An Englishman or a Frenchman?"

"You can ask, but I won't answer."

"You really won't tell me?"

"Not tonight. But perhaps one day I will."

"One day?"

"Yes. When I'm back in Philadelphia. I'll write you."

"You'd put an ocean between us before you told me?"

"Absolutely."

"Why?"

"Because I would rather be half a world away than be vulnerable in front of you."

The honesty in her words caught him off guard. Although she was still smiling, there was something genuine in her face that gave him pause. She was being purposely flippant yet sincere as if the only way she could tell him these things about herself was if she added a dose of self-deprecating humor.

Yet it also made Derek wonder why being open was such a struggle for her. Leona wasn't like that. Her sincerity came quickly. What had happened then to Mabel that made her so guarded? Did it have something to do with her marriage?

"I think I should get back to my room," she said, shaking him from his thoughts. "And I think you should figure out some way to take Alfred away, maybe for a day or two. A little distance should prove... A good idea, no doubt." Her words seemed to possess a double meaning, and Derek only nodded. "Goodnight."

"Goodnight."

Half horrified and half desperate to follow her, Derek let her leave. It had been shocking to realize that everything that had previously exasperated him about Mabel had switched to everything he suddenly found attractive. From her forwardness, to her sharp mind and tongue. And on top of all of that, there was a thread of tenderness that seemed to wrap around her, and it left Derek thinking of her well into the night.

Chapter Seven

MABEL WASTED NO time writing to the Duchess of Combe to organize a shopping trip to Bond Street with Leona, as the duchess probably knew all the most expensive places to go. This would aid in Mabel and Derek's plot to make Leona appear to be a frivolous spender. To justify her reaching out, she added a line in her letter expressing a desire to become better acquainted with the earl's friends since she would eventually leave Leona in their care when she returned to Philadelphia.

It wasn't necessarily a lie, Mabel told herself the morning after she received the duchess's response. She quite liked the duchess. But the truth was it didn't matter whether she found the duchess to be a wonderful person or a monster. Mabel was counting mainly on her expertise in spending money, which needed to happen immediately. With the entire Trembley household set to disembark to the country at the end of the week, Mabel would have to move quickly to help along whatever discord she could. That way, she and Leona could hurry home and put some proper distance between themselves and the Trembley men.

Not that Mabel was willing to admit that she needed an ocean to curb the desire she had for the earl. What she *would* admit was that kissing him had been a mistake. When she entered the dining room for breakfast, she was relieved to see that Derek was not in attendance.

"The regatta will be held a week from today, and we will absolutely host a ball at that time," the dowager countess said to Leona as she brought a teacup to her lips. "You'll love it, my dear. Boxwood Park has a wonderful view of the river. They've done the regatta several times before, but they're thinking of making it an official occurrence. Supposedly, the Crown has become interested and is looking to patronize the event."

"Is that so?" Leona asked as Mabel fixed herself a plate at the sideboard. "What does it involve?"

"Oh, it's a fine competition," Alfred said. "A public draw is held in the town, and rowers are done up into teams. Then, they're set on either side of the river to compete. It's divided into the Bucks and the Berks. Mother always bets on the Bucks—"

"Alfred!"

Alfred smirked at his mother before popping a strawberry in his mouth.

"It's a right good time," Fredrick said. "Eton was keen on trying to make a club of sorts for students, but it hasn't happened yet. Although, we all did a bit of racing ourselves while at school." He glanced at his brother. "Some of us better than others."

"I wasn't very good," Alfred admitted sheepishly to Leona. "But Fredrick and Derek were."

"Not very good?" Fredrick continued. "You were the whole reason we had to be visited by that Dutch fellow from the Society for Recovery of Drowned Persons." He buttered a piece of toast. "We all had to spend a week learning how to rescue people from drowning."

Mabel's brow raised as she spun away from the buffet.

"So, you *did* drown, Alfred? Leona mentioned it to me, but I thought she was exaggerating."

"Only for a moment or two," he said with a wink, as the countess rolled her eyes.

"Um, what are Bucks and Berks?" Leona repeated, confused.

"You mentioned it before, but I'm not familiar with the terms."

"Bucks for Buckinghamshire and Berks for Berkshire," Fredrick explained as Mabel sat down. He faced her. "Violet tells me you're off on a shopping trip this morning with her and Clara."

"Oh, yes," Mabel said. She was unaware that the duchess had invited her sister-in-law, but she had no objection to the addition. "It should be an exciting experience. I'm eager to see what sort of things London has to sell."

"I'm sure it's no different than what we have in Philadelphia," Leona said.

"But we shan't know for sure unless we go see for ourselves," Mabel answered as another body entered the dining room.

"Where the devil is Alfred?" Derek asked before surveying his surroundings. Seeing his youngest brother, he stalked toward him, though his shifting glance caught Mabel's eye just as she sat down.

She swallowed and dropped her gaze to the plate of food before her, trying hard not to remember their kiss. Instead, she chose to focus on the task at hand. Today, their plan would commence. Derek would take his brother away for an undisclosed amount of time, without offering anyone any explanation, while Mabel would force a spending spree onto her sister.

"Derek, manners," his mother chided him.

"There's no time for niceties, Mother. We've an appointment this morning."

"Do we?" Alfred said, standing up.

"Yes. We've appointments all over town actually," Derek said, his eyes meeting Mabel's for half a second before returning his gaze to his brother. They mustn't appear to be in cahoots with one another. "Shall we?"

Alfred was clearly unaware of what plans his brother had for him, but he put forth no objection, merely wiped his mouth with a kerchief and hurried after Derek, who had already bowed and left the room.

"I wonder what they're up to," Leona said as she watched her fiancé leave.

"Who knows," Mabel said quickly. "But let us discuss what we will be doing today. Where shall we go? Oxford Street? Saville Row?"

"For what? We already have everything we need."

"Oh, but I should like to find something to take home with me when I return home. Let us find something special to commemorate this trip."

Mabel took a sip of her tea, her concentration on the plate before her, when she noticed the silence. Glancing to her side, she saw Leona's crestfallen face.

"I forgot you were planning on returning to Philadelphia," she said, shaking her head as if trying to dislodge the sudden sadness from her features. "I guess... Well, it's just that the Trembleys have been so accommodating," she said. "I assumed..."

"Leona, you couldn't have thought that I would stay here once you were married. Surely not."

"No, no, I knew you were going back, but well, I just assumed that you would stay for a few months."

"Months? Goodness no, I plan on leaving immediately after the wedding."

Leona's eyes widened in surprise. "Immediately? But why? Surely there's no need to rush away."

"My dear, Papa is expecting me before the season is over. And as obliging as your future in-laws have been, they can't be expected to house me forever. Besides, I miss Philadelphia."

"Yes," Leona said sadly. "Of course."

Mabel nodded, but a stone felt suddenly lodged in her stomach. It had been a different kind of difficult when she had left America the first time to marry the comte. Leona had still been so young at the time, and while they had been close, Mabel had craved a romantic life and believed she had found one. As sad as she had been to leave her home and family behind, she'd been full of hope for the happiness she expected to find in France. But when her marriage fell apart, and she returned to Philadelphia, with the shame of divorce hanging around her neck like a weight, Leona had been there to help her ease the pain of a broken heart and bruised ego. She and Leona had been inseparable ever since. Now her sister was going to marry Alfred and stay in England forever.

Well, not if Mabel could help it.

"Come, let's not be all doom and gloom this morning," she said, straightening her back. "Let's go see what London has to offer."

"Yes, I think that's a grand idea," the countess said as George entered the room.

"The Duchess of Combe and Lady Violet," he said with a bow as the fair-haired countess and her sister-in-law entered the room.

"Good morning," the duchess chirped as Mabel and Leona rose from their chairs. "I'm so glad you suggested this outing, Miss Meadows."

"I'm so pleased that you accepted my invitation, your grace," Mabel said, curtsying to both women.

"Oh, none of that," Violet said, taking Leona's arm. "We're to be family in a few short weeks after all."

"Yes, I suppose we will be," Leona said.

"Lady Trembley, are you sure you don't wish to join us?" the duchess asked, peering over Mabel's shoulder.

"Goodness no. I've much too many appointments myself today. George?"

The footman came forward from the door.

"Yes, my lady?"

"Have the carriage readied for our guests," she said. The footman bowed and left. "Be wary of time though, ladies. We've the opera tonight."

"Yes, my lady," Leona said as she stood, and the four women made their way out of the dining room and into the foyer.

An hour later, Mabel, Leona, the duchess, and Violet were on their third store and had already saddled their accompanying footman with several boxes. Sheet music, gloves, luxury luggage, and a crystal tea set had been purchased during their excursion.

Leona and Violet kept close to one another, whispering secrets and chatting merrily. For a moment, Mabel was glad to see that her sister had made such a friend, but then, remembering that the whole point of this excursion was to create a rift between Leona and Alfred, she glanced down to inspect an invisible speck of dirt on her glove.

"Mabel?" her sister called, causing her to glance up. "What do you think of this?"

Leona held up a tin of mint sweets. "They're so much like the ones Alfred bought in Philadelphia. The ones he sent home, remember? He liked them so."

"Oh yes," Violet said. "The earl gave them to Gavin, who very much enjoyed them."

"They were not to the earl's liking?" Mabel heard herself ask.

"Unfortunately, no. He said as much at a dinner party several months ago."

Mabel made a point to remember that information as her sister placed the tin back down on the shelf.

"My dear, why not buy them for Alfred if he enjoyed them?"

"Well, we aren't yet married, and it's untoward to buy a man a gift, isn't it?"

"But you will be soon enough," Mabel said, picking the small tin up and placing it in her sister's hands. "In fact, I wanted to encourage you to buy gifts for the entire family."

"Oh, I couldn't possibly."

"Why not? It will be a lovely gesture. They will be personal thank-you tokens, for each and every one of them. For housing us during our visit and welcoming us so generously. I'm sure they will be very well received."

Violet and the duchess did not speak—likely because they knew her words were untrue. To buy gifts for everyone in the

Trembley household would be seen as excessive and unnecessary.

But Mabel had to push.

"Are you quite sure?" Leona asked.

"Of course."

Leona beamed as she and Violet picked out an assortment of trinkets and gifts.

"I hope you don't mind me saying so," the duchess said quietly when Leona and Violet were out of earshot. "But there isn't a need to bestow such gifts on the Trembleys. They would appreciate the thoughtfulness of the gesture, I'm sure, however the earl may well be embarrassed to receive gifts from his guests."

"Will he?" Mabel feigned surprise. "Well, he needn't be."

The duchess's unwavering stare set Mabel's nerves on edge, but she would not cower. She and the earl had a plan.

"You know, Derek has been somewhat out of sorts these past few weeks," the duchess said slowly, her fingers trailing down a length of silk ribbon that hung from a hook on the wall. Several dozen silken lengths hung down, in varying shades of blues. The duchess examined them carefully as she tested one after another. "I'm sure he's too much of a gentleman to speak of it with ladies, but I wonder if he's not perhaps somewhat nervous about his brothers' upcoming nuptials."

Mabel glanced at the duchess.

"Do you think so?"

"I do. Perhaps you can relate? I don't have any siblings myself, but I can't imagine what it would be like to lose a beloved sister to a man who lived on the other side of the world."

Heat began to creep up Mabel's neck. The duchess was a perceptive woman, but she wasn't exactly someone Mabel could confide in.

"I'm only glad that my sister has found love," she said evenly, turning around to gaze across the room. "She and Alfred seem very happy together."

"They do. They really do," the duchess said, pulling one of the ribbons down. "I hope they stay that way."

"As do I," Mabel said, unsure if she was lying. She *did* want her sister to be happy. And Alfred too, she supposed. She just didn't see how they could stay happy if they chose to stay together.

"Mabel?" Leona called from across the shop. "What about this cameo pin, for the countess? Or maybe a silk fan would be better."

"Buy them both," Mabel said, pushing along with her plot.

"Violet helped me pick out this very handsome pen for Fredrick," she said, coming over. "But I'm at a loss as to what to get the earl. Maybe a cravat? Oh, but that's too personal."

"A book," Mabel said offhandedly.

"A book? What sort of book? One on horses?"

"No, this one," Mabel said, holding a small, green leather-dyed book. "*Precaution* by James Fenimore Cooper."

"What's it about?" Leona asked, taking the book from her sister.

"The domesticity of life, what else?" Mabel said. "But it's written by an American, who pretended to be an English woman and wrote about this country."

"Really?"

"Yes. I think the earl will find it entertaining."

Leona bought the book, as well as several other odds and ends, all at the insistence of Mabel, who began to feel a wight of sorts around her shoulders as they made their way to the next shop and then another. It didn't help that she quite liked Alfred. Mabel believed he would make someone a fine husband. But it would be best if he made some British bride happy. Just as she had discussed with the earl.

For the rest of the day, Mabel had to continue assuring herself that what she was doing was for the best. And when she wasn't busy making justifications to herself, she was struggling to keep her thoughts from turning to the earl. It seemed every subject reminded her of him, simply because she wondered what his opinion would be on it.

It was a struggle to keep her thoughts free of him all morning and even still when they returned that afternoon. The duchess and Violet left after they returned to Mayfair, and Mabel began to dress for the evening out to the opera.

When she finished readying herself for the evening, she left her room and descended the stairs, only to find the countess and Leona alone in the foyer. Mabel arched a brow.

"Is something amiss?"

"No," the countess said, tugging on her satin gloves. "Except that my sons seem to constantly want to vex me."

Mabel studied Leona, curious to see her reaction.

"The earl and his brothers sent their regards, but they won't be able to make it tonight."

"Oh?" Mabel said, trying to sound curious. This was precisely what she had asked the earl to do. "Are they all right?"

"Quite," the countess said, sounding annoyed as she brushed past them. "Shall we depart?"

The sisters followed, eager not to upset the older woman any more than she already was. Once they arrived at the Opera house, however, Leona made a show of her slipper coming undone. Dragging Mabel away, they made their way to the ladies' waiting room to see to it. To Mabel's surprise, a visibly upset Leona gripped her hand once they were out of the countess's sight.

"What's happened?" Mabel asked, genuinely worried.

"I overheard the countess speaking with George. Apparently the earl and his brothers are staying at the gentleman's club tonight. Whites."

"All night?"

Leona nodded.

"Yes. Evidently there's some large bidding going on and, and..."

"And what?"

"And it seems that Alfred is too busy to be bothered to come and keep his plans with us."

So that was it. Well, Mabel had to give the earl credit. A gambling game was the perfect lure to use on his brothers. While it wasn't lovely, and Mabel felt rotten for causing Leona to be so melancholy, she told herself it was for the best. A sudden zing of guilt cut through Mabel's heart at her and Derek's plan, but unfortunately, it needed to be done.

Swallowing the lump of guilt that had formed in her throat, Mabel spoke.

"Well, it's to be expected of their sort, isn't it? Men of the peerage often find themselves with too much money and not enough to keep them busy."

Leona's brow pinched together.

"But Alfred isn't like that."

"No? Oh, well, then I guess you've nothing to worry about." Mabel tried to sound flippant. "Come, let us not tarry and leave the countess by herself for too long."

Leona nodded and after a moment's hesitation, she walked out to find the countess. Mabel followed, and while a sour taste formed in her mouth, she ignored it.

This was what was best for everyone. Or at least that's what she kept telling herself during the days to follow.

♣

THE HAZE OF an early morning fog fell over London in the early hours, two days, and three nights after the missed opera show. Derek and Fredrick helped carry Alfred down the steps of Whites, where the three of them had spent the last few days drinking and gambling in the name of celebration. Derek had pressed the idea that his brothers should have a stag party that lasted two full evenings, as they were to have a double wedding. And then after that, he was somehow able to convince them to stay for a third night, which had obviously proven to be too much for Alfred.

"Poor bloke," Fredrick said as he missed a step, nearly causing all three of them to fall. Derek hoisted him back up, shoving Alfred toward him. Fredrick hiccupped. "Never could hold his liquor."

"You're still three sheets to the wind yourself," Derek said as they reached the bottom of the steps.

He and Fredrick dragged their semi-conscious brother to the vehicle, where the waiting driver yawned loudly before hurrying forward to help load Alfred inside like a sack of flour.

With a grunt, Alfred all but fell onto the floor of the carriage as Derek climbed in after him, fighting off a raging headache. Fredrick nearly followed him but grimaced.

"Actually, I think it would be safer if I rode with the driver," he said before closing the door.

Derek understood. He wasn't looking forward to the ride home and whispered a silent prayer not to be sick as the carriage lurched forward.

He would deserve it, he mused miserably as the carriage jolted from side to side down the cobblestone road. It had been bad form not to send word to his house about their whereabouts after that initial missive stating that they wouldn't be coming to the opera, but that was the idea, wasn't it? To make Alfred appear inconsiderate. Keeping him away for two whole days would likely solidify that impression.

The first night had been easy enough. With Fredrick, Silas, and Gavin, along with dozens of friends, Alfred had had little chance to argue. They had all come to celebrate his pending marriage, and it would be rude to argue that he had other plans. It was far easier for Alfred to allow himself to be plied with drink and enticed with gambling, particularly since he hadn't indulged for some time. A grand night was had by all.

The second night, however, was more difficult. Alfred had been ill from the first night of drinking and carousing, which meant, thankfully, that he had slept in. Derek had kept him at the club until five o'clock, offering him food and headache powders as Fredrick riled the rest of their friends to celebrate again. Soon enough, another celebration was taking place, but Alfred, who never could drink very much, had expressed his desire to leave.

"We really should return home," he had mumbled from a club chair, hand on his head. "Leona is undoubtedly worried."

"Nonsense," Derek said. "I'm sure she knows that you're just having some fun. She'll have to come to expect that you'll visit the club when you're married."

"Yes, but not for an entire night and day…and now another night again?" he said, struggling to stand. "Come, let's go."

"How about a bit of the hair of the dog?" Derek offered. "It wouldn't do the womenfolk any good to see you sick from one night of drinking. Really, I thought you would be able to hold your own for a more than a day. Take Fredrick for example."

"I've held my own plenty of times," Alfred snapped, but after a moment, he glanced at his brother. "Do you think a bit of drink will cure this insufferable headache?"

"It's worth a try."

And so, Alfred drank, ate, and eventually began a game of cards, which evolved into a second wild night of revelry. Derek had tried to keep a distance from all the whatnot, but it couldn't be helped. Instead, he and his brothers had fallen into the haze of debauchery.

All three Trembley men had been ill the next day and decided it would be best to recover at the club before returning home. Then at some point during the evening, they each came down for a game of hazards, which had quickly become one of the best games of Alfred's entire life.

It was incredible to watch as he threw nines and elevens almost repeatedly for an hour. They had all won an exorbitant amount of money and hadn't fallen asleep all night. Now, in the cold grey light of early morning, they were left with pockets full of banknotes and headaches so vicious they each swore never to drink again.

What had surprised Derek the most during their three-day celebration was Alfred's devotion to his fiancée. At least a dozen times each night, he would wax poetic about his betrothed's many charms. He was not always especially coherent when he was deep in his cups, but his fervent admiration was crystal clear as he praised her. How kind and brilliant she was. How beautiful and amiable Leona always proved to be.

It almost made Derek regret what he was doing. But this was the best for everyone.

As the carriage careened down the empty London streets, he wondered what Mabel had been doing these past few days. Had she needed to comfort her sister while they were away? Would she be annoyed that he had caused her so much discomfort, or would she be grateful that he had followed the plan?

Derek doubted he would be met with much excitement upon their return. His mother would undoubtedly be furious with him and his brothers, an unfortunate consequence of the plan, but one he could rectify quickly enough.

Leona, however, would be a different story entirely.

Folding his arms across his chest, he stretched his legs out and closed his eyes as a wave of nausea washed over him. He was in desperate need of a bath and a change of clothes. He also needed a proper night's sleep, one not interrupted by gambling or drinking. But as he rested his eyes, a familiar image popped into his mind, just as it had for the past several nights.

Mabel, dressed in her nightgown, seated next to him at the gaming table. It was a picture he had fought hard to forget. But the memory of her seated next to him, cards shuffling in her hands, and the soothing tone of her voice had lulled him to sleep each night he had spent at the club.

It was ridiculous how much he had been affected by that kiss in the library. Even with a club full of beautiful and willing women, Derek had gone to bed alone, confounded by his desire to remember the taste of Mabel's lips rather than muddle it with a kiss from another.

But he needed to stop. It wouldn't do to keep thinking about his feelings of desire that would only complicate things.

Thankfully, by the time they reached the Trembleys' house, the world had barely woken. He hoped to sneak in and put Alfred to bed before the rest of the household roused, and he was grateful when George appeared.

"My lord?" he asked, coming forward as Derek and Fredrick entered, carrying Alfred.

"Take him to bed, George. And try not to wake anyone."

"Yes, my lord," he said. "Ah, but I think you'd better visit your office."

Derek frowned as he handed off Alfred.

"Why?"

"There's a lady asleep in there," he said as he and Fredrick helped the nearly sleeping Alfred toward the staircase.

Momentarily confused, Derek turned and quickly headed for his office. Upon opening the door, he saw Mabel curled up on a chaise lounge positioned near the window, fast asleep.

Dressed in a nightgown and robe, she looked rather innocent. As if a curse had never dropped from her lips nor an ill thought crossed her mind. Derek wondered if she might have always looked like this before the world had given her such a problematic shake.

While he had always been vocal about his aversion to divorce, he wondered if sometimes it was for the best. Silas had undoubtedly needed to get out of his marriage, and by the sounds of it, Mabel had been delivered her fair share of misery with the comte, as well. Perhaps he had been too judgmental of her and of her past.

Approaching her slowly, Derek raised his hand to her face and brushed a wayward strand of hair away from her cheek. The warmth of her skin beneath his fingertips caused his breath to catch for some reason. She was so perfect in this moment and a part of him desperately wanted to see her in this state of rest for years to come.

But that wouldn't happen. It couldn't.

Letting out a heavy breath, Derek's hand moved to her

shoulder.

"Mabel," he said to her, gently shaking her. "Mabel, wake up, love."

"Mm?" she spoke.

Mabel lifted her head, as if following a tune. Her eyes flittered open, and when she saw Derek, he half expected her to recoil. Only she didn't. Instead, she examined him with such a soft, welcoming smile that he was nearly convinced he had met her in a dream.

"Derek?"

It was the first time she had said his given name, and the way his heart thudded wildly at her sleep-heavy voice was another thing to add to the list of responses to this woman he was going to have to learn to ignore.

"It's late. Or rather, early. You need to return to your room."

"When did you get in?"

"Just a few moments ago."

"Oh." She sniffed the air. "Goodness, you smell like you fell into a bottle of bourbon."

He frowned.

"Yes, I know," he said. She closed her eyes and tried to roll over. "No, no, no. You have to get up. The house is almost waking up."

"What time is it?"

Derek quickly gathered his silver pocket watch out of his coat and clicked it open.

"Nearly six in the morning."

Mabel's brow furrowed.

"Oh goodness, no."

"Yes, now come on. It would be unseemly to be caught down here."

Mabel yawned as she rolled back to face Derek. Lifting her arms, he gathered her hands in his and helped her stand. Derek tried his hardest to ignore her silhouette in the tightly wrapped velvet robe, but it was impossible. His whisper turned husky.

"What are you doing down here anyway?"

"I told you, sleeping evades me at night."

Yes, she had said as much, and once again, Derek found that he was curious as to why. But there was no time to ask about that now. He needed to get her upstairs so that he could wake the house and alert everyone to Alfred's return. Then he could put on an apathetic front.

"Hurry," he whispered, helping her to steady herself on her feet. "You have to get to your bedroom."

She nodded slowly, covering her mouth as she yawned and walked toward the door. She paused and spun to face him.

"Are you coming?"

God, did he want to follow her. But he couldn't.

"No."

Seemingly hearing the depth of that word, Mabel's face took on a strained expression. But she simply nodded before leaving quietly.

Derek stood there, unsure why he felt so suddenly lost.

Chapter Eight

THE RIDE TO the parish of Henley-on-Thames was always a welcome change from the hustle and bustle of London. The ancestorial home of the Trembley family, Boxwood Park, stood on the east bank of the Thames some fifty miles west of the center of London.

It was previously a private hunting ground of Edward the Confessor some seven hundred years earlier. It had belonged to the Trembley family since 1685, when one of Derek's ancestors married the illegitimate daughter of Charles II and his mistress. The deer park had been a gift from the king before his death the same year, along with a generous dowry, which had been used to build Boxwood into the home that it was today.

The country air was a gentle balm to Derek's crumbling conviction. He knew, logically, that his brother would be better off in the future if he ended his engagement to Leona, but the way the wind had left his sails since he and Mabel began their plot had been causing him an uncomfortable notion, one he had little experience with.

Could he be wrong?

Logically, no. It was ridiculous to consider, and yet his brother's mood had changed significantly since the previous day after he had slept off his hangover. He evidently had a bit of a row with Leona, who hadn't appreciated being left behind without any word of when he was going to return. She had explained her expectations about their marriage—but Alfred, being only a man, had not taken too kindly to Leona's domineering tone, or the display of her headstrong side.

Evidently, the two decided to make amends that morning, but there was still a palpable tension in the air that seemed to put everyone on edge, including their mother.

"What's wrong?" she asked Alfred, who was in their carriage on the way to Boxwood Park. "I thought you and Leona made up?"

"We did," Alfred said stonily, gazing out the window.

"And yet you're clearly still upset."

"Mother, as much as I'm sure you have a wealth of advice to give on the topic of relationships, I'd rather not talk about it right now."

The countess's brow arched.

"Oh? Forgive me," she began sarcastically. "I forgot that I was in the company of such learned men. Men who, without anything more than the barest note to inform your family of your whereabouts, disappeared for two days, leaving his fiancée alone to…what? Gamble and drink your days away?"

"Mother—"

"Do not pity yourself, Alfred. Everything that happened was of your own doing."

"It wasn't even my idea," he said, glancing at Derek. "He dragged me out to begin with."

The countess squinted at her other son.

"Yes. Why is that, Derek? You've not behaved so poorly since before your father passed away."

Derek shrugged.

"It was a stag night. Besides, I was feeling nostalgic, I suppose. It won't be long until Alfred here is married and I'll be without either of my brothers to gallivant the night away with—nor do I imagine I'll be able to carouse with anyone else, since everyone I know is getting married and settling down."

"It's not as though Fredrick and I won't still come to the club even after we're wed."

Derek shook his head.

"It will not be the same and you know it. There's no use in denying it."

"Well, perhaps you might consider marrying someone soon as well, then. The earldom does require you to have some offspring, Derek."

"There's plenty of time for that, Mother," Derek said, choosing discretion over bringing up the fact that he would likely not marry for several years. Although the idea had recently been more prominent in his mind. But his mother didn't need to know that. "Besides, all is well. Just explain to Leona that it was my fault."

"I did," Alfred said, lifting his chin.

"Oh." Well, that was quick. "And she didn't believe you?"

"She said it was the sign of an unreliable character to blame others for my actions."

Derek studied Alfred, then also his mother.

"She isn't wrong," Derek admitted. "And rather a clever girl if you ask me."

"Quite right," the countess said with a firm nod. "Nevertheless, you should apologize again to make things right. Maybe give her a token to demonstrate your sincerest regret."

"A token? Like what?"

"A bouquet of sweet pea flowers," Derek said, the words nearly sticking in his throat. "I'm sure any woman would forgive a man who gave her a pretty posy. I believe there are some growing in the potager garden at Boxwood."

"Sweet pea flowers… Do you think that will be enough to satisfy her?"

"Whether it will be enough or not, who knows? But it's worth a try, isn't it?"

Alfred nodded.

"I suppose."

Derek's mother didn't say anything, but he knew she was staring at him intently, and he sensed her gaze on him for the rest of the way to the estate.

When they reached Boxwood Park that afternoon, everyone seemed eager to stretch as they climbed out of their carriages. Leona was instantly set upon by Alfred, who offered her his arm. Derek, meanwhile, was watching Mabel, who was peering up at the large house, her mouth slightly ajar.

Boxwood Park was a red brick building that had begun from a simple base but that had been added on quite a bit during the eighteenth century, with the new additions in a neoclassical style. The hall faced west, as it was situated to look over the water. A series of carefully placed hedgerows framed the vast lawn that had a stunning view of the river Thames.

Derek took great pleasure in seeing Mabel's clear blue eyes widen as they made their way into the foyer. All the floors in Boxwood Park were in a black and white checkered pattern, and the walls were cream-colored and adorned with vast paintings of river scenes. Black marble pillars could be found in most of the grand rooms, such as the ballroom and library, and seasonal flowers filled nearly every vase, as per the countess's standing request for when the family was in residence. Their London home was finely decorated, but there was something about Mabel's assessment about this home that stirred a feeling of pride in Derek. Before he could think too deeply about that, he approached her with the idea to give her a tour himself.

"If you would like, I could show you and your sister around. After luncheon that is."

Mabel gazed up at him, a knowing smile hovering on her lips.

"Do you think that wise?" She glanced around them, her voice lowered. "We wouldn't want to appear too at ease with one another, lest anyone guess at our partnership."

Derek smirked. "I doubt very much that anyone would suspect that we were in each other's confidences. Besides, it might give us a chance to evaluate the situation thus far."

"I suppose that is a good idea," she said as Leona appeared at her side, causing Mabel's expression to shift to one of concern. "Leona, are you well?"

"Actually, I'm feeling a little tired. I may go rest for a bit," Leona said softly. "I think the ride here did not agree with me."

"Oh, dear. Do you wish to go upstairs?"

"No, thank you," she said, facing Derek. "Please, do not let my absence deter you from any activities you may undertake."

Leona smiled briefly before Alfred appeared by her side.

"Here, let me help you," he said, reaching for his fiancée. "I'll show you to your rooms."

"I'm quite able to manage myself, thank you," she said coolly as she moved around him.

Undeterred, he followed her, leaving Mabel and Derek alone at the bottom of the stairs.

"Oh dear," Mabel breathed. "She is not pleased."

"I suppose it's working then," Derek said.

"Yes," she answered, but she didn't sound entirely happy about it.

Derek offered her his arm, and she took it, causing a sense of pleasure to curl through him. He escorted her to the dining room, where a luncheon had been laid out. The meal was a quiet affair, and the fare was excellent—consisting of roasted chicken, freshly baked bread, seasonal vegetables, butter, and jams. Alfred appeared a quarter of an hour later, a satisfied grin on his face. Derek wondered what exactly he was smiling about when his mother stood up.

"I'm going to rest for a bit. The trip always takes it out of me, I'm afraid. Alfred?"

"Yes, Mother?"

"Have you received news from your brother? I don't understand why he couldn't come with us this morning."

"He had a meeting with the Duke of Carberry about breeding one of his thoroughbreds for racing. Have no fear, Fredrick will be here tomorrow with the Combes."

"Very well then," she said, shaking her head. "Why he needs to involve himself in such a silly pursuit, I'll never know."

"He has a talent for it."

"I hope he does—otherwise, his fixation will make him look like a fool," she said, turning to the rest of them. "Now if you'll excuse me."

The countess left as Derek and Alfred stood. Mabel took one last sip of her tea before also standing.

"Now to go out and find a dozen or so sweet peas," Alfred said. "Excuse me."

With a nod, Alfred disappeared, leaving Derek and Mabel alone once more.

"He seemed rather pleased with himself when he came in," Mabel said. "I wonder why."

"Well, hopefully the posy of sweet peas will throw off whatever reconciliation has settled between them."

"Yes," she said, and again, her tone sounded vexed. He glanced at her.

"I hope you are not having second thoughts about our plan. It's for the best, Mabel. Truly."

"Yes. Yes, I know that, it's just…" But she shook her head. "Never mind."

Derek understood her apprehension. It felt odd trying to wedge Leona and Alfred apart, mainly because of how genuine they were with one another. But Derek and Mabel had a plan, and it was for everyone's betterment in the long run.

"Come," he said, offering her his arm.

They began the tour in the portrait gallery—a long, wood-paneled hallway set in the west wing of the house. At the end of the hallway, two large French doors were kept open on fine days so that a gentle breeze could waft down the narrow space.

Hundreds of paintings hung from the walls, including dozens of Trembley family members. Derek eagerly explained the history of each and every family member as well as their family's lineage of being descendants of a royal mistress, unsure why he wished for Mabel to know. But he *was* relieved to note that his stories seemed to dissipate her melancholy state.

"A mistress? How shocking," she said mockingly.

"It is," he replied, noting the warm humor that shone in her eyes. "Are you amused by it?"

"I am. To think, the beginning of your line was because of a love affair. It makes me think a little better of you because of it."

"Really?" he asked, examining the portrait. "I always thought it was something to be, if not ashamed of, then at least apologetic."

"But why?"

"Well, most peers come by their titles from their ancestors' gallant accomplishments. Battles fought and won, services provided to the crown, that sort of thing."

"I think it was gallant of the king to give his children titles. It was his way of supporting them."

"Yes, but there's always the connotation of the land and title being a consolation prize in lieu of being in line to the throne."

"Had you been in line to the throne, my grandfather would have been treasonous against yours," she said with a wink, which caused him to laugh.

The referral to the war with the colonies was a valid point.

"I suppose so."

"Would you really wish to be in line for the throne? It seems such a heavy burden to bear. I think ruling would be a dreadful thing to have to do."

Derek shrugged.

"Dreadful or not, it would be my duty."

Mabel's eyes lifted to study one vast portrait. Derek glanced up as well. It was a family in a natural setting, with several children and a severe-looking man and woman. They were outfitted in court garb from the English Civil War period.

The severity of these paintings always made Derek somewhat uncomfortable. No one appeared happy. By contrast, he remembered how his mother always insisted that they smile when their portraits were being painted. She didn't like the harsh faces of the past either and always beamed herself so that she might be remembered as a happy woman.

"It seems much better to be outside of that world," Mabel continued, bringing him back to the present. "No choice is your own. Every minute of your day is planned out. Countless people depend on you, need you. You must be present at all times."

She seemed to trail off at that moment, and Derek glanced at her. The curiosity he had toward her had grown three-fold in the past few days, and he couldn't stop himself before asking, "May I ask you something?"

"Of course."

"What was your life like, when you were married?"

Silence followed. The question had certainly caught Mabel off guard. But whether she would answer him honestly or fend him off with a vague answer remained to be seen.

"It was a marriage," she said vaguely. "No different than any other, I suppose."

She was electing for a vague answer then. That was a pity.

"No different?" he repeated, his voice skeptical.

She shrugged lightly. "Perhaps a little different, but who's to say? I'm not sure what goes on in other marriages. My parents' marriage wasn't like mine and I suppose I always took their relationship as the standard."

"And what exactly led to your divorce?"

She glanced at him.

"Why are you so curious?"

"Because I am." Mabel squinted at him, as if she was weighing his sincerity. He sought to reassure her. "You don't have to tell me if it is unpleasant to recall."

"I'm actually rather indifferent to it."

"Then?"

Mabel gave him a speculative glance before nodding.

"Very well. I didn't leave for frivolous reasons, if you must know. I know how the papers have made it sound. They've made me out to be a right devil. But I assure you, I tried very hard to stay in that marriage."

Derek remained silent until she sighed.

"Very well. I met my husband in Philadelphia just before my official coming out. He was terribly handsome, well-groomed, and attentive. He spoke several languages and was rumored to be a great-grandnephew of General Lafayette. He was welcomed into every home of prestige in Philadelphia, ours included." Her attention drifted to the ground. "I was so taken with him, as was everyone, that I fell in love with him at first sight.

"I assume he relished that I said yes so quickly to his proposal. I was thrilled to have won his heart—or rather, I *believed* I had won it. He was quick to tell me he loved me, but then he was quick to say a great many things, most of which were untrue. His name and his title were real, but everything else?" She shook her head. "He was so terribly indebted, he and his family, that the only way they could get out from beneath their debts was to marry an heiress. He knew that in America, he would be far enough from his creditors that he could pass himself off as a wealthy man without anyone calling him out on his lies. Moreover, he knew that we would be impressed with his title and his heritage—and in that, he was quite correct. My father was more than happy to make the match, and I was the envy of everyone I knew. Meanwhile, my very large dowry was transferred to him the moment we wed.

"His attitude toward me changed drastically as soon as we left Philadelphia, on the ship to France after the wedding. I'm not fond of water, and had a terrible time on the ship. I thought he might stay in our cabin, to comfort me but…"

She shook her head as if the memory pained her. Derek wasn't sure why, but the image of Mabel, alone and scared in a tiny ship cabin, made him irrationally angry.

"It was my own fault, I know that now," she said quickly, recovering. "With no mother to advise me, I didn't know that husbands preferred their wives away from them. Particularly when they became ill. I suppose I shouldn't have expected so much from him." She paused, her gaze unfocused as if she was peering into the past, revisiting her memories. "You know, he was repulsed by me the first time we laid together. He couldn't stand the sight of blood, and he made me swear never to go near him when my courses started."

Mabel froze as soon as the words were spoken, snapping her mouth shut. It was beyond crass to mention something so private, but it seemed she had forgotten who she was speaking to. Either way she blushed crimson and in spite of the growing loathing Derek was feeling toward her former husband, he couldn't help but appreciate how well the flush on her cheeks suited her. She peeked up at him nervously, as if she expected to be scolded for mentioning something as outrageous and inappropriate as her monthlies in front of a man. But he wasn't deterred by the realities of womanhood, and he waited for her to continue.

"I realize now that it was my fault. I should have realized that being sick in front of him would make me unattractive to him."

"He sounds like a bloody idiot," Derek muttered, which for some reason made Mabel smile.

"Actually, Pascal quite prided himself on his cleverness. Or at least, he liked to believe he was more intelligent than others. It gave him particular pleasure to make others appear foolish."

"He should have stayed with you, if you were sick."

"No. It wasn't a pretty thing to watch—"

"What sort of fool would expect anyone to be attractive when they're ill? He was your husband and as such, he should have protected you, if nothing else, consoled you when you were ailing. It was not good of him to abandon you."

Mabel shook her head again as if agreeing with him would somehow break the conclusion she had come to about men. Still, she continued.

"It didn't get any better once we landed. We travelled east to his family estate, which I soon discovered wasn't the grand castle that he had described. Or rather, it might have been at one time, but it had not been well maintained over the years. What I saw was a dilapidated medieval castle with a leaking roof, drafty rooms, and moldy, moth-eaten furnishings. It also happened to be crowded with a great deal of family that all thought very little of me. I spoke some French, but whether I spoke it correctly or not, I cannot claim to know, because they never acknowledged me."

"They ignored you?"

Mabel shrugged, but also nodded.

"That wasn't the worst of it though. Upon arriving, Pascal introduced me to my lady's maid, Yvette. I thought I might gain a friend for a moment, but it wasn't long before I realized that she was Pascal's lover, positioned as my maid so that she could serve as a spy and make sure that I didn't inform my father or sister about the conditions in France. I was devastated at his infidelity, of course, but I was not yet ready to give up on my marriage. I took my vows seriously and believed that I could win his heart if I just wanted it enough." She let out a sad *harrumph*. "Wasn't I pathetic?"

"No," he said firmly, but she didn't seem to hear him.

"For a while, he let me believe I was succeeding in winning his affections. I don't know why he bothered with the lie, unless it was to enjoy my devastation when he revealed the truth all over again. He would always wait until I had sunk low enough to beg for his love, and then he'd snatch it away and tell me how pitiful I was. And I was."

"It's not pitiful to be a devoted wife."

Mabel's shoulder lifted and dropped again.

"Whether it is or not, who knows? But I did stop caring eventually. The scullery maid, Juliette began to attend me once Pascal and Yvette's relationship was exposed and she stopped even pretending to be my maid. I was very lucky to have Juliette. She was married to one of Pascal's servants, a brutish man named Jean. He was just as cruel to Juliette as Pascal was to me. I suppose that's why we became such fast confidants.

"With time, I was finally able to find the strength to realize that my marriage was never going to get better. Pascal was never going to love me. And if I wanted to have a good life, it would only be possible if I got far away from him." She paused before adding, "I guess that's why I'm not particularly interested when people tell me that I should have stayed and worked on my marriage. I did everything I could to please him, to get his family to respect me. But after a year I realized that nothing I did would bring them to care for me. So, I told him I was going to leave."

Derek tried not to appear so affected by her story, but he was sure he failed.

"What did he do?"

"He flew into a rage. He berated me. Told me he would lock me away before he would allow me to embarrass him. That he'd rather see me dead than leave. I was able to calm him down by promising not to go anywhere. What he didn't know was that I had already made up my mind and I was determined. I began plotting my escape. Juliette happened upon me during the night I left, and she begged to come with me. She helped me make my way back to Nantes and we took the first ship to America. It was an awful experience. It rained nearly every day for weeks. I was sick the entire time. By the time I reached Philadelphia, my father almost closed the door on me because he didn't recognize me, I had become so gaunt. Once he realized it was me, he brought me in and called a doctor. He proceeded to file for divorce on my behalf."

Derek was quiet as he absorbed all her information. What a horrific experience. He had half a mind to travel to France at once and beat her former spouse to a bloody pulp.

"Dreadful, isn't it?" she said, her tone tinged with humor as she smirked. "Yes, I suppose it is. But I'm not one to wallow. I never was. So, for a few months I licked my wounds, and nursed my bruised pride until I became the woman you see today." She lifted her hands up, as if to show herself to him. "Too brazen to care about people's opinions, not demure enough to win over anyone. But safe."

"Safe?" he asked. She nodded slowly. "You mean, safe from him?"

"No. I mean safe in the sense that I am alone, and no one can hurt me." Her smile was tinged with sadness.

Derek watched her, noting the melancholy behind her words. He realized that Mabel's flippant nature seemed to emerge most strongly when she spoke of unfortunate things. It seemed to be her way of distancing herself from all that tragedy.

"I'm sorry."

"You needn't be. It's not your fault—"

"No, I'm not speaking of your divorce," he said, halting. "I'm sorry I judged you for it."

Mabel's eyes widened, and her mouth fell open slightly, appearing more startled than anything.

"Excuse me?"

"What I mean to say is, I don't blame you for it. I know marriage can be difficult. Or at least, I assume it can be. I've witnessed it in friends and family. I always expected whatever hardships were found there, that they could be mended, but I suppose that would only work if both persons were willing to do the work to fix it."

Mabel closed her mouth and bobbed her head in acknowledgment, almost too stunned for words. Suddenly uncomfortable, Derek cleared his throat.

"Come. I'd like to show you the fish folly."

Mabel silently followed Derek to an ornamental brick building with several open breezeways. It was only partly visible because of the wood and scaffolding encircling it that was presently being taken apart by several workers.

Some of the men—the bricklayers—wore leather aprons over brown pants and white linen shirts, and most of their fronts were covered in red dirt. The decorative bullnose that wrapped around the steeple of the folly spiraled up to the spire. It was as if a giant had come along and twisted the top half of the ornamental building.

"My, what talent," Mabel murmured as two men carrying a ladder walked past her to load it into a horse-drawn cart. "How did they get it to twist like that?"

"They used red builder bricks. They're fired at a lower temperature for longer in the kiln so they're baked rather than burnt, like most bricks," he said, picking up a broken one from a pile. He lifted it and broke it in half. "They're far softer than regular bricks and therefore can be cut to very specific proportion, allowing for the twisting effect."

"But wouldn't it melt away then or something? Crumble from the elements?"

"It might if it weren't for the sealant that gets put on it once it has been fitted into its shape," he said, tossing the broken brick back into the pile. "These men are just finishing up. I had hoped for it to be finished before the regatta and I dare say it will be."

"But the regatta is tomorrow."

"Yes, but it should be finished by tonight. I'll probably be down here inspecting it all evening to make sure it's ready for tomorrow," he said as he pointed upriver. "You will be able to see the rowers start from a little way upstream. Because we're one of the homes to line the river, it's our custom to host a Wanderers party."

"A what?"

"A Wanderers party. Crowds cheer on the rowers and some people try to follow them all the way from start to finish. It's become a bit of a custom to offer Wanderers food and drink as they go. Of course, a proper ball will be held later and only invited guests will attend that."

"I see. That all sounds rather charming."

"I'm glad you think so."

Mabel smiled at him and to Derek's surprise, it made him feel rather breathless to be on the receiving end of such a sight.

"I think I should like to rest now," she said, glancing back at the house.

"Let me escort you."

They returned to the house, Derek feeling like he was walking on unstable ground. Everything he had learned about Mabel had surprised him, yet he wanted to know more. He was nearly desperate to hear her speak when they reached the house, but when she turned to him, his mind went blank.

"Thank you for the tour," she said.

He nodded at her as she climbed the stairs up to her rooms, leaving Derek unsure why he felt so empty without her company.

Chapter Nine

Mabel had been lucky enough to be put in a bedroom with two large bay windows overlooking the river, fitted with alcove benches. Sunshine was the theme, as the bedding, lounges, and wallpaper were all shades of yellow. It was a rather cheerful space, but Mabel couldn't help but be disengaged as she toyed with the king of hearts from her deck of cards.

Placing the card back down onto the top of the deck, Mabel continued to fidget. Her index finger pushed into the center of the deck as her middle and ring fingers held one side in place, then her thumb pulled back, causing the cards to flutter against her palm.

She was struggling to stay focused on her sister as she listened to Leona go on and on about Alfred.

"—I couldn't believe that he had followed me into the garden, but then he said he was desperate to speak with me. He said that he couldn't stand that he had made me so upset and promised to spend a lifetime making it up to me," Leona recounted, smiling. She was leaning against the wardrobe, gaze lifted to the ceiling as she rocked slowly back and forth. "It really was the most romantic thing anyone has ever said."

"I'm sure it was, my dear."

"Oh, I'm so glad I've decided to forgive him."

"Have you?"

"Yes, although I haven't told him that yet. I think I'll tell him tomorrow, during the regatta." Leona gave a light little laugh and then pushed off from the wardrobe. "How was your tour with the earl?"

"Oh, fine, I suppose," Mabel said, putting her brush on the table.

"Just fine?"

"Yes," she said. Leona frowned. "What is it?"

"Hmm? Oh nothing. It's just... Alfred and I were speaking earlier and... No, really, it's nothing."

Leona hurried toward the door.

"Wait, Leona," Mabel said, standing up. "Tell me what were you speaking about."

"Well," she said, dropping her gaze. "It's just, we both thought you two might have found some common ground. You know, you were so hesitant to befriend him when we first came here, but lately, you seem to be getting along better."

Mabel couldn't tell her sister precisely what she and the earl had in common. Instead, she shrugged and Leona leaned her back against the door.

"Have no fear, my dear," Mabel said. "The earl and I will maintain civility while we're in each other's company."

Leona's smile widened.

"I'm very glad to hear it. You know, Alfred told me that you would have a permanent invitation to stay with the Trembleys whenever you wish to visit. He said he understood what it was like to be away from his family, particularly what it was like to be separated from his siblings and, well, he wanted to make sure that you knew you were always welcome. And now that you and the earl have become friendly, maybe it will be easier for you to visit."

The grain of guilt Mabel had been experiencing seemed to grow into a pall-mall-sized ball. While she firmly believed that Leona would be better off back home in Philadelphia, Mabel couldn't squelch a growing worry that perhaps that opinion was driven more by what *she* wanted rather than precisely what Leona needed. The longer she spent in her sister's company, the more unsure she became of what would be best.

She wondered if Derek felt the same.

"That is a very kind thing for Alfred to say."

"Oh, but he didn't just say it. He meant it. Alfred cares about you just as much as I do."

Mabel pushed the uncomfortable feeling of being cared for out of her heart.

"It's getting late, dear," Mabel said.

"Oh, of course." Leona turned and opened the door. "Goodnight, Mabel."

"Goodnight," she replied as she closed the door behind her sister.

Well, if that wasn't enough to make her question everything about her arrangement with Derek, she didn't know what would. Why did Alfred have to be so accommodating and caring? It was enough to make her question whether it was right to tear Leona away from someone so sweet and kind.

No. She wasn't just questioning—she knew. It wasn't right to separate them. It wasn't right at all.

Sighing, Mabel walked toward the window bench, and sat on the yellow silk cushions and bolster pillows as she gazed out the pane glass. The last of the laborers were leaving, packing up their carts with tools and whatnot. She could see Derek, in a waistcoat and shirt sleeves, inspecting the bricks himself as the last of the light from the workers' oil lamps faded, leaving him in darkness.

For a moment, she thought about going down to speak with him. She couldn't ignore this growing fear that she wasn't doing right by her sister and Alfred. She wanted to stop meddling in their affairs, and she resolved to tell Derek as much.

As the last of the workers waved to the earl before leaving, Mabel decided to confront him. Standing up, she wrapped herself in her aubergine robe and quickly left her room.

It was nearing midnight, and most everyone had retired early to prepare for tomorrow's festivities, so the household was fast asleep. Without making any sound, Mabel hurried down the stairs, halting abruptly as she heard footsteps. Twisting quickly around the baluster, she ducked out of sight as a pair of footmen marched across the foyer. Once they had disappeared into the dining room, Mabel continued toward the front door and exited the house.

The midsummer night air was warm and comforting as she crossed the drive to the lawn. She knew that it wasn't terribly clever to go traipsing around an unfamiliar property at night, but she couldn't help herself. She needed to speak with Derek immediately.

The moon was full and low in the sky, shining a good amount of light across the grass as she walked down to the small bridge that led into the folly.

Derek was leaning against one of the brick pillars, gazing up as if he were trying to spot something. His shirtsleeves had since been folded up over his forearms, and Mabel ignored the simmering heat that coursed through her at the sight of them.

When he glanced at her, he started at first to look away again before doing a double take when recognition struck. Smiling, even with his brow knit together, he cocked his head to the left.

"Mabel? What are you doing here?" he asked, pulling out his pocket watch. Leaning his hand out of the shadows, he read the face in the moonlight. "It's nearly midnight."

"I wanted to speak with you."

"It couldn't wait until tomorrow?"

"No, unfortunately. I believe it's something that cannot be delayed." Derek folded his arms across his broad chest, and Mabel made a point not to let her gaze linger on his exposed forearms. "It's just that... Are you feeling, maybe, a little guilty about what we're doing?"

He frowned.

"Guilty? No, not really."

"You don't?" she asked again, shifting from one foot to the

other, unsure. "You aren't at all ashamed of all our meddling?"

"Meddling? I wouldn't call it that."

"No?" she asked. "I think trying to break two people apart may be the definition of meddling."

Realization appeared on his face.

"Oh, you're speaking about Leona and Alfred? Well then, yes, I suppose I have felt somewhat guilty about it, but it's what we decided what was best, wasn't it?"

Mabel shook her head.

"Yes, but I don't know if I'm doing it for the right reasons. I think perhaps we were too quick to judge Leona and Alfred's relationship by our own wishes. When you look at them together, without any preconceptions in the way, it's clear that they are quite devoted to one another."

"They are," he said, unfolding his arms as he approached her. "But I thought we decided that separating them was for the better?"

"Yes, but, well… I think I've changed my mind."

"Have you?"

"Yes," she said, moving past him to scan across the river. A handsome white stone estate sat across the water on the opposite bank. "It's just, from what I've witnessed, Alfred seems perfectly capable of keeping Leona happy. And as much as I'd rather have her return to Philadelphia, I'm almost positive that if I was able to bring that about, she would be miserable."

"Leona does seem to bring out the best in Alfred."

She twisted back to face him.

"Then perhaps we should resign our attempts at separating them."

Derek nodded slowly.

"I suppose you're right. I don't relish the thought of Alfred being hurt if he is not able to marry Leona. Besides, my mother is rather fond of her."

Mabel smirked.

"Yes, I noticed that too."

"Very well then," he said. "We will dissolve our previous agreement."

Mabel stuck out her hand, and Derek took it after a moment. The warmth of his fingers wrapped around hers nearly caused her to shiver. When she glimpsed up, she saw that the humor floating at the edge his lips had disappeared. His face was solemn now, and the hairs on the back of Mabel's neck begin to stand up.

Just then, a tremor went through his hand, and he dropped hers immediately as if to hide it. Considering that they were alone and rather more coconspirators now than acquaintances, Mabel wanted him to know that the shaking of his hands did not bother her.

"I don't think anyone else notices it," she said softly, uncertain how he might respond. Would he be upset with her for bringing it up? But she felt it needed to be said, even if it *did* upset him at first. "Your hands, I mean." Evidently, he was stunned, for he just gaped at her. She swallowed before continuing. "It's not noticeable, it what I meant to say."

He stayed silent as an uncomfortable flush of embarrassment crawled up her spine. She shouldn't have said anything. It was apparent he didn't want to discuss it, and yet—

"*You* noticed it."

Mabel's mind raced to try and think of something clever or witty. Something charming that would deflect from the moment. Something that might make him laugh and put him at ease at the same time, but all she could say was, "Yes."

"So, it is noticeable."

"Oh, no," she said quickly. "No one else seems to even notice your hands when it starts and if they do, you're rather quick at hiding it." She paused. "Is it... Do you know what causes it?"

Derek shook his head.

"No."

Mabel's hand came up to her head as she silently scolded herself. She had no right to ask him such a question.

"I'm sorry. It was unkind of me to ask."

"No," he said. "It's all right, I suppose. I've just never discussed it out loud."

"Not even with your mother?"

"My mother?" he asked before realization dawned on him. "Oh. Because she gets it as well? No. My mother's tremors seem to come on during anxious times for her. But my own never come during one particular time or another—at least, not that I've noticed. It happens when I'm annoyed, or happy, or excited. Even when I'm tired." He inhaled and exhaled slowly. "There seems no rhyme or reason for it."

"Oh."

"Yes," he said, gazing up.

The profile of his face was outlined in moonlight, and the line of his jaw was predominantly severe. Mabel nearly bit her lip as she strained to keep herself from giving in to the urge to touch it. Instead, she gave him an uncomfortable smile. She needed to escape him immediately, or she might find herself in a dangerous predicament.

"Well then," she said, dipping her chin. "Good evening."

But before she could walk past him, his hand touched her elbow, and she stilled.

A warm, near-tangible electricity vibrated between them. They both seemed to breathe momentarily, acutely aware of the heat between them. When Mabel lifted her gaze, Derek leaned forward with deliberate slowness while she remained perfectly still.

She racked her brain searching for something to say, but as the seconds dragged on, no words came to mind. Mabel's heart hammered within her chest, unsure why he had stopped her if he had nothing to say. She nearly pulled away when his hand came up and, for the briefest of moments, touched her cheek.

Like a thread snapping, all clear thinking evaporated as Mabel leaned in and kissed him. The moment their lips touched, Mabel was flooded with the same familiar, intoxicating sensation that had swallowed her the first time they kissed.

Mabel's hand rose against the side of his head, and her fingertips barely grazed his scalp as she scratched through his hair, causing him to shiver. His fingers tightened on her wrist, and the sharp intake of breath from her mouth at the corner of his lips made his solid body press against hers. It was outrageous, and yet she could sense the demanding need of his body. She deepened her kiss, her tongue swiping against his. He shifted, and her body pressed against the railing of the folly, pinned there by his weight and his strength.

Derek's mouth drifted downward as Mabel gasped out. His lips trailed over the length of her neck as his free hand drifted upward. The one holding her wrist raised it gently, pinning her arm over her head while his other hand drifted slowly over her breast. Mabel let out a shaky breath and arched her back as if begging for his touch, and blessingly, he complied.

Slowly, he fingered the edge of her robe, moving up and down with excruciating deliberateness. He peeled back the silk only to tease the peak of her breast through the thin fabric of her night rail. Mabel's skin was hot and aching, and the utter torment of his determined, unhurried movements caused her to growl. It was as if he thought he might miss something, causing Mabel to become desperate. She didn't need the gentle touch of an experienced man to carefully lead her toward orgasm.

She knew what she wanted.

"Derek, please," she said. "Faster."

"Not for all the stars in the sky."

She exhaled.

"This is torture. I'm not some young miss who needs you to waste time with—"

"My love, you speak as if this wasn't something to savor," he said as his head dipped. "I'd pay a fortune to be allowed to spend forever watching you squirm like this."

"Please," she breathed as his hot breath skimmed her nipple through the cloth. "Derek, please."

"Yes," he murmured softly. "My god, is there anything lovelier than your pleas?"

"Derek..."

Without warning, Derek's mouth fell to her breast, his wet mouth soaking the fabric as he sucked. Mabel's entire body quaked as his teeth toyed with her, lightly nibbling on her flesh beneath the nightgown.

What torture, yet what bliss. Every moment, every breath in his presence was exquisite, and he refused to hurry that which he seemed to feel demanded his meticulous attention.

"Derek," she moaned softly as his hand drifted lower between them. "Ah, we, shouldn't..."

"Do you want this?" he asked, as she began to shake in his arms.

"I... Yes..."

Evidently, that was all he needed to hear. Derek suddenly lifted her up and pushed her against the brick column while simultaneously bending his head to take the tip of her breast into his mouth to taste her more thoroughly. Though he didn't hold all of her body weight up, she was decidedly higher as he no longer had to bend his neck.

Her arms wrapped around his head, holding her tight as he feasted upon her. He changed between sucking and nibbling, and her erratic breathing only seemed to fuel him more. She ran her fingers through his hair, pulled and pressed him against her chest as her hips bucked forward, other parts of her wantonly desperate for his touch.

The need for him, as well as the desire, scorched her inhibitions as she released her hold on him. She slipped to her feet, several inches lower than she had been, but then he dropped lower and lower. His palms smoothed around the flare of her hips through her thin, muslin nightgown until he was on one knee, touching her ankles. Mabel's mood swung from disappointment to confusion to sheer shock.

"Derek, we can't—"

"Hush," he commanded.

"But—"

"Mabel, I cannot possibly live another day on this earth without tasting you. And I intend to do so, right this minute."

Her mouth dropped open at his words, and she knew in that instant that she would never forget this image of him, bathed in moonlight, mouth agape and eyes wide with equal parts need and desire.

Gathering the hem of her nightgown in his hands, he pushed up. Finding the part between her draws, he slowly, almost reverently, kissed her as her entire body jumped. Mabel hadn't ever experienced this sort of tenderness. He tasted her, licking deeply as she twitched and squirmed. One hand pressed against her hip bone, pinning Mabel's lower half against the brick column, while the other hand came underneath her, where her buttocks met her leg, and held her still as he continued to consume her.

Almost immediately, she began to shake, and then cry out. Surprisingly, she wasn't terribly worried about how loud she was. She had no fear of being heard, as her world had shrunk to this fish folly. The taste of his mouth still lingered on her lips, and her heart seemed to beat with the idea that this man would devour her. Every inch of him, every flavor, every word he spoke, was hers, and satisfaction rolled through her at his ability to make her squeak.

"Derek!" she cried, her body chasing a need that would not stop until it was fulfilled. "Yes! Please, yes."

A mighty swarm of pleasure swept through her as her body involuntarily clenched. Derek only deepened his fingers and maddeningly licked at every drop as her orgasm broke.

Moments, minutes, or months could have passed before Derek wrapped his arms around her thighs. When her limp body sagged against the column behind her, he squeezed around her legs before he drew away and came up off of his knees. When she saw him, dark hair rumpled, lips lustrous in the moonlight, she sighed. Never had a man been so tantalizing, and she was desperate to taste him as he had tasted her, to share all the wild need she had for him.

He stepped forward, looking as if he intended to have more of her, when the gentle sound of clanking, like tin on glass, caught his attention. Mabel barely heard it as she gave him the tiniest of smiles. She hadn't been bashful in years, and yet, beneath his intent and hungry gaze, she almost felt like a virgin again.

"That was—"

The clanging noise sounded again, and the lustful gaze he gave her cooled into something more alert. His brow pinched together.

"What was that?"

He put his hand to her mouth and shook his head as he surveyed the area around them. The moon was bright, but there were no signs of activity around the folly save the rushing water of the river. Mabel pushed off the column and squinted, gazing into the dark as Derek's hand came up from behind her to caress her cheek.

Mabel crooked her neck to press a kiss against his fingertips. His attention was temporarily on her, and it unnerved her how endearing she found it. But then he held his index finger to his lips as he gazed back over the water. Squinting, she doubted he would be able to see much, even with the moon so bright, and twisted again to see if she could see anything. Shadows stretched out from beneath the trees across the yard of Lord Nesby's property.

"What is it?" she whispered. "Do you see something?"

But he didn't answer. Shaking his head, he stared at her.

"No. But I did hear something."

"Me too," she said. "Maybe it was something in the river?"

"Maybe," he said as the wind blew. "Either way, to continue here would be dangerous. We should go inside."

"Oh," she said, somewhat disappointed. "I thought we might…"

"Yes, I did too," he said, gazing down at her. "But I'm afraid I let myself get carried away by the moment."

"I didn't mind."

Derek smirked.

"No, neither did I," he said. "But heaven forbid someone did see us," he said as the weight of that reality began to sink in. "You would not be pleased with the outcome of such a scandal."

"Nor would you," she said, almost too quickly in response.

Of course, she knew what the end result would be if they were caught. He'd be honor-bound to marry her—and even she, as brazen as she was, would have to accept his proposal, or she'd never be accepted in decent society again. She had vowed that she would never wed again…and yet for some reason, she couldn't quite reconcile with herself that marriage between them was the worst thing that could happen. Still pushing the idea out of her mind, she spoke again.

"You're right. We should not take any further risks. We would not want to cause any trouble for Leona and your brother, now that we've both consented to them marrying."

"No, especially considering what it would mean for your sister."

Mabel frowned.

"My sister?" she repeated. "Why especially her?" If there was a scandal, surely it would subject *both* of their families to gossip and derision.

"You know that it is the lady in these cases who is always the subject of the most speculation," he said, his tone even. "Leona would be the sister of a fallen woman."

"Fallen?" she repeated, evidently annoyed. "I'm not an innocent. I've been married before. Have known the touch of a man."

Though she said it matter-of-factly, Derek's mouth set in a hard line. It was almost as if he disliked being reminded of that fact. Whatever his reasons, Mabel didn't appreciate his reaction to it.

"Yes, but that hardly allows one to do what we just did out in the open."

"I wasn't the only one participating," she said, pointing her finger into his chest. "You, however—"

He encased her finger in his hand.

"Easy, love. There is nothing here that I regret. I only think we should go inside."

Mabel bit the inside of her cheek, conflicted. She didn't regret anything either, but the highhandedness of his remarks irked her.

As they approached the front door, a pair of stable hands came across the drive. Before she knew what was happening, Mabel was swept up in Derek's arms and hauled out of sight. In an instant, she was pressed against the hedge as the two stable hands laughed, their voices fading away as they walked, oblivious to the presence of their master mere steps away.

When they were well away, Derek released her, and Mabel stumbled slightly, only to grip his forearm. She couldn't quite settle why she had become suddenly unsure of their situation, but when they reached the house, Mabel left his presence as quickly as she could, without so much as a goodbye. She turned toward the staircase and climbed the steps to the second floor, leaving Derek behind.

Chapter Ten

THE WEATHER ON the day of the regatta was perfect as puffy white clouds rolled lazily by a blue sky and the sun shined. The air was almost abuzz with excitement as guests arrived at Boxwood Park. As Mabel dressed in her favorite amethyst colored gown, she couldn't keep a cheeky smirk off her face. It was one of those mornings where anything felt possible, and she was wholly ready to meet the day.

The countess's ability to procure blooms in quantities that should not have been feasible had extended to the country as the whole house was covered in a sea of colorful petals. It was as if every available flower in the county had been delivered that morning as the staff hurried around the house, preparing for the guests that would arrive momentarily. Luncheon would be provided outdoors during the race, and the regatta ball would be held later that night. It would be a grand affair, and some of the Trembleys' closest friends began to arrive just after breakfast to try and get a premium spot in the fish folly to watch the race.

The Combes and the Bairnsdales arrived within an hour of each other around noon. The duke and duchess were, of course, accompanied by Violet and Fredrick, dressed in their best day clothes; Mabel peered down from her room, watching them exit their carriages.

"It's a lovely day, isn't it?" she asked her sister, whose hair was plaited and pinned into an intricate style.

The wistfulness of Mabel's tone, however, seemed to catch her sister's attention.

"Lovely? You haven't described any days in this country as lovely."

"Well, today seems to be the first one," Mabel replied with a shrug, moving around the room. "The heat has diminished since leaving the city and this really is beautiful country. I think being on the banks of a river has helped."

"Indeed," Leona said, turning back to the mirror so her maid could finish her hair. "Well, hopefully, today will be better than yesterday, though it is not off to a very promising start."

"Why, whatever do you mean? Were we not just agreeing that it's a lovely day?"

Leona managed a weak smile. "It *is* lovely, but I'm afraid my mood is not similarly bright. Alfred brought me a bouquet of sweet peas this morning," she said, shaking her head. "I can't believe he would be so careless. Particularly after I told him how much I detest them."

"Did you?" Mabel asked, her voice slightly high.

"Yes."

"Well, I'm sure it was just an oversight," Mabel began, hoping to rectify the situation. "I believe I heard the earl say that Boxwood Park is quite famous for their sweet pea blooms. Yes, I think he even suggested to Alfred that a posy would be a thoughtful gesture."

"That may be so, but even if it was the earl's suggestion, Alfred should have told him my dislike for them. And don't think I'm not aware of what this lack of attentiveness to my tastes and preferences might signal."

Guilt dropped into Mabel's stomach.

"What is that?"

"Just what you've always told me. That when a man stops listening, trouble is afoot. After this and abandoning us for three whole nights, I have begun to question if we are suited for one another."

Shame bubbled within Mabel's chest at her sister's confession. After realizing that Leona and Alfred's relationship was genuine and that Mabel's own selfish wants had clouded her vision of their happiness, she had hoped her and Derek's meddling would pass without consequence. But had they been too late in calling off their agreement? Had they already done too much damage to the relationship of their siblings?

"And yet," Leona started again, gaining Mabel's attention. "The only dream I have of a life without him is a nightmare. I do love him so, but I fear I'm perhaps the only one who feels so deeply."

"There, there," Mabel said, coming to her side. "I'm sure he loves you equally. These past few days have merely been a hiccup of sorts."

Leona peeked up at her sister.

"Do you really think so?"

Mabel bobbed her head earnestly.

"Yes, of course. And I'm sure from this day forward, Alfred will be nothing less than perfect when it comes to your relationship."

Leona stood up.

"How can you be so sure?"

Mabel couldn't tell her it was because she and Derek wouldn't be interfering anymore. Instead, she only smiled brightly.

"Because, I just am."

"I don't know what I would do without you, Mabel. I'm so grateful you are here. And I dread the day you'll leave for good."

Mabel gave her a tight hug before releasing her as they left her room. As much as she would miss her sister, she realized that returning to the States was the only thing she could do, particularly after last night.

As much as she hated the thought of leaving her sister behind, Mabel knew the only place Derek Trembley belonged was an ocean away from her. She simply wouldn't be able to help herself otherwise. No. She would take her leave the day after her sister was married.

Yet, as she followed her sister down the staircase to greet the Combes and the Bairnsdales, she wondered if she would be able to forget him, even once they were far apart. Every memory she had of the earl seemed to be her favorite thing to replay at night, and she worried she would never truly rid herself of Derek's image.

Shaking the thought from her mind, Mabel greeted the duke and duchess.

"Your graces," she said with a low curtsy. "A pleasure to see you again."

"I wish you wouldn't stand on formalities," Clara said, coming forward. She took Mabel and Leona by the arm, coming between the two. "We are nearly family. Come, let me introduce you both to everyone."

"Oh, um, perhaps just Leona should go with you," Mabel tried to pull away.

"Why is that?"

"Well, she's going to be a part of this world very shortly and I think she should be the center of attention." Mabel waved her free hand in the air. "I think it would be good for her."

"But aren't you going to be with her? Where are you going?" Clara asked.

"I'll be returning to America just after the wedding takes place."

The duchess's face fell slightly.

"So soon?"

"Yes. My father is expecting me to return promptly with a full report of Leona's happiness," Mabel said.

"Still, that shouldn't deter you from meeting everyone. On the contrary, it would help fill out your report to him. Come."

Without a viable excuse to remove herself from introductions, Mabel allowed the duchess to escort her out of the house and down the broad front steps of Boxwood. Across the drive, in between the curved hedgerows, were several blue and white striped tents set up by the servants.

Elegant ladies and gentlemen, dressed in their absolute best day clothes, mingled, and glided across the lawn as an air of enthusiasm buzzed through the crowd. The chance to gamble, even on rowing, seemed to be at the forefront of everyone's excitement. Mabel herself was eager to gather information on whom she should place her bet. She considered seeking out Derek to ask his opinion, but then she hesitated, feeling unsure about approaching him.

Having shared what they had last night, Mabel wasn't certain how he would behave upon seeing her. Would he be happy to see her, or would he rather keep her at a distance? She could understand both. Still, it wasn't up to her to discern Derek's thoughts or to determine his actions. Perhaps he would act like nothing happened. That would probably be the best thing to do, but then the image of his bare forearms cased in the moonlight made her shiver. She had touched him, held him close to her as he…

She swallowed and closed her eyes as Leona and the duchess spoke about the loveliness of all the seasonal flowers growing along the hedges. Mabel sighed. She needed to force herself to feel neutral about the situation. Otherwise, she was liable to make a fool of herself.

Why did she care, though? Derek was not anyone to her, and yet, even as she thought it, she knew that wasn't exactly true. She wasn't sure when it happened, but somewhere between first meeting the earl and last night, she realized that Derek had become someone she cared for.

As Mabel peered across the crowded lawn, she saw the fish folly packed with guests. To think, only a few hours ago, she had been there with Derek, in a state of blissful frenzy. Why, it was enough to make even Mabel blush. It had been an outrageous thing to do, to make love out in the open like that, but they hadn't been able to help themselves.

Glancing at Leona, Mabel knew that even without this latest scandalous act on her part, she had already tainted her sister with her marred reputation. Even after she left, Mabel would be remembered as some sort of harlot, thanks to her bold manners and history of divorce. And while money and position awaited her in Philadelphia, this was an entirely different world, and Leona would have to deal with their rigid morals and standards. The least Mabel could do for her sister was not to make things worse in the little time she had left in England.

"Miss Meadows?" A familiar male voice called to her, shaking Mabel from her thoughts. Turning, she saw Mr. Bentley beaming at her as he came forward. "I'm so glad to see you again."

"Mr. Bentley," she said, mirroring his smile. "A pleasure indeed."

"Your grace, Miss Leona," he said, bowing to the others before returning to Mabel. "Would you allow me to escort you to the river's edge? I believe we'll have a fine view of the race when it comes by."

"Of course. Perhaps you can help me choose which team to bet on."

"Oh, I'm not very good at betting, I'm afraid," he said as they left the others' company and headed across the flat lawn to the carefully manicured slope. "I must say, I was worried that you would not appear today."

"Why is that?"

"Though it has been a week since we last spoke to one another, I had become convinced that I had dreamt you up. I was so pleased to see you exit the house just now with the duchess and your sister."

It was a sweet thing to say, and the blush on the crest of his cheeks proved that he was sincere, which made Mabel feel oddly abashed. Her flirting with Mr. Bentley had evidently caused the young man to develop an infatuation. Mabel had only meant to have some fun, but it seemed he had interpreted their relationship differently.

"Oh, Mr. Bentley, that is a kind thing to say," she said gently. "But I assure you, I am no dream."

"I disagree," he said earnestly, following her across the bridge that led to the folly. Several ladies and gentlemen were there. "I see your face every time I lay down."

Oh dear.

"Please, Mr. Bentley—"

"Ah, Miss Meadows," Lord Nesby said, his stare roaming over her in the same, obvious way he had done so at the red tulip ball. "What a pleasure. Come, nephew, bring our American friend closer. This is a fine spot from which to witness the race."

It wasn't lost to Mabel that they were all standing in the exact spot where she and Derek had been last night. Just the idea of it began to make her feel warm.

"Lord Nesby," she said with a head bob. "It's wonderful to see you again."

"Ah, uncle," Mr. Bentley said, his brow knit together. "I didn't expect to see you here." He glanced over his shoulder across the river. "Are you not hosting an event today as well?"

"Yes, I am," he said, his steady gaze on Mabel. "But I thought I'd be neighborly before the event. Besides, I was hoping to speak with Miss Meadows."

"Oh?" Mabel said. "What about, my lord?"

He leered at her, and for some reason, the prickling of doubt settled in her spine. Something was not right.

"It is a private matter, I'm afraid," he said as he glanced over the crowd. "Nephew, why don't you go and fetch me something to drink, so that I might have a private word with our Miss Meadows."

He seemed hesitant at first, but then Mr. Bentley nodded.

"Of course. Would you like something, Miss Meadows?"

"No, thank you," she said, unsure what Lord Nesby wished to speak to her about.

After Mr. Bentley disappeared through the crowd, the older

gentleman leaned in and spoke so softly that no one but Mabel could hear.

"A nice lad, he is. But not quite worldly."

Mabel tilted her head.

"Worldly, my lord?"

"Yes. He's a gentle sort, not really aware of what sort of company to keep or what company to avoid."

Vaguely aware of what he was implying, Mabel steeled her spine as she pushed her shoulders back. She stepped forward to gaze out over the river as a warning began to beat through her. Her hand fell to the railing, almost as if to brace herself.

"Why, Lord Nesby, that almost sounds as if you were implying something."

"Oh, come now Miss Meadows," he said, leering at her. "There's no need to be coy with me. A lady of your...history, shall we say? It isn't so very surprising that you would start an affair with the earl."

Mabel's eyes went wide as her insides turned to ice.

"Excuse me?" she breathed.

"My dear, there's no reason to sound so worried," he said as his meaty, short-fingered hand crossed over hers on the rail. "It was rather, exciting, in a plebian sort of way, watching you two last night. In this very spot."

Mabel tried to drag her hand away, but before she could, his stubby fingers gripped her wrist firmly. She leaned heavily onto the metal rail.

"Easy, my dear. I'm simply interested in offering you a similar experience."

"Absolutely not—"

"Ah, I wouldn't be so quick to answer, Miss Meadows," he said lowly. "We wouldn't want rumors to go around about what I saw. Would we?"

Fury, like she had only experienced with Pascal, flooded her veins. Whirling around, Mabel opened her mouth to tell Nesby precisely what he could do with his proposal when the brick cracking suddenly sounded. Mabel yelled out, surprised that her entire body tipped forward as she toppled over the broken railing and into the water.

SPLASH!

The instant submergence of the cool water was panic-inducing enough, but the rushing river was dragging her downstream, and the weight of her dress would not let her surface. Frantic, she tried to claw through the running water to the surface as muddled sunlight edged with dark waters clouded her vision, but the river was too swift.

Kicking her legs, she tried to find something beneath her to push off, but her skirts were too heavy and made it nearly impossible to move.

This was it. She was going to die. Unable to keep her mouth from opening, her lips instinctively parted, trying to draw air into her lungs, but she only inhaled water, which caused her to cough as the icy water filled her lungs.

Blackness edged her vision, as if her mind were swimming itself, but then the next thing she knew, she was violently slammed back into reality. She barely had a moment to realize that she had somehow been removed from the water before her lungs seized as the muscles in her body contracted. Sharp, painful breaths coursed through her chest as she coughed up water. She could hear shouting and distant voices. A woman crying? But the deep, centering voice of Derek was close to her ear.

"Mabel? Mabel," he repeated, an urgency in his tone. "Can you hear me?"

The darkness that had engulfed her faded away as the world seemed to solidify around her again, her mind gradually sharpening out of its fear-filled daze. What had happened? It felt like she was waking from an hours-long nap. Only she was drenched to the bone.

Mabel blinked several times before her brain was able to understand her surroundings. Above her, staring over her, was a shadow of a man's silhouette outlined by the warm sun. She squinted as her lungs contracted, causing her to cough some more.

"D-Derek?" she sputtered, gasping once more for air.

"God above," he said, as he held her tightly to his chest.

She was halfway across the yard before she realized she was being carried by Derek, who was just as soaking wet as she was. Had he jumped in the river to pull her to safety? She coughed into his chest as the warm touch of his mouth pressed softly on her temple. Was she dreaming that? Indeed, she must be, because he would hardly be so brazen as to kiss her in front of witnesses.

"I…I fell," she said as she scanned beyond his shoulder. Mortification dawned on her as she realized that all the guests were watching her being carried into the house.

"Blasted railing," he spat. Mabel's hand gripped his coat, hoping to distract him from his anger. Sensing her anxious nerves, he spoke softly. "Easy, love. I don't want you to worry. You were unconscious for several minutes."

"Was I?"

"Shh," he cooed as the servants rushed to open every door. "Have the doctor come up at once," he spoke to everyone and no one in particular as he climbed the stairs. A herd of maids followed them, carrying towels and kettles to fill the bath with steaming water.

Everyone was moving so quickly. When they reached Mabel's bedroom, Derek brought her to the yellow silk chaise and gingerly set her down.

"Oh no," she said softly. "I'll ruin it."

"Hush," he said as Juliette came forward.

He peeled off his wet coat as Mabel's maid fussed over her, demanding to know what had happened.

"Mademoiselle! Qu'est-ce qui s'est passé?"

"Elle est tombée dans la riviere," Derek said, causing Mabel and Juliette to look up. Noticing their glances, he paused in his undress. "What?"

"You speak French?"

"Of course," he said as if she had just stated that the sky was blue. He addressed Juliette. "She needs to undress, or she'll catch a cold."

"Oui," Juliette said quickly, as she put her hands on Derek's chest, trying to make him leave the room. "Vous devez partir maintenant."

"No—"

"Absolument."

"But—"

"She won't help until you're gone," Mabel said just as Leona appeared.

"Mabel!" she said, rushing toward her, nearly bumping into the earl's shoulder. "I couldn't get through the crowd. Are you all right?"

"Yes—"

"She can't be sure," Derek interrupted. "She's not seen a doctor yet. And she needs to get into the bath."

"Then let's hurry," Leona said, reaching for Mabel's dress, but Juliette only glared at the earl.

"Sortez," she said, pointing toward the door.

Derek's mouth flattened into a hard line, and he glared back at the maid, but his amber-flecked brown eyes flickered at Mabel. As if waiting for a signal from her, Mabel gave him a short nod.

"Very well," he said to the maids. "I want a fire started and for that water to be hot. Have her out of there before the doctor arrives."

A series of "yes sirs" followed him as he stalked out of the room.

"Ce comte est un problème," Juliette said as she assisted Mabel to her feet while Leona helped undress her.

"Yes," Mabel said, her gaze on the door. "He certainly is trouble."

Chapter Eleven

DEREK SAT IN a deep brown leather club chair, staring absently at the billiards table later that night as the regatta ball carried on in the ballroom. He had accompanied the doctor into Mabel's room when he arrived and hadn't left until he was satisfied that she was perfectly fine. But even with the doctor's guarantee, Derek was left feeling shaken.

He had noticed her the moment she came out of Boxwood. She and her sister were arm in arm with Clara, and Derek had had to force himself not to go to her side immediately. The previous evening had been an experience. Derek hadn't ever come away from a coupling feeling as overwhelmed and transported as he had last night. It was unequivocal what was between him and Mabel, and every fiber of his being had called out to her the moment he saw her. But just as he began to approach, he saw that he had been beaten to the mark by an eager Mr. Bentley.

Derek had stopped himself, partly out of self-preservation and curiosity. There was no threat from Mr. Bentley, and as he gazed at Mabel's face, he saw an obvious discomfort, but to his surprise, she appeared almost bashful.

Derek took a sip of scotch as the events of that day replayed in his mind. Fredrick had interrupted Derek's staring along with Silas. They had wished to speak about horses or something. It had been a challenge to even pretend to pay attention to their words when every bit of him wanted to seek out Mabel.

And then, all of a sudden, he heard a scream, which caused everyone around him to look up. Before he could even question how he knew it was Mabel who yelled, he was racing toward the folly, only to realize that the crowd was gazing downstream, pointing, and shouting.

Derek's steps had slowed as he'd realized that someone had fallen into the water and was being dragged away by the current. Spinning around abruptly, he'd run as fast as he could, pushing through worried guests as he'd neared the bank of the river. In three giant steps, he'd crashed into the water before diving beneath the surface. The water had been moving fast, and it had taken him a moment before he saw the shimmer of Mabel's gown.

Swimming as quickly as he could, it seemed like hours before he reached her, but it was likely only minutes. When he'd grabbed her skirt, he'd held on tightly and dug his heels into the bed of the river as the water tried to force his body to topple over. But Derek would not move, and he drew her toward him, holding her to his chest as he began to make his way back toward the river bank. Thankfully, dozens of people had witnessed what happened, and by the time Derek reached the riverbank, several gentlemen had come to aid him.

But Derek had barely allowed the others to help before she was laid on her back in the grass. Fear had iced through him when he'd noted that she wasn't breathing, but he hadn't been willing to give up on her. Having once been a classmate of Granville Pattison, who had studied under the renowned Scottish surgeon Dr. Allen Burns, Derek and his schoolmates had all been taught about resuscitation.

He'd placed his palms over her chest, one atop the other, and then he'd pressed firmly into her chest several times before dropping down to breathe air into her mouth.

"My lord!" a woman screamed. "He's assaulting her!"

"He is not," Fredrick spat, reaching them. "He's helping her."

But the seconds had stretched endlessly, and every moment, she'd become paler until, blessedly, she'd coughed and then coughed again as a bubbling stream of water came from her mouth. Placing his arm around her shoulders, he'd sat her up immediately, thanking the lord above that he hadn't taken her.

"Are you all right, Trembley?" Silas asked, shaking Derek from his thoughts. The duke was sitting next to him in an identical leather club chair. Derek nodded at the question as Fredrick and Alfred argued over a shot taken on the snooker table. Gavin was leaning against the wall, watching the game intently, but Silas seemed entirely focused on Derek.

"Yes," he said, trying to put enough certainty in his voice to convince his friend—and himself, as well.

"Well, I must say, it was a very heroic thing you did," Alfred said, chalking the end of his cue stick. "Poor Leona was besides herself."

"Yes, it was rather a spectacle," Fredrick said, leaning over the table to line up a ball for his next shot.

The term caught Derek's attention.

"It wasn't on purpose," he said defensively. "She fell."

"I know that," his brother answered, standing up. "I didn't mean anything by it."

But Derek's worry for Mabel had soured his whole mood. Though the events of the day had still carried on, from the race to the ball that evening, he had elected to stay away from his guests rather than participating, wanting to be available should Mabel need him. His mother had been understanding, and even supported the idea of him not attending, as she too had concerns for Mabel. But after the fourth visit to Mabel's room since the doctor's departure, he was practically hauled off to the billiards room and forced to calm his nerves with a dram of whiskey.

"I know you don't, Fredrick."

"I suppose it is to be expected, however. Considering…"

When he didn't finish his sentence, Derek looked up. Suddenly alert, like a deer who had just heard a twig snap, Derek leaned forward.

"Considering what?"

"Well," Silas said, glancing at Gavin before looking back at Derek. "Isn't it obvious?"

"I'm afraid not."

"Really?" Fredrick asked, coming forward, a disbelieving frown on his face. "You don't see it?"

Alfred elbowed their brother, which only added to Derek's rising agitation. Standing up, he glared at those around him.

"See what, exactly?"

"Derek," Silas said quietly, gathering his attention away from the others. "It's obvious you care for the woman."

Derek let out an annoyed snort of laughter.

"Excuse me?"

"It's true," Gavin said. "Holly's been pointing it out for weeks now."

"And your wife is an expert on such things?" Derek asked.

Gavin smirked. "Yes."

Derek scoffed. "Let me assure you all that I'm not at all interested in Mabe—eh, Miss Meadows. I admit that we had a partnership of sorts that has recently come to an end. Now, all I wish is for her to get better so that she might enjoy the rest of her trip and return home promptly."

Neither Silas, Gavin, or Fredrick spoke. Alfred, on the other hand, took a slow step forward and cocked his head.

"Partnership?" he spoke, honing in on the word. "What sort of partnership?"

Derek nearly groaned but only exhaled loudly. Silas was studying him intently, causing Derek to feel exposed. He needed to leave. Now.

Taking a final swig of his drink, he stood and stalked out of the room.

"Where are you going?" Gavin called after him, but Derek didn't heed him.

He had already said too much. He didn't want to even be tempted to confess to his friends during some weak moment of self-reflection. Instead, he would check again on Mabel.

As he climbed the stairs, he wondered if his feelings regarding Mabel truly were so obvious.

Coming to the door that led into her bedchambers, Derek nearly knocked when a maid opened the door, jumping a little at seeing him.

"Oh, my lord," she said with a quick curtsy. "I did not think you would come again."

Oh good. It seemed everyone was keeping count of his visits. Well, she *was* a guest of his household, after all. He had every right to make sure that she was on the mend.

"Is she well?"

The maid gave him a cheeky wink.

"Go on, my lord. She'll tell you herself."

Derek started to step forward, but then a thought gave him pause. "Ah, as to her lady's maid, Juliette…"

"Yes, my lord?"

"Is she in there?"

"No," the maid said with a little chuckle, moving around him to step into the hallway. "She went down to the kitchens for something to eat. It's where I'm headed, myself."

"Ah. I wouldn't usually ask this, but if you could—"

"I'll keep her busy, my lord. She's a stern one, she is."

Derek nodded his thanks as the maid disappeared down the hallway. He leaned into the room, noting the oil lamps that had been dimmed to give the room a peaceful ambiance. Yet the lamp on the end table closest to the head of the bed was turned up, and Mabel was using the light of it to read by, tucked beneath a thick brocade of blankets. Derek found that the image of her absorbed in her book, mouth slightly open with a dark braid falling over her shoulder was perhaps the most exquisite vision he had ever seen.

Her silver-blue eyes lifted then from the pages, and a grin

broke out on her face. What should have broken the spell only illuminated it.

"What are you doing here? Isn't there a ball going on?"

"There is," he said, stepping into the room. "But I wanted to check on you."

She tilted her head.

"You've already made sure that I have everything I need, half a dozen times thus far. And I do. If this persists, I should require the doctor to visit again."

His heartrate picked up.

"Why? Are you unwell?"

"No, but I'm afraid you'll drive yourself mad with worry."

Amused by her gentle teasing, Derek smirked as he came toward the edge of her bed, absently moving his fingers over the curve carved into the wood of her bedpost.

"I promise, I'll not visit again tonight."

"Oh, but," she said quickly, propping herself onto her arm. "I don't mind. Really." Warm satisfaction simmered in his chest.

"I wanted to apologize to you, Mabel," he said softly. "I don't think you'll ever understand the guilt I have about what happened to you."

"It's not your fault," she began, but he held a hand up.

"It *is* my fault though. I pressed the laborers to have the repair work on the folly completed before the race and the mortar hadn't had enough time to set. I was impatient."

"You were told it was safe."

"I should have known better."

"How could you have? Are you a master builder?" she asked. When he didn't answer, she continued. "No, of course not. And all is well. I'll be back on my feet and out of bed in no time, I'm sure. Although..."

His eyes snapped to hers.

"Although what?"

She gave him a sad sort of smile.

"I'm afraid my playing cards were ruined," she said, nodding at a palm sized, mushed up ball of paper that sat on the end table. "They were in my pocket."

He reached for it and squeezed as an excess amount of water dripped onto the floor.

"I'll replace them, of course."

"There's no need for you to do that," she said, lifting her body slightly.

"I want to. And you need to rest," he said, as his free hand came to her shoulder and gently pushed her back.

"I won't rest for long, I assure you."

A quick quip about keeping her in bed surfaced, but he pushed past it.

"Goodnight, Mabel," he said, turning to leave.

"Goodnight," she said.

And for the most part, it was a good evening. Derek ventured to the ballroom, where everyone was eager to talk to him about how Miss Meadows was faring after her ordeal. To his surprise, Mr. Bentley was adamant about visiting Mabel the next day should she recover so soon. Lord Nesby was equally insistent that he be allowed to visit. Derek, of course, agreed, but when they showed up the next day, he was filled with a feeling of frustration.

Mr. Bentley arrived just after breakfast. It was hours before the appropriate calling time, however, Mabel had told the countess that she was eager to accept visitors so as to lessen everyone's worry about her. Derek tried to object, but he found that both his mother and Mabel seemed determined to carry on with or without his consent.

"Good morning, Trembley," Mr. Bentley said upon entering the foyer, dressed in a fine grey suit, holding a bouquet of bright-colored wildflowers. "I've come to see how Miss Meadows is faring."

"Yes, so I've been told," he grumbled. "I believe you'll find Miss Meadows in the family parlor."

"No, dear, Miss Meadows will be visiting with guests on the terrace this morning," the countess said as she approached the men. "My, what lovely flowers Mr. Bentley."

"Thank you, countess."

"The terrace?" Derek interrupted. "Miss Meadows shouldn't be outside. She's likely to catch a chill."

"In this weather? I doubt it and besides, Miss Meadows insisted, and I think the fresh air will do her good. Come, Mr. Bentley, I'll escort you to her."

Derek was about to open his mouth to argue further when another visitor showed up, followed by another. Every bachelor from here to London had heard about the American's plight and came to give their condolences. To his chagrin, Mabel allowed each and every visit from where she held court on the terrace while Derek lurked just inside the house. He still felt it was unnecessary for her to hold court outside, given the traumatic events from the day prior.

Derek was determined to stay out of Mabel's way as she was fawned over by visitors, deciding it best to keep his growing annoyance in check, but he was unable to do so. Every time he thought up something to busy himself with, he would find himself by the open doors that led out onto the terrace, positioning himself so that he could just make out what Mabel was saying. She was seated at the stone bench, surrounded by at least four gentlemen. A wooden table had been carried out and covered with a tablecloth and dozens of plates of teacakes, scones, and more.

"—and I'm simply overwhelmed by all the well wishes that have come my way," she said, burying her face in a large peony, one of dozens Mr. Bentley had brought her. "It truly has made me reconsider my thoughts on the British gentleman."

"I hope for the better?" one gentleman said.

She smiled, and Derek rolled his eyes. Must she be so damn flirtatious? She seemed practically on the verge of inviting all these men to write her poetry. It was appalling how they flocked to her, practically begging for her attention.

A moment of self-reflection might have brought him to the

uncomfortable realization that he acted the same way with her, but that wasn't something he cared to think about, so he pushed the thought away.

"When you are well, you must let me take you rowing. I'm an excellent boat man."

"That is kind of you, but I think you'll understand, especially after my latest experience, that I'm not particularly keen on water."

"But that is why you must give it another chance—so that you may overcome your fear before it becomes too entrenched. And of course, you will be entirely safe when you're with me. I don't mean to sound arrogant, but I'm probably the best row man for a hundred miles."

"Is that so?" she asked, not sounding at all sarcastic.

Why not just dismiss the prat? he wondered. But Mabel only tilted her head and appeared coquettish.

"You must let me—"

Derek nearly stalked out onto the stone patio to deal with the gentleman's impertinence, but his plan was interrupted by the clearing of a throat from behind him. Turning around, he saw Lord Nesby, who gave him a crooked grin.

"My apologies, my lord. I did tell my nephew that he was likely hunting the wrong prey if you will."

Derek frowned.

"Excuse me?"

"Well, I don't mean to pry, obviously, and you know how I loathe gossip," he said, coming closer. "But the night before last? Before the Regatta? I was out back, inspecting the grounds when I saw, well…"

The man's brows wiggled up and down as a surprising amount of ferocity swelled in Derek's chest.

"You saw what?" he asked quietly.

"Let's not say what it actually was." The man winked. "But good for you. I thought of sampling her spirits myself, to see if there was any contrast with the English whores, but I doubt an

American will be much different, no?"

A sudden ringing sounded in Derek's ears as the man's words sunk in. Nesby had seen them together and now thought to bring it up in conversation? On top of which he had the gall to compare Mabel to a whore?

Derek's fingers curved into fists at his side as he tried to steady himself.

"You're mistaken, Nesby."

"I don't think so, Trembley. As old as I am, my eyesight is still very keen and I—"

"You what?" Derek hissed. "Think to insult a guest of my household?"

The old man blinked, confused.

"Come now, Trembley, there's no need to pretend to be indignant. She's a divorcée and we're all adults, after all."

The shakes that had haunted Derek for months began to shiver through him as his hands trembled. He tried to focus, but his fury at Nesby's words would not subside.

"Leave my house. At once."

Nesby frowned, then let out a little chuckle.

"Goodness me. If I'm not mistaken, it seems you're rather taken with the little trollop—"

Vehemence slammed into Derek's chest, and before he realized what he was doing, he had his fingers wrapped around Nesby's throat as the old man clawed at Derek's fingers.

"Get out."

Nesby sputtered and coughed.

"Take your hands off me!"

But he would do no such thing. Instead, he began to haul the old bastard down the hall, deciding to throw him out. The scuffle had been loud enough that Mabel and the others entered the house.

"Uncle!" Mr. Bentley said, rushing after Derek as he dragged the man out of his house. "Lord Trembley, please, unhand him!"

"Miss Meadows has had enough visitors for today," he

snapped over his shoulder. "You all may leave."

"Excuse me?" Mabel said, annoyed.

"Surely she can decide that for herself!" someone said, but Derek didn't much care what anyone was saying.

All he knew was that he needed to remove Nesby, or else he would kill him.

As they reached the front steps, Derek hurled the older man to the ground. Nesby stumbled somewhat on his way out, before falling onto the stone drive. After a moment of coughing, Mr. Bentley helped him up. Fixing his jacket, the old man glared at Derek.

"I've a mind to challenge you!" he spat.

"Do it then and meet your end," Derek countered.

"Stop, please!" Mabel said, coming forward as the other gentlemen hurried out the door and down the front steps to avoid Derek. She spun on him. "What are you doing?"

But he ignored her.

"Very well, Trembley," Nesby said. "Have it your way."

Derek turned his back on him and the others, reentering his house with Mabel hot on his heels.

"What was that about?" she asked, following him. "Have you lost your mind?"

He had gone too far, obviously, removing Nesby as he had, but the bumbling fool was out of line. "I was helping you."

"By scaring off my visitors?"

He scoffed. "You didn't really want to hear those idiots continue with that drivel, did you?"

"Whether I did or not is none of your concern," she snapped.

Just then, Alfred and Fredrick came down the staircase, while Leona and the countess came out of the parlor.

"What's all the commotion about?" Alfred asked. "It sounds like someone's having a brawl."

"What happened to Mr. Bentley and the other gentlemen?" the countess asked, concerned. "Derek?"

"Do you know what he..." Derek started, only to glance

around. He was making a spectacle of himself. Spinning around, he spoke out loud, addressing everyone. "I require a private audience with Miss Meadows."

"Absolutely not," she said, but no one moved.

Everyone seemed either too frightened by the tone of Derek's voice or else they were too curious to see what would happen next. Either way, they would not budge—so it would be up to him to relocate. Derek stalked over to the closest door, the study, and held it open as he waited for Mabel to enter. She glanced around once more, searching for someone who might argue on her behalf, but finding none, she sighed and entered the study, followed by Derek who closed the door behind them.

But if he had hoped to speak his peace, he was mistaken.

"What in God's name is wrong with you?" Mabel started, launching into an argument. "What on earth could that man have said that would cause you to lay hands on him? And his poor nephew. He looked appalled. Not to mention the others."

"Mabel, listen—"

"I don't know what has come over you, but this certainly isn't the behavior of a sane person."

Derek stalked over to her and, placing his hands on her shoulders, he stopped her.

"Listen to me. Nesby saw us."

"Saw us? Saw us where? When?"

"By the folly, the other night."

Mabel's blue eyes stared for a moment before realization dawned. She blinked, then winced as the information settled. "Are you sure?"

"Yes."

"But how can he even be certain it was us? It was dark out, and he was a fair distance away."

Derek nearly growled.

"From his words, he seems quite sure."

Mabel drew back from his grasp.

"What did he say?"

"Nothing worth repeating. But we do have to deal with this."

"How?"

He regarded her, and she swallowed, seemingly able to read from his expression the solution he was about to offer. Indeed, it appeared to him to be the only step they could possibly take. Anything else held too much of a chance of leading to her disgrace.

"No. No, absolutely not," she said, clearly trying to sound firm, but he didn't miss the tremble in her voice.

"I don't see any way around it," he countered.

"I do. Put me on a boat to America immediately. And pay off that man."

"He has no need for my money. He didn't come to me to ask for a bribe—he came to…it doesn't matter," Derek said, his hand going through his hair. "Besides, even if you did leave, what of Leona?"

"What about her? Surely your brother wouldn't abandon her."

"No, but he would not be able to stifle the whispers. She would face some cruelties—"

"Nothing she couldn't handle."

"Their children might be tinged with it as well."

"Ch-children?" Mabel said, looking as if she'd taken a physical blow at his words. "What can we do?"

"The only thing we can do," Derek said slowly. "We must marry."

But Mabel was already shaking her head. When she spoke again, her voice was chilled.

"I swore never to marry anyone ever again."

From what she had shared about her marriage to the comte, Derek could understand her apprehension. But surely she didn't mean to spend her entire life alone? She was too young, too beautiful, and too strong a woman to be unwed. She deserved a husband that would care for her, a man who would do anything to keep her happy all her days. And after having spent so much time with her these past few weeks and sharing all that they had with one another, Derek couldn't ignore a prickling urge, deep in his stomach. An urge that asked the question, why not him?

Yet, he couldn't ask her that and so settled only on one word. "Why?"

"Because I will not bring myself to be someone else's property once more. I prefer scandal and freedom to propriety and subservience."

Derek stared at her.

"I would never require you to be subservient."

She rolled her eyes, clearly not giving his words as ounce of credence. "Every husband requires that."

"Not me," he said, coming forward.

His hand came to rest on her cheek, and for a blinding moment, she seemed to soften, as if she was finally ready to let go of the past. But then her spine straightened and her gaze hardened.

"I don't think I can," she spoke honestly.

For a moment, neither moved. But then, he did—lifting her chin with his hand.

"I do not pretend to understand all you've experienced with marriage, but I would ask that you not equate anything from that time to now. Yes, there is a situation at hand that needs to be dealt with, and I'm not the sort of man to ignore my responsibilities, which now include asking you to marry me."

"But—"

"That said, I want you know that I'm quite dedicated to this match between us. There's no denying that we are attracted to one another."

"Attraction does not make a happy marriage."

"No, but respect does." Mabel's gaze snapped to his. "And I do respect you. I think you are intelligent, and amusing—though often rather insulting and a bit of an instigator."

"As are you."

"Even without romantic inclinations, I believe we could have a proper marriage. You would not crumble beneath the pressure of this position and I doubt either of us would ever be bored with one another."

A humorless noise escaped her lips.

"That's true," Mabel admitted, glancing down.

"Do you… I mean, would you…" she began.

"What is it?"

"It will not bother me however you answer, but I would like to know if… if you have a mistress?"

She didn't meet his eyes, and he was curious as to why.

"Not for well over a year," he said honestly. "I suspect that's half the reason why I'm so taken with you." She let out a small laugh, but then he continued, quite serious. "If you do not wish for me to have a mistress, I won't."

Her stare turned skeptical.

"As if it were that simple."

"It is," he said. "If my needs are met by you, I should have no reason to seek comforts outside our marital bed." He paused before adding, "And I believe we are quite suited in that respect."

Mabel's cheeks burned.

"Are you blushing?" he asked, oddly charmed by the thought.

"Absolutely not."

"I believe you are," he said, touching her cheek and feeling its warmth.

Mabel swatted his hand away and turned her back to him.

"Very well," she said.

"Very well what?"

"Very well, you may ask me."

This was it, then. "Mabel," he began, his tone suddenly solemn. "Will you marry me?"

"Yes."

Few moments in Derek's life had ever compounded so many emotions. Apprehension, desire, worry, satisfaction, lust, and excitement. They all seemed roll together, expanding and contracting simultaneously as he gazed into Mabel's blue eyes, but one surged above the rest and it was that one feeling he decided to lean into with his whole being.

Hope. Hope that this was not only the right decision, but a deeper hope, that spoke to a quiet fear he had possessed as of late. He had been putting off the idea of marriage for years now, not because it had an aversion to it, but because he hadn't been able to find any one woman that would not only be compatible for him, but one that would also be good for the earldom. But as he gazed down at this woman, he felt a surge of hope.

Bending down, he brushed his lips against hers and was equal parts eager yet hesitant. She leaned forward, hoping to deepen their kiss, but he pulled back, and unable to resist, he smiled at her.

"Then I believe we have some work to do."

Chapter Twelve

Mabel sat in a chair in her sister's bedchamber, dressed in a silk plum gown embroidered with white rosettes along the hem, a week after returning from Boxwood House. The earl and his brothers had left that morning at the request of the countess so that she could see to the final wedding arrangements. Violet was dressed in a pale-yellow gown, while Leona wore silver. All three were being attended to the morning of their collective weddings, though Mabel perhaps was the least excited.

"It will be all right," Leona said, bending down to kiss her sister on the cheek as Mabel stared out into the ether, a new deck of cards clutched in her hand. "I'm sure the earl will be a wonderful husband."

"Of course he will," Violet said, shifting away from the mirror as she fixed an emerald diadem at the crown of her head. It had been a gift from her brother. "Trembley is not the most sought-after gentleman in London without reason. Mabel will surely be the envy of every lady in town."

It had certainly been a shock to society that Derek and Mabel had decided to marry, but supposedly it hadn't been as surprising to some within their closest circle of family and friends. From what Derek had said, both Silas and Gavin had been unsurprised. Deeply amused, but not surprised.

"I've no wish to be the envy of anyone."

"Mabel," Leona tried, her voice strained. "Please. What's done is done. You accepted him yourself."

"Under duress," she argued. "He made it seem so much worse than it would be."

"Really?" Violet said. "Have the papers not been cruel enough?"

Mabel's cheeks burned. The papers had been exceedingly harsh since their return from Henley-on-Thames. Reports of Mabel's recovery seemed to dominate the gossip pages, as her fall had been discussed far and wide. Still, two separate and contradicting articles reporting on the issue had only been squashed by the news of Mabel and Derek's nuptials.

The Times had reported a scathing article about the lack of care Mabel received from the lecherous villain that was Derek. Of course, no one believed it as Derek had long had a reputation for upstanding behavior, but he had been furious by the article, and it had spurred a flurry of people into whispering what sort of things the earl had done to garner such ill comments.

The other article had been quick to center the blame around Mabel instead, insinuating that her fall into the water had been some sort of well-orchestrated plot to compromise the earl and force her attentions on him. Her "scandalous" behavior had been the subject of a great many prudish reproaches—as if she had *wanted* to nearly drown.

"It will be all right," Leona repeated, trying to jostle Mabel out of her hostile mood. "I promise."

Mabel sighed deeply. It wasn't Leona's responsibility to mollycoddle her sister, particularly on her wedding day. Mabel gave her a forced smile, and, placing her hands on the armrest of the chair, she pushed herself up to stand.

"Of course, it will be, my dear," she said, brushing out the nonexistent wrinkles of her skirts.

Just then, the door opened, and the countess entered. Dressed in a pink striped gown with a stunning amount of lace trim, she came into the room, followed closely by Juliette, who was carrying two small wooden boxes on top of a large wooden box that she had gone to gather from the countess at her request.

Mabel swallowed. She had avoided her soon-to-be mother-in-law for days now, having noted the uncertainty on her face when Derek announced their engagement.

All three ladies curtsied.

"Good morning," the countess said with a nod, her reddish-brown curls bobbing against her cheek as she did so. "I trust you are all are well this morning?"

"Yes, my lady," they all said in unison.

The countess came forward and inspected each one of them up and down. "My, what lovely gowns. This will be a wonderful day, to be sure," she said, her eyes lingering on Mabel. "Mabel, dear, I wish to speak with you. Alone."

Tension piled on Mabel's shoulders.

"Yes, of course," she said, as Leona and Violet regarded one another. They began to leave.

"Oh no, dears, you stay here. Juliette has something for you both. Mabel?" she said as the others were handed the smaller wooden boxes. "Come with me."

Mabel followed the countess out of the bedchamber and down the hallway. While she had always been an accepting sort of lady, particularly of her new American daughters-in-law, Mabel couldn't help but wonder what the woman truly felt. Of course, she had put on a good show publicly of supporting her sons in their matches, but Mabel sometimes wondered if the show of acceptance had been the poor lady constantly trying to demonstrate to the rest of the ton just how proper her family really was, despite every example leading to the opposite conclusion.

Entering into a small room that Mabel had never entered before, she was surprised to find a cheerfully decorated space with peach blossoms painted on the wallpaper and a cherry wood desk. The countess made her way to it, and as Mabel came closer, she saw dozens of miniature paintings, all set on her desk so that she was surrounded by them when she wrote letters. They were all different sizes, and when the countess picked up a particular one about the size of her palm, she handed it to Mabel.

"This was Derek's father," she said, her tone warm. "He was a stoic sort, but he loved his children very much."

Mabel studied the miniature painting. He was a serious looking man with strong shoulders, not unlike Derek in his bearing, though it was Fredrick and Alfred who had inherited his coloring.

"He was quite handsome."

"He was," she said affectionately. "You know, Derek is so much like him."

Mabel tilted her head.

"Is he?"

"Oh yes, although I like to think a bit of my practicality rubbed off on him."

"Practicality?"

"Yes," she said. "Has he told you the story of how his father and I met?"

"No."

"Come," she said, sitting down as she patted the settee next to her. Mabel obliged, seating herself beside the countess. "I met Harry at my coming out ball. He had a bit of a reputation and my mama made it clear that I was not to be caught even talking to him."

"Was he that bad?"

"Oh, not really, not at heart—but appearances were rather against him, so I suppose everyone else truly believed that he was. But he was playful and he made me laugh, which was quite a blessing. I was so nervous for my season, you see. But he turned it all into a game, and that eased my mind tremendously. I did love games."

"Did he ask to court you?"

"Yes. My mother wasn't pleased about it, but my father allowed it. He was very sweet then, always sending me poems. He couldn't write them himself of course, but he had his favorites. I'll have you know that the Trembley men all turn poetic when they fall for someone."

Mabel chuckled.

"I believe that. Your son Alfred recited nearly an entire book of poetry by John Dryden on our voyage across the Atlantic."

"Oh, I can easily imagine that, considering how he feels about Leona. John Dryden was on of Harry's favorites. *Happy the man and happy he alone, he who can call today his own…*"

Mabel chuckled. "I wonder what Derek might quote if he… I mean…" She cleared her throat.

"I know what you meant. And Derek has always had a soft spot for Robert Herrick, I believe."

"Herrick?" Mabel repeated, surprised. "That doesn't seem likely."

"No?"

"No. I mean, from all our interactions, I would have assumed he would be partial toward someone more, well, grounded in reality. Herrick is too philosophical. Don't you think so?"

A small smirk spread across the countess's face.

"Perhaps," she said, with a tiny chin dip.

Suddenly unsure, Mabel began to chew on her bottom lip.

"But then again, who am I to claim to know your son?"

"Oh, but my dear, I think you're quite the right person."

"How so?"

"Well, you are a lady of propriety, regardless of our countries' differing ideas of what that entails. What I mean to say is, you're a lady who has been educated, one who is poised and well-spoken and who has seen something of the world." She scooted closer to Mabel as if to tell her a great secret. "May I speak candidly?"

"Of course."

"We, my sons and I and everyone in London really, live in a condensed world, if you will. There are other countries, other courts, but to us, none is more important than our own. As it should be, with any loyal servant to their country. But because we all live within a stone's throw of everyone who, in our opinion, truly matters, we might appear rather daunting to others. Now you, with your outside view, may have the ability to judge us, without worrying about the ramifications of those judgements."

Mabel's brow knit together.

"You mean, because I'm not one of you, it's easier for me to see your true character?"

"Exactly. And I would very much like to know what conclusions you have reached on that matter."

Mabel fumbled a little for words. "Well, from what I can tell, my lady, your family is a genuinely lovely group of people—"

"No, no," she said, shaking her head. "I would like to know your opinion of Derek."

"Derek?" Mabel repeated as the countess bobbed her head. "But why?"

She straightened her shoulders.

"Because I wish to know," she said, with a slight tone of authority.

"Well," Mabel started off guard. "He is a fine, honorable gentleman—"

"I do not wish for you to wax poetically about things you think I wish to hear about my own offspring. I want your genuine opinion. What do you think of him?"

"I…well, he's kind and generous—"

"Miss Meadows," the countess interrupted. "What do you think of Derek?"

"I think he's arrogant," she spit out before quickly covering her mouth with her hand.

Only the countess didn't seem too upset. Instead, she seemed pleased.

"Go on."

Emboldened, Mabel continued.

"I think he's closed-minded. And particular. He's also brilliant, but not in a way that's humble. No. He lets everyone in the room know exactly how brilliant he is, which is conceited, if you ask me."

But the countess didn't ask. She only waited patiently, as if urging her to continue.

"And he thinks he's terribly clever," Mabel continued, standing up. "Smarter than everyone. Yet if he wasn't so worried about others' opinions he might realize that they don't matter anyway."

"I quite agree with that," the countess said.

"But the most particular thing I have noticed about him is his inability to realize that someone else, anyone else, might have a better idea then himself." She shook her head, annoyed. "It's exasperating."

A moment of silence followed, and Mabel worried that she had said too much, but then the countess chuckled.

"He is so much like his father."

Mabel turned.

"Is he?"

"Oh, very much so," she said, standing herself, as she smoothed out the creases of her skirts. "Unfortunately, I wasn't always successful in my attempts to break his father away from an older way of thinking."

"In what way?"

She sighed then.

"Harry and I agreed on most things, but not everything. He believed our union was a prosperous one because of our similar heritage and upbringing. In other words, because we were both from good stock, born to proper, well-to-do families. But I always held the notion that we were meant to be. That regardless of our class or our pedigree, that Harry and I would have found each other and been happy together. He used to laugh at that of course, but I never wavered in my belief. Harry and I were meant for one another, and the fates had been generous enough to put us in the same place at the same time in a position where it was easy for us to come together and be wed. But even if it had been harder—even if it had been shocking or scandalous—I still think we would have wed all the same."

Mabel grinned.

"If we are speaking candidly, my lady, you don't really believe that just because you and your husband were happy together that it was somehow meant to be, do you?"

"Of course I do."

"But that's... Well, forgive me, but I find that a bit absurd."

"Why?"

"How likely is it that if your circumstances in life had been different, that you would have even been able to find one another, much less be married? If your husband, God rest him, was a born during the age of the Vikings, instead of when he was born, it wouldn't be a tragedy. He would have married someone else as would have you."

"So soulmates are not something you believe in?"

"I'm sorry, countess, but no."

The countess smiled widely then.

"Well, I'd ask you to explain more about your opinion, but we have a wedding to get to," the countess pointed out. Mabel nodded, trying to appear happy but failing. "Come. You must return to your sister's room to have the finishing touches done."

"Finishing touches?"

"Yes, yes. Now go."

The countess rushed Mabel from her private sitting room and back down the hall. Feeling guilty about admitting all she had to the older woman, Mabel took her time returning to the bedchamber. When she did arrive, however, she found both Leona and Violet beaming.

"Come see," Leona said, coming up with her wrist out. "The countess has lent Violet and me bracelets."

Leona wore a gold and citrine cuff bracelet, while Violet raised her own wrist to display one made of diamonds and silver.

"It was very kind of her," Violet said, admiring the piece. "The countess has always been a generous woman. I can't wait to see what she leant you."

"Me?"

"Yes, there's a third box," Violet said, motioning toward

Mabel's maid with her hand.

"Mademoiselle," Juliette said, coming toward her. "La tiare de Comtesse Trembley."

"Oh dear," she breathed as Leona and Violet came around to flank her. "She really didn't have to send this over."

"Mais oui," Juliette said as she opened it.

All three women gasped.

Set on a purple velvet pillow was a tiara that would make the grandest of queens green with envy. Ten perfectly oval cabochon cut amethysts, each encircled by dozens of diamonds, had been fixed to two circular pieces of silver. The stones were just larger than robins' eggs, and for a moment, Mabel feared the weight of such an impressive piece of jewelry.

"Allons-nous?" Juliette said, rotating to place the wooden box on a table as she moved to help Mabel put it on.

"No," Mabel said quickly, causing the others to look at her. She knew she didn't have a choice, but she was nervous. "I mean, I suppose we must."

"Oui," Juliette said, her tone slightly condescending.

Where most maids might have been chastised for such a tone, Mabel had the utmost faith and trust in Juliette. She sat once more in the chair and waited for her maid to fix the piece to her head. Unsurprisingly, it was cumbersome, and it took several minutes of Juliette yanking, tying, and braiding her locks around the piece to secure it well enough that it wouldn't shift. Yet despite the literal and metaphorical weight of the piece, she couldn't deny that she felt a sense of pride from wearing something that represented Derek.

It was difficult to admit how she felt about him. For the longest time, she had been certain that any relationship she had after Pascal would only be surface level. She never wanted to trust or believe in another man ever again. And yet, every day that passed in Derek's presence, she sensed the ways in which she was slipping more and more into the same dangerous traps she had fallen into during her time with Pascal.

She knew they weren't the same person, but the trepidation she had that morning was palpable. Pascal had been sweet and seemingly sincere until she said *I do*. Then, like a candle being blown out, she had been left out in the cold.

Would Derek do the same?

Chapter Thirteen

While the marriages of the Trembley brothers were wildly reported on, considering their unique circumstances, the wedding ceremony itself was a small affair, particularly when bearing in mind that there were three brides and three grooms. Double weddings were uncommon enough, but a triple wedding was practically unheard of, and while only a few had been invited in to watch, there were many people gathered outside who had come out just to see the fanfare.

But that had been expected. Though Derek never much minded crowds, he wasn't particularly pleased when he had seen the crowd upon his arrival at St. George's Church. The pews were filled with family and friends, and for the first time in a long time, Derek was nervous. But all that disappeared the moment he saw Mabel being escorted down the aisle. Silas, who had graciously offered to give away the Meadow sisters alongside Violet, walked behind the three women. Mabel was in the middle, and when she reached Derek, he was at a loss for words.

Her plum-colored gown matched the Trembley tiara perfectly, and the amount of pride he had from seeing her in it did things to him that he never expected. His heart thudded almost painfully in his chest and squeezed when she reached him.

Leona and Violet peeled off to each side of Derek, taking their prospective husbands' hands while his own bride waited for him.

Attentively, he reached out his hand, and Mabel took it, standing next to him while they waited for the bishop to step forward and begin.

All throughout the ceremony, Derek could barely follow what the bishop was saying. All he could manage was to stare at Mabel, who appeared lovelier than any woman he had ever seen—but who also seemed to be carrying an alarming amount of tension. Her apparent worry, the slight downward turn of the corners of her mouth, and the anxiety in her silver-blue eyes concerned him. Something was bothering her, and once they were away from everyone, he would discover whatever it was and promptly find a way to set her at ease.

But as soon as the ceremony was over, they were loaded into an open barouche and were paraded through Mayfair back to the Trembley Manse. Derek had barely been able to ask her how she was doing when they were being unloaded in front of the house.

If anyone had believed that the dowager countess's tulip party had been over-the-top, the sheer number of roses that had been brought into the manse that morning would have shocked them. Indeed, they'd have seemed excessive to even the most extravagant party throwers.

Every available inch had been covered in peach and white blooms. The dowager countess had somehow managed to have the house transformed while they were at the church. To see Mabel's face glow with wonder at the sight made Derek's heart expand. As they made their way through the foyer and into the dining room where the wedding breakfast was to be held, he picked up a single, half-unfurled peach rose placed on a hallway table and handed it to Mabel.

She seemed stunned momentarily, but then a small grin curved her lips, setting off a wave of gladness through Derek as she cupped it with her fingers. If he could make her smile, perhaps he could obliterate her anxiety before tonight.

Derek exhaled. He would be lying if he said he hadn't thought about their wedding night ever since she had said yes to his proposal. They had only been together once, yet Derek had been unable to sleep peacefully since. He longed to hold Mabel.

But he couldn't think about that now. Instead, he focused on the table as people congratulated them.

The food was decadent, and the guests were cheerful, but while Derek's bride appeared pleased, her body language conveyed the opposite. Mabel was a woman of contradictions, and there was still so much he didn't know or didn't understand about her. The situation was not helped, of course, by their animosity when they first met. He had to admit that neither he nor Mabel showed the other person their best versions of themselves. Derek had been haughty and arrogant; Mabel had been biting and conniving. They had lived down to each other's worst expectations, bringing Derek a tremendous amount of comfort. Because if that was the worst of Mabel, he couldn't help but be excited at the prospect of getting to know more of her.

"And another toast to my brother, Derek," Alfred said, lifting a flute full of champagne with his arm around the waist of his bride. "While the start of this journey was unconventional, I couldn't be happier for you."

"Here, here!" Fredrick said as everyone murmured their agreement.

It was not lost on Derek that this was not a situation that anyone in the house had anticipated. Yet still, Mabel, who had been perhaps too vocal in her protests the days leading up to the wedding for his liking, was all smiles. She displayed her most pleased personality for everyone else. It was a convincing act, but Derek noted the tension that still held her rigid, and it made him uneasy. He held his tongue and talked with his family and friends as they filtered in and out of the morning room that had an excellent view of the garden.

"It was a lovely ceremony," his mother said behind him. Turning, Derek saw her, eyes glittering. "Imagine. All my boys married on the same day. What were the odds?"

"It was certainly a Trembley wedding. Nothing quite like it in all of London."

"And I suspect all of you will be very pleased with your wives."

Derek took a sip of his champagne.

"I hope so."

His tone didn't explicitly betray his uncertainty about Mabel, but his mother frowned with concern.

"Oh, Derek," she said softly, stepping toward him. "Do tell me that you believe you've made the right choice."

"Little I could do about it now."

"I'm not questioning that," she said. "I mean, you believe that Mabel will be a dutiful wife, don't you?"

The idea of Mabel being docile and obedient almost made him laugh. But he didn't need to worry his mother about such things.

"I'm sure she will."

Placated, his mother nodded.

"Good. You know, I thought it would be a shame for such a woman to disappear from our shores when I first saw her."

"Did you?"

"Yes. She's a spirited woman, but she isn't foolish," she said, lifting her chin. "She reminded me of myself actually, in my younger years."

"Is that so?"

"Yes."

"Well, you've managed to say the exact opposite of what every son wishes to hear on their wedding day—that apparently I've married my mother."

She swatted his arm.

"Sharp-tongued devil," she chastised him. "And you should be so lucky. But no. She is entirely her own person in many ways, though I do believe we share a clever, lively sort of spirit. But your wife comes off as far stronger than most, even to a fault. *That* is a trait I never had. I was never so bold as to go about believing that I didn't need a husband."

Derek faced her.

"You think she doesn't need me?"

"No. I think *she* thinks she doesn't need you. Which is a conundrum in and of itself."

"How so?"

"Well, whether she thinks she needs you or not, she has chosen you. And that is far more important than marrying someone because she needs to."

"But she didn't choose me. It was a result of—"

"No, my dear," his mother said. "She could have left and found a fine life in America."

"But her devotion to her sister wouldn't allow it—not when her leaving without a marriage would tarnish Leona's reputation."

"Her devotion to her sister has nothing to do with your marriage," she said softly. "She chose it."

His mother gave him a comforting look and went about her way, engaging in a conversation with an elderly lady, an ancient aunt who had attended the wedding.

Derek glanced across the room to see Mabel laughing and chatting with one of their guests. She appeared so effortlessly engaging and beautiful that he foolishly felt somewhat jealous that he wasn't in her presence at that moment, but that was ridiculous. Mabel was his wife, and he would have the pleasure of her company for the rest of his life.

He certainly wouldn't give her a reason to leave him as her last husband had.

After breakfast, everyone saw the others off. Alfred and Leona were taking their honeymoon to the continent, and Fredrick and Violet were going north to Scotland.

Only Derek and Mabel were staying in London. In response to this, the dowager countess had decided to visit her cousins for the remainder of the summer. It was a tactful way to leave the newlyweds alone, and one Derek appreciated.

The crowd came to the foyer and out onto the front steps of

the Trembleys' Mayfair home. Two carriages taking the couples to their different destinations were waiting on the quiet street, and those walking by stilled to watch it all play out.

Alfred smirked at his brothers and patted Fredrick on the back. He grinned up at Derek.

"Well, to new adventures," he said as his bride kissed Mabel on the cheek.

"Goodbye, Mabel," Leona said, her eyes filled with joyous tears as she hugged her sister. "I can't believe we won't see one another for two entire months."

"It will go by very fast, I'm sure," Mabel said, her voice tight. "Besides, you'll be too busy to miss me."

"As will you," she said, facing Derek. "Take good care of her."

"There's no need for all that," Mabel said, but Derek took her arm and met Leona's gaze with calm determination.

"I will," he said, so seriously that he was sure it conveyed all he wanted.

Mabel peered up at him as their siblings hurried away and all too soon, the rest of the newlyweds had departed. The remainder of their wedding guests left, and soon enough, they were left alone—the only two people in the house, aside from the servants who were far too busy cleaning up to pay them any mind.

Mabel and Derek made their way up the staircase for their first night together as husband and wife. As they reached the second story, Derek let himself lean toward her.

"How are you?" he asked gently.

"As good as one can be, I suppose. How are you?"

"There's no need to worry about me."

"I'm not worried," she said. "It's just that you've never had a wedding night before."

The gentle reminder that this wasn't her first marriage made Derek stop in his tracks. Mabel's cheeky grin melted away at once.

"I'm sorry. I don't know why I said that."

"I know why."

Her eyes snapped to his.

"Do you?"

"Yes. It's because, despite everything, you're nervous."

"Nervous? Ha. What do I have to be nervous about?"

"A fine question and one I'd like an answer to myself," he said, holding up her hand. He pressed his mouth to her knuckles, and she shivered. "I noticed it this morning, in the church. What's worrying you?"

Mabel visibly swallowed as if trying to consume her own emotions. But he squeezed her fingers, urging her on.

"Tell me."

"It's just... the last time, I was left quite alone, almost immediately." She spoke with her eyes lowered as if meeting his gaze would expose too much. "And I suppose I'm just waiting."

"Waiting for what?"

She lifted her blue gaze.

"Waiting for you to tire of this situation. To realize that you've won—that there's no challenge left here—and then... I don't know. I suppose I'm waiting for you to leave."

Derek stared at her. He couldn't possibly tell her how his heart ached at her words, but then he couldn't let her keep believing such nonsense.

"Mabel, I'm not going to tire of this situation."

"Aren't you?"

"No," he said, somewhat more forcefully than he had meant to. "I'm not Pascal."

"I know that," she said.

"Do you?"

She nodded. "I didn't mean to upset you. It's just where my mind has been all day."

"Then will you grant me the chance to change it?"

She cocked her head. "How so?"

"Come," he said, taking her hand as he led her away. But he didn't take her to his bedroom. Instead, he led her back down the stairs and down the hallway.

"Where are we going?" she asked, perplexed.

"I'm assuming that once you and Pascal were on the ship that you boarded after your wedding, you retired to a private cabin?"

"Yes, of course."

"Well, that's the thing of it. I don't think you should have quite the same experience."

"You don't?"

"No."

"So where are we going?"

He didn't answer and only led her to the library, where they had first had a private conversation. Derek wished he could eradicate all of Mabel's painful memories but knew it was impossible. He could, however, help her make new memories.

When they reached the library, he cocked his head to glimpse at her over his shoulder and found that she was smiling. Emboldened by that, he dragged her into the room, releasing her as he closed the door. Spinning back around, he saw her watching him with fascination.

"This is rather unconventional, isn't it?"

"It is," he said, stalking toward her.

She laughed, and his entire body pulsated. Her giggling faded, however, when he reached up and touched her cheek. Taking a deep breath, she stared into his eyes. Her sole focus was on him, and he had never been so sure of himself in his entire life.

"I have something for you," he told her.

"You do?" she asked.

"Mm-hmm." He turned away from her as he headed for his desk.

A small wooden box sat alone in the center of his writing table. Picking it up, he handed it to her. Confusion flooded her face as she slowly raised her hands to take it.

"What is it?"

"Open it."

Her mouth scrunched to the side as she viewed her gift before opening the top. He waited, anticipating her reaction. At first, she frowned, unsure what she was seeing, but then, it happened. Mabel's eyes widened, and her nostrils flared slightly. She looked up at him, then back down.

"What... How?"

Satisfaction rolled within Derek's chest as pride filled him. He had surprised her. It was a glorious fulfillment, knowing he could amaze her. Even before she had touched it, he was already devising ways to make her light up like this again.

"Derek," she breathed as she scooped out a deck of Flemish Hunting cards. "How did you find these?"

"I made an inquiry or two," he lied, unwilling to admit just how difficult it had been to find them. "Do you like them?"

She opened her mouth to speak but closed it, obviously uncertain how to respond. He basked for a few moments in being particularly pleased with himself, before his heart sank at the slight, sniffling sound she made.

Oh dear. He had made her cry. *Bollocks.*

"Are you all right?"

"Yes," she said, shaking her head as she gripped the deck of cards in her hand, placing the wooden box down on the desk. "Yes, I'm quite all right."

Taking a step toward her, he reached out, then hesitated—wanting to touch her, but uncertain if his touch would be welcome.

"Listen Mabel, I want you to know that I'm aware you're not particularly pleased with this arrangement—"

"That's not true."

He didn't believe her. "You needn't lie."

"I'm not lying," she said, shaking her head. "It's just that, it's all rather sudden, isn't it? And I have had years of believing that this was not something for me."

"What? Marriage?"

She nodded.

"Because of the problems with your first marriage? But those were hardly your fault. Why should they mean you could not find happiness with someone else?"

"Because I don't deserve it," she said. "I was too brash in my youth. Too confident in my choices. In the end, I chose poorly, and I suffered the consequences. The experience...it changed me. I'm not as kind as I once was. It might even be said that I'm mean, particularly to you. I'm jaded, distrusting. Those are not the things any man would want in a bride. So, I had made peace with the idea of spending the rest of my life alone."

She was being too hard on herself.

"But my love, if you spent the rest of your life alone, who would I spend my life with?"

The softness of his question made her want to reach out to him, and almost before she was aware of it, she found her hand reaching out to caress his face.

"I think there would have been at least a hundred women better suited for you than myself. This marriage may prove a risky gamble."

He shook his head.

"I doubt it," he said, dipping his head down closer to hers. "Besides, I can't help but think that lady luck has smiled on me today."

With that, he leaned in and pressed his mouth to hers. Out of the corner of his eye, he saw Mabel drop the cards to the table. Her fingers came up into his soft hair as she kissed him deeply. Like a man touched by Aphrodite's spell, he peeled back his coat as he kissed her, untying his cravat while she clawed at the bottom of his shirt.

Derek reached behind Mabel as she undid his vest buttons. Her gown was tied at the waist, with a series of clasps held the gown together at the back, and once she was finished with his vest, he turned her in an effort not to tear the garment from her body.

She twitched her right shoulder up, escaping the sheer sleeve of her gown. Slowly, he watched as she loosened her other arm from its sleeve and drew the garment down. He made short work of the long corset with ties down the back as the piece of clothing fell to the floor with a soft thud.

Embarrassingly, though, his eagerness was apparent as his hands began to shake. Pausing for a moment, he flexed his fingers, trying to get a handle on his tremor. But he was not able to repress it soon enough. Mabel turned, reaching for his trembling hands, but he drew away before she could make contact.

She frowned.

"What is it?"

"It's nothing."

"If it were nothing, I'd not be curious about it," she said softly, reaching for his hand again. This time, he let her. "They did not shake the night in the fish folly."

"We weren't…"

She was not his wife then, and as ridiculous as it was, being married, bound to one another, made the moment heavy with meaning in a way that was entirely new to him. Still, he did not wish to admit his feelings at that moment. Thankfully, recognition spread across her face at his silence.

"Oh."

For a moment, he was sure she was going to press the issue. Instead, and quite suddenly, she gathered the chemise she was wearing in her grip and swiftly heaved it up over her head before tossing the piece to the floor, leaving her gloriously bare.

While most everyone believed that a virginal wife on her wedding day was something to be admired, Derek had never been so grateful that the opposite was true. He had worried somewhat that Mabel's previous relationship might tarnish their time together, but in actuality, he could only be delighted that it left him with a woman who knew her own desires.

She stepped toward him, so there were barely inches between them, and once more reached for his hand. She placed it at the center of her chest, between her rounded breasts, and held him there until, to his surprise, the shaking relaxed.

As distracting as it was that she was standing naked in front of him, he couldn't help but be amazed. Usually, the only thing that would stop him from shaking was a forced meditation he practiced when he was alone.

Profoundly grateful, and nearly blistering with his clothes still on, Derek quickly undressed, never taking his gaze off Mabel. Her gentle smirk faded once he was undressed, and for a moment, they only stood there, staring at one another.

With a painstaking slowness, Derek's hand approached Mabel's face, grazing her cheek. She closed her eyes and leaned her face into his palm as the softest of moans escaped her lips. God, she was perfect. Once again, he was grateful that he would not have to go slowly as he pulled her close and kissed her.

Mabel's palms were instantly at his shoulders, her fingertips digging into his skin. She held onto him as his tongue searched her mouth, kissing and nibbling at her lips, tongue, and chin as he gathered her up into his arms.

Skin against skin, he brought her over to the gaming table. He placed her down in a half-leaning, half-seated situation before lowering himself onto his knees before the table's edge. A gasp came from somewhere above his head, but he was too desperate to take any note of it, filled with the need to taste her once more.

When his mouth found her core, Mabel's leg spasmed, which oddly made him gleeful as he feasted on her. Never in his life had he been so desperate to taste a woman again, and yet he knew at that moment that he would likely be desperate for her for the rest of his life.

The slickness increased as he shifted. His middle finger came up and moved in and out, pumping in a slow, near-torturous way as her soft murmurs became moans. He wanted to give her every pleasure, and when he had found the rhythm that suited her best, he carefully maintained it as she crumbled and came.

Mabel was shaking against the green felt of the table as Derek stood on unsteady legs. He thought he had never seen anything so beautiful. Her dark hair was spread out around her head like a halo, with one hand by her head and the other at her breast. One leg was bent up while the other hung over the table's edge.

Consumed with need and desire, Derek leaned over her only to be stilled by a hand on his chest.

"My turn," she breathed as she hoisted herself up while dragging him down to the table.

Before Derek's shoulders were even pressed against the table, Mabel was on her knees and her mouth was on him, causing a ferocious tremor to tear through him. His hips bucked as his fists balled at his sides. Lord above, he wanted to hold her, to touch her, but he held back, more desperate to see what she might do on her own.

Mabel's tongue swirled around his cock, in between short bursts of rapid sucking as his mind went blissfully blank. God forbid she ever ask him anything while performing this task, for he would promise her the world and deliver it, if only for the promise to be at her mercy again.

Mabel was generous, if not wicked. Just as the primal build of his desire became uncontrollable, she drew away and rose so that she was face to face with him. To his surprise, she was smiling. He opened his mouth to speak, but before he could, she shifted, moving so that her leg came over him, and in a stunning second, he was in her.

Slowly, she pumped her hips back and forth as Derek silently swore his undying allegiance to her. It was mad, the things that raced through his heart as she gyrated above him. For a moment, he wondered if he should shift, but then her breathing became short and sporadic, as did his own, and in the next moment, they were both shaking from expended pleasure.

Mabel's limp form fell over his chest, and Derek held onto her tightly as he kissed her shoulder. The fiercest sensations cascaded over him as her breath slowed and evened. He wanted to protect her, to keep her happy and content for the rest of his days, if only for the pleasure of seeing her smile.

He was devoted to her, far more than any man should be to his wife, and yet, even knowing that he couldn't stop himself.

After many minutes, Mabel lethargically lifted her head. Her eyes were half closed, and a satisfied grin appeared on her lips.

"Derek," she whispered.

"Hmm?"

"Take me to our bed."

The gentle command and the promise of things yet to come filled his heart with spirits he couldn't quite name. Instead, he pressed a kiss to her forehead.

"As you wish."

Chapter Fourteen

IN THE FOUR weeks since their wedding, Mabel found that her marriage to Derek was entirely different from her marriage to Pascal. She was slowly but surely becoming a believer in Derek's theory, that marriage, given the proper circumstances, could be a wonderful thing. And while it had only been a month, Mabel's confidence grew every day.

Marrying Derek had been the right choice.

Where Mabel's first husband had all but cast her away the moment their marriage contract was signed, Derek proved to be the exact opposite. Not only was he curious about her and her opinions, but he sought her out to share with her nearly everything he did. He was attentive and considerate, and to her disbelief, she found that she wanted to please her husband—of course, she would hardly admit to such a thing.

Derek had explained that because she was the new countess, she was entitled to know how the estate was run, but even Mabel knew that it was highly unusual for a man to seek out his wife's opinion on such things. Most husbands handled whatever business they did while their wives tended to things like running the household, but in her marriage with Derek, there was no definitive line between their works. He would offer his opinions to her as well, though he made a point to explain that she had the final say in most house-related issues. Mabel had experience with keeping house for her father, but while her childhood home was comfortable, it couldn't begin to compare to the Trembley estate, and there was much for her to learn. Fortunately, her mother-in-law had run Trembley household exceedingly well for years, and the staff was well trained and diligent in their work. Still, there were instances where Mabel sensed she was quite out of sync with her new role.

Upon the first morning, when she first began to receive guests as the newly minted Countess Trembley, Mabel found that her forwardness was nearly scoffed at. When Lady Bettina Cole, freshly married to the elderly Lord Cole, came to offer her felicitations, she had to hide her mouth lest Mabel see her snicker at how she received her. To Mabel's frustrations, the British upper crust had the fantastic ability to deliver crushing criticisms with a mere expression.

For nearly two hours, Mabel bumbled her way through receiving guests. It was like that all morning until, blessedly, the Duchess of Combe came just as the Viscountess Montcliffe left.

"Thank goodness you're here, Clara," Mabel said, greeting her friend. "It's been a harrowing morning to say the least."

"Has it?"

"Yes. It's so unbelievably difficult to say or do the right thing. It seems every word I use is the wrong one. Every topic I choose isn't delicate enough. And every lady I meet appears wholly unimpressed with me."

"My word, it sounds as if you've had quite a trying morning. Tell me, who has come to greet you today?"

"Well, the Viscountess Montcliffe was not pleased at all with my inquiries about the confinement of her sister, Lady Delphinia. And Mrs. Franklin found my knowledge of shipbuilding to be, as she put it, masculine. And Lady Bettina Cole snickered at everything I did, yet she did it so subtly it would have been madness to accuse her."

"Oh, bother," Clara said as they took a seat. "The Viscountess Montcliffe is something of a hysterical sort. She's petrified of anything that isn't wrapped in lace. Mrs. Franklin is a conservative woman, so while I disagree with her sentiment, I understand why she would feel that way. And Bettina Cole, formerly Bettina Moppet, has been a snob since the day she was born. Don't pay any attention to her."

"But how can I just ignore what's so obvious to everyone?" Mabel said, her voice strained as she slumped against the back of her chair. "It's plain to see that I've no idea what I'm supposed to do. And even the ladies who've shown me kindness are only acting so generously out of charity."

"My goodness, I've never known Americans to be so self-deprecating," Clara said, sitting up. "Now I've had my fair share of cuts and snubs in society since I wasn't born a duke's daughter. But I've managed since marrying Silas and I've found it's quite easy to fit in, once you know the trick of it. Watch." She pressed her shoulders back to demonstrate a perfect posture. "Now all you have to do is lift your chin like this," she said, tipping her head back. "Keep your tone soft and arrogant, like this." She sighed, appearing bored as her voice became slow and haughty. "And talk about how wonderful or terrible the state of the weather is."

Mabel studied her with suspicion, though she couldn't help but grin.

"How can that be all?"

"Until you get the handle of things, this will work. No one will bother you. As long as you appear annoyed with everyone around you, you'll be left alone. I promise. Although, you should have the dowager or your sister with you whenever you can."

"I'm afraid the entire house has abandoned me and not without reason."

"Yes, I assume it's because they wanted to give you and the earl some privacy."

Mabel's cheeks warmed. It was true, but it was somewhat uncomfortable to address it so openly.

"Even so. I wish someone had left me a rule book or something about the topics on which I'm allowed to speak about during these meetings."

"Well, have no fear. I'll remain for the rest of the morning and next week, Holly will come once she's returned from Lincolnshire. She's very well versed in the decorum of ton behavior. More so than me at least. But I wouldn't worry too much about what these people think."

"No?"

"No. After a few weeks, you'll be old news and they'll be onto the next topic that arouses interest. They're only interested in the latest gossip. I lived through it myself, you know."

"Really? Even as a duchess?"

"Oh, yes. Silas's divorce was infamous before we married. His previous wife had seemed to everyone to be the epitome of a fine British lady. I was considered quite a step down, socially."

"At least you're English," Mabel said, unsure if she should feel buoyed by Clara's words or worried by them. "I'm just afraid I won't be able to ever accustom myself to this sort of life. It's as if every move I make, even the correct ones, are scrutinized and commented on. Just this morning, I was walking alone in the park, and—"

"Alone?" Clara interrupted, her brow crunched.

"Um, yes," Mabel answered. "I always walk alone. Accompanied by a servant, of course."

"The earl doesn't wish to walk with you?"

"No, it's not that," Mabel said, her gaze dropping. "It's just that, I walk to clear my head and if Derek were with me, I'd be distracted. It would negate the purpose of the whole thing."

"I suppose I can understand that," Clara said. "But be wary. Gaining a reputation for walking alone in the mornings, especially as a countess, may cause you some unwanted speculation."

"What sort of speculations?"

"I couldn't begin to imagine," Clara said. "But if nothing else, the ton will mark you down as peculiar."

"Well, perhaps I am peculiar," Mabel said stubbornly.

Clara smiled gently at her.

"Perhaps you are. And that will suit me quite well, as I'm decidedly peculiar myself."

Mabel couldn't help but return the countess's smirk. She was exceedingly patient with Mabel, and it was kind of her to lend a helping hand.

The rest of the day was spent attending to guests, making menus, picking out new linens, and several other domestic things that called her attention. By the time evening fell Mabel was exhausted and happy when Derek suggested having dinner in their room.

In a glaring contrast to the days, their evenings were spent with each other, and Mabel was grateful for the nightly reminder of Derek and his unwavering interest in her day, as well as his soothing support for everything she did.

Lying in bed together later that evening, Derek was half propped up by pillows, holding the book *Precaution* in one hand while the fingers of his other hand flittered up Mabel's spine as she lay on her stomach. They both were nude as neither felt a particular need to be otherwise. She was re-reading a letter that had arrived from Leona, describing her time in Scotland. It was late, and while it would have been an excellent time to fall asleep, it seemed neither person could come up with a reason to do so.

She cocked her head to the right and watched her husband as an increasingly common fluttering sensation took hold of her chest. He really was an attractive man. Every time she gazed at him, she practically swooned. It was rather embarrassing, particularly because everything about his face had once bothered her so. But now, she could barely hesitate from touching him.

Obviously sensing her staring, Derek glanced down at her, and Mabel inhaled.

"Is there something I can help you with, wife?" he murmured, his brown eyes warm with implication.

She simmered with pleasure at being called that.

"When will you take me to Scotland?" she asked, shaking her

letter teasingly in the air. "Leona says it's the most beautiful place on earth. I want to see if she is correct."

"Anytime you like, I suppose," he said, leaning down to brush a kiss against her forehead. Mabel trembled as he kissed her temple, her cheek, and the corner of her mouth as his book closed. "After parliament lets out."

"When will that be?"

"Less than a fortnight now."

Mabel rolled onto her back and wrapped her arms around Derek, who slid further down in bed to hold her in turn, his long torso pressed against her breasts. His fingers tangled through her dark locks and tugged slightly, sending a pleasurable pain through her. She let out a soft gasp, and he inhaled deeply at her response.

"Parliament doesn't meet tomorrow, does it?" she asked, knowing very well that it didn't.

"No."

"Then I think we should spend the day in bed," she said as she leaned to kiss him, only to find air.

She blinked, realizing that he had shifted backwards. He had an apologetic expression on his face.

"Unfortunately, I have to go to Boxwood Park tomorrow."

"Tomorrow?" Mabel repeated. He nodded. "But why?"

"The final inspection of the fish folly. After the last time, I insisted that I inspect it myself before signing off on the work."

"Oh," she replied, somewhat deflated. "Should I go with you?"

"I had planned on riding horseback as it's faster than the carriage. I should be back tomorrow evening." He paused. "Unless you wish to come? If we're going together, I've no objection to taking the carriage."

She stopped to consider it, then shook her head. "No, I don't suppose so. Not if you'll be back tomorrow evening. I have plenty to do here, as well as an engagement with Holly tomorrow. She's going to introduce me to her lady's salon."

"Ah, then I hope you'll take comprehensive notes," he said,

bending his head to kiss the tip of her nose. "I've never been privy to a lady's salon before."

"I'll let you know all about it," she said, smile deepening just before he kissed her.

That was the most direct change in their relationship since marrying. Derek appeared far more at ease than she had remembered. Even the tremors in his hands seemed to disappear, at least in her presence. Mabel doubted the shakes had gone completely.

She hadn't asked about it, not wanting to pry. If Derek didn't see a reason to explain it, she wouldn't poke, even if she was curious about it.

Regardless, though, the Derek she had first met and the Derek she was now married to seemed to be two completely different people. Yet, Mabel was still wary. Fears from her previous marriage still kept a hold of her, and deep down, a warning haunted her, saying that all was not well and that happiness was not meant to last. Not for her, anyway.

Rising early the next morning, Mabel felt a strange dread about the day. She wished to stay in bed with her new husband, but he was already up and preparing to depart by the time sleep left her.

"I'll be back tonight," he said as he leaned over Mabel to kiss her.

Derek pressed his mouth to hers as his hand touched her chin. Mabel closed her eyes, enjoying the sense of safety and comfort she found in the display of affection. Her arms wrapped around his neck as she held him close to her, unwilling to let him go.

"Mabel," he breathed against her lips. "I must go."

"Not yet," she mewled, kissing his freshly shaved chin.

She inhaled deeply. He smelled of soap and the leather that sharpened the blade that shaved his stubble.

Slowly, her kisses lead down his neck as she gently nipped at his skin. He shivered in her arms.

"You're going to provoke me, love," he whispered.

Mabel dragged her fingernails down his spine, and around his hip, grazing against the front of his buckskin trousers. Her hand curved around the length of him, and he hissed into her ear.

"Mabel," he warned.

"Derek," she teased back, only to suddenly inhale as his arms snaked beneath her back and caught her in his strong embrace.

She smirked against his cheek as he rolled over her, hauling her body on top of his. Her tousled hair hung down over her shoulders as she looked down at her husband, his own gaze warm and intense as he stared up at her.

Bending at the waist, she came down, moving her mouth gently over his, though she didn't kiss him. No, she was feeling playful and wanted to tease him. Shifting her legs so that she straddled his leg, her hands went to either side of his head to brace herself above him.

With a determined intent, Derek moved to undo the buttons on his vest, but Mabel put one of her hands over his to still them. He obeyed, as one straight brow lifted slightly. Mabel's fingers trailed down painfully slowly, until they pressed again over the front of his trousers.

Derek breathed through his clenched teeth as she found one row of buttons on the side of the flap. With her gaze locked on him, Mabel felt a heady rush of power course through her. Derek would let her do anything she wanted at that moment and she relished that feeling as her hand slipped beneath the fabric of the front flap of his trousers. Gripping the length of him, she squeezed gently, sliding her hand up and down. It was almost intoxicating how focused he was on her. With the slightest shifting of her shoulder, her nightgown fell off, exposing her left breast. Wondering how far she could push him before it became too much, she rebalanced herself so that she could lift her other hand and use it to lightly caress herself, teasing the peak of her nipple under his lustful watch. She began to methodically grind her hips against his leg.

His breathing became strangled at the sight as her hand worked faster. It was nearly as enjoyable as orgasming herself to see the man she cared for being brought to the edge. Her own breath was becoming short by the time she felt his strong hand find her knee and then begin to move upward, kneading her straddling thigh as his thumb found the center between her legs. She gasped as his finger entered her, both of them moving their hips in sync, searching for the same ecstasy.

"Mabel," he whispered, but her name on his lips was almost too much. "God, you're beautiful."

His sweet words undid her and to her slight embarrassment, she began to shake. Derek found release at the same time.

Mabel went limp and fell onto her husband's chest. Her ear was directly over his heart and she closed her eyes as she listened to his heartbeat come back down to a more regulated pace.

"You, my lady, will be the death of me."

He couldn't have known, but his words didn't sit well with her. After several more moments of silence, Derek tried to shift out from under her, but Mabel held onto him. She didn't want to let him go and the earnestness in her touch must have alerted him that she was troubled.

"Mabel?"

"Hmm?"

"Are you all right?"

"Yes."

"You needn't lie."

"I'm not lying," she said.

It was obvious that Derek didn't believe her—and he was right not to, because she *was* upset, though she couldn't say why. Something just felt wrong. He bent his head and kissed her on top of the head.

"I have to go," he whispered.

She nodded and lifted her head. His warm, dark eyes were watching her with concern.

"I know."

"If you'd like to come with me, you can."

She wanted more than anything to go with him, but she knew she was being silly. Besides, the feelings she was experiencing in that moment needed some further exploring, because quite honestly, she wasn't sure she had ever felt like this before.

Shaking her head, she moved off of him so that he could get up.

"No. I'm much too busy."

He nodded, rolling to the side as he stood up. He crossed the room, taking off his shirt and vest to replace them since they were now stained with his release. He gave her a mock scolding look, before dressing in another vest. Pulling on his coat, he buttoned it up and headed for the door, but before he could reach the handle, Mabel spoke.

"Derek."

He turned.

"Yes?"

But what could she say? There was no reason for her sudden trepidation that morning, and she certainly didn't want to give him any reason to worry. Perhaps she was just being foolish.

Mabel shook her head.

"Have a safe ride," she said, as her face fell when he closed the door behind him.

What was wrong with her?

Pushing the covers off, Mabel got up and decided to dress. She should take her morning walk early. That always seemed to clear her mind. Yes, that would likely shake off whatever faux concern she was experiencing.

Dressed in a handsome mauve walking dress with chocolate piping, Mabel was surprised to hear her door open as Juliette entered.

"Juliette, it's early," Mabel said as the maid pointed to the chair before her vanity table, silently directing her mistress to sit. "You needn't worry about doing my hair. I was just going to braid it and pin it myself."

"Non," Juliette said, fighting off a yawn as she brushed Mabel's hair.

For several minutes, Juliette worked in silence as Mabel chewed the inside of her bottom lip, pushing down the sense of dread that seemed unwilling to let go of her. After Juliette finished, Mabel stood, but her maid had a disapproving countenance about her.

"Quelque chose ne va pas," she murmured.

Her words mirrored Mabel's anxious feelings so exactly that she shivered. But she tried to push those concerns aside, pretending she didn't know what Juliette was talking about. "What's not right?" she asked, studying herself in the mirror. "My hair?"

"Non."

She turned to Juliette and noted the crease between her brow. "Well, whatever it is," Mabel stated firmly, "let's not wallow. I'm sure whatever is bothering you will melt away at some point today."

Juliette frowned, evidently not agreeing with Mabel's optimism. She left the room as Mabel pulled on her gloves. Within minutes, she met George, who had been awake since Derek's departure. He had taken it upon himself to order the coach to be readied, and soon enough, he and Mabel were making their way down Grosvenor Street.

Deciding that she was being ridiculous and superstitious, Mabel exhaled slowly as she began to pay attention to things around her. The softness of her kid gloves against her fingertips. The sound of the horses' hooves clip-clopping along the cobblestone road. The smell of rain that seemed unsure if it should fall from the sky. Concentrating on things in her immediate vicinity always helped bring her mind into focus.

As she climbed out of the carriage with George's help, she began her walk. Briskly, she strolled along the Serpentine, wary not to get too close as the footman followed her.

Her thoughts drifted to the situation between George and

Juliette. Their recent interactions had become somewhat strained, and whenever Mabel mentioned George in Juliette's presence, she would grow quiet. Which was rather unlike her, considering how vitriolic she had been toward him in the beginning.

Was there a romantic connection blossoming between them? Mabel, thankful for the sudden distraction, glanced over her shoulder to see if she might speak to him when she saw the wary look on the footman's face. Looking to see what had caught his eye, she spotted a well-dressed man approaching them from several yards away. That dread she had been experiencing all morning suddenly flared, and she felt a flash of warning wash over her as if some internal instinct was telling her she should turn around and run.

Staring at the man, her feet slowed as he lifted his head to reveal his face from beneath the brim of his hat. Their eyes met, and Mabel's stomach dropped as the last person she expected to see glared back at her.

Pascal.

Mabel lost a step for a moment before correcting herself.

"My lady?" George said behind her as she stopped in front of Pascal. He smirked at her and bowed gracefully.

"My dearest Mabel. How good to see you," he said, his accent curling around his words.

"My lady?" the footman repeated, coming forward.

"It's all right, George," Mabel said softly, waving her hand behind her.

"Who's this?" Pascal said, bending slightly to peek around her. "Your new husband? I thought you married an earl, not a footman."

"What the hell are you doing here?" she asked quietly, stepping away from George so that he might not overhear them. "Have you lost your mind coming to London?"

"Well, when I read in the paper that your sister was coming to England, I had the good manners to visit. But then I heard that you were here and, to my surprise, remarried."

"Stay away from me," she said shortly, turning on her heel.

"I would not walk away from me so quickly, ma cherie," he threatened softly, causing her to stop. Rotating back, she saw him glaring daggers at her. "We've much to discuss."

Curiosity mixed with the apprehension engulfed her.

"Like what?"

"I'm in the business of finding capital. Capital you will help secure for me."

She huffed.

"Are you mad? You took my entire dowry. It's not my fault you sank a sizeable fortune into whatever failures you've had. No doubt the pile of rubble you call a home."

A flash of fury showed in his blue eyes. He was dedicated to his ancestral home, and Mabel knew it.

"Be careful, ma cherie," he said with a quiet threat in his tone. "As I was saying, when I learned of your sister's engagement, I thought to contact you through her, but when I learned that you had accompanied her, I thought I might see what you had to offer."

"Nothing for you."

"But I have something for *you*," he said, reaching for something within his coat pocket.

It was a folded piece of paper that he held it out to her.

"What is this?" she asked, taking it to read. She frowned. "I don't understand."

"It's not quite legitimate, but it will cause you a great deal of time and energy, as well as money to deal with it."

"What is it?"

"A statement declaring our divorce invalid."

Mabel's eyes snapped to his.

"Our divorce was perfectly valid. My father handled it himself."

"Oui, that's true. But a very dear friend has written this up for me and it will cause quite a bit of a public scandal here for you, and your new husband, should you choose to ignore me."

"So, you're trying to blackmail me with faux documents?" she hissed. "Unbelievable."

"Believe it."

"What do you want?" she snapped at him.

"I require some money."

"Perhaps you should work for a living then if you're in such dire straits."

The flash of impertinence shone in his eyes.

"Once the regime is back in place, I will be handsomely rewarded."

"What regime?"

"Do you not follow the papers? Oh no, of course you don't. Well, for your information, Charles X of France will be ruling the country soon enough. His ascension to the throne is eminent, if only he has the resources to manage it."

"What do you want of me then?"

"Funds. From your new husband."

Mabel stared at him for a moment before a choking sound came from her throat. He had lost his mind.

"Ha," she laughed. "You must truly be mad. Derek would never give you a farthing."

"Oh, I think he will. Especially because if he doesn't, I have plans to sue."

"On what grounds would you sue him?"

"Not him, ma cherie. You. If I don't get what I want, Mabel, I will go to the papers and expose you as a bigamist."

"A bigamist? Surely you're joking."

"I am not."

"It wouldn't up hold in court."

"No, but it would ruin your reputation for a time. And even if you're vindicated in the end, will everyone truly believe it? It's so much more delicious to think of someone as guilty, whether they are or not. You wouldn't be able to show your face once everyone reached the conclusion that the Countess of Trembley was actually just a whore." He said the word loud enough that

George could hear, and rage bloomed within Mabel's chest. "And I don't think your husband would appreciate his good name being dragged through the mud by the likes of you."

"My lady, I believe we should leave," George said firmly.

"Burn in hell, Pascal," she snapped at him as she spun away.

Before she got several steps away, she heard him yell after her.

"Then so be it!"

Chapter Fifteen

Derek's return to London was not nearly as eventful as he had expected, mainly because he had spent so much time during the ride home imagining what sort of homecoming he might enjoy with Mabel. By the time he arrived, it was already well past sunset, and he hurriedly handed off his horse to a stable hand and entered the house, climbing the stairs two at a time to reach his bedroom as quickly as possible. He might appear eager, but then again, he was, and there was no use denying it. He simply couldn't wait to see his wife.

It was rather fascinating how much he had changed since their wedding. During the long trip back and forth to Henley-on-Thames that day, Derek had enough time to examine his new life, and he realized how much more at peace he felt having Mabel as his wife. It wasn't something he had been expecting when he'd proposed to her, yet he couldn't deny that she had altered his moods for the better. He was less sharp with himself and more patient with others. Hell, even the shaking of his hands had lessened.

Derek had been equally surprised by how much he craved not only the physical aspects of their relationship but the mental and emotional ones, too. He was well and truly obsessed with Mabel, and he couldn't ignore how his body reacted to being so close to hers again. He wanted to undress, bathe, and lay with her a dozen times before the morning.

But as he reached the bedchamber, it was apparent that he wouldn't be engaging in such activities.

Mabel was already sleeping soundly, tucked beneath the thick brocade comforter of their bed. Her deck of cards sat on the edge of the end table. It was odd to see them as she usually kept them in their box, but then he assumed she had used them to soothe herself because she'd missed him.

Touched, he began to undress. While he had been eager to hear about her day, he guessed it was too late. He would have to wait until tomorrow. The ride to Boxwood Park and back had been long and exhausting. As soon as his head hit the pillow, Derek was fast asleep.

His dreams were ambiguous and vague, with pale versions of people moving in and out of his mind as the night wore on. Eventually, he realized he was standing in a dark pond, with the water waist-deep, surrounded by nothing but blackness. He thought he could hear Mabel's voice, far away, but he couldn't make out what she was saying.

Thankfully, the dream faded, and soon, he was opening his eyes, searching the bed with his hand. The soft, broad curve of Mabel's hip met his hand, and he sighed peacefully. Rolling to his side, he saw his wife, her mouth partially open with her hair covering her closed eyes. A soft snore escaped her, and Derek couldn't help but smile.

It was strange how much his opinions of her had changed in the days since he first met her. As each day passed, he became more convinced that he'd made a brilliant decision in choosing to marry her. They were ideally suited, and if he was a pessimist, he might be worried that something terrible was on the horizon—a counterbalance to how perfectly his life had fallen into place. But as far as he could tell, all was well and seemed likely to continue so.

Even now, as Mabel snored next to him, every inch of him wanted to wake her. To love her and show her just how much he found her irresistible. But something gave him pause. Perhaps it was her peaceful countenance, or maybe it was his desire for her to be fully rested, but he restrained himself from waking her and decided to rise and get dressed instead. As quietly as possible, he left the room before he could disturb her.

He was descending the stairs on his way to the dining room for breakfast when George appeared at the bottom of the steps, looking eager to gain his attention.

"My lord," he said with a quick bow. "I sought to speak with you last night, but by the time I learned you had arrived, you had already retired and I didn't wish to disturb you—"

"It's all right, George. What was it you wish to speak to me about?"

The footman fidgeted as Derek walked around him, continuing to the dining room.

"Well, um… Did the countess not mention anything?"

The worry in his man's voice gave Derek pause. He faced him.

"No."

"Oh."

A sense of dread began to fill Derek's gut. "What would she have to mention?"

George squirmed, looking as if he didn't know what to say. "Ah, well, um… I do not wish to betray her confidence."

Impatience rose, and it took everything Derek had to keep from snapping at the lad. "George. What happened?"

"Well, the countess was approached by a man yesterday morning in the park during her walk. A man who, well… She addressed him as—"

"Who?"

"Comte de Retha."

Derek stared at the footman, unsure if he had heard him clearly. The Comte de Retha? Why would Mabel's former husband be approaching her during her morning walk?

"Excuse me?"

"He did not stay long in the countess's presence, and I was not close enough to catch everything they said, but I know I heard him mention their marriage. She was quite displeased when we left the park."

"What business would the Comte de Retha have with Mabel?"

"I do not know, my lord."

That wasn't the answer Derek wanted to hear. What purpose would the comte have for seeking Mabel out? And wouldn't that be something worth telling him? Granted, she had been sleeping when he returned home, but it seemed very much something to stay up for.

Derek turned and took several steps into the dining room. After a moment of silence, George spoke up.

"M-my lord? You should know that the countess was most distressed."

Derek delayed lowering himself into his chair as an arrow of discontent shot through him. Shaking it off, he sat and glanced at George, unsure what to say.

"What did they speak of?"

"There were only a few words I overheard. Money, regime and well," George stalled, visibly swallowing his distress. "Um, bigamy, my lord."

"Bigamy?" Derek repeated as his discontent evolved into silent outrage.

His hands gripped the armrest of his chair, and he nearly stood up, wishing to go upstairs right then and shake Mabel awake to demand an explanation, but he stopped himself. He could not act when he had so little control over himself. He was furious and worried for reasons that weren't entirely clear to him.

As George waited for him to speak, Derek took a deep breath.

"Thank you, George."

"My lord, do you wish me to—"

"That will be all."

Visibly unsure, George bowed after a moment and left the

room. After several minutes of sitting at the table without getting up to make himself a plate, a servant came forward to plate him some food, but Derek held his hand up.

"I'm waiting for the countess to join me."

"Yes, my lord," the servant said, instantly replacing the plate on the sideboard.

"Have the papers not been delivered yet?" he asked.

"Ah, not yet my lord."

"Bring them at once when they do."

"Yes sir," the servant said as he left Derek alone.

How long he sat there, Derek wasn't sure, but he kept his eyes on the door as his mind raced. What reason would Pascal have to corner his wife during her morning walk? Blast those walks. Why was Mabel so dedicated to them? He should have forbidden them the moment she arrived on his doorstep. But even as the thought passed through his mind, he knew she would have bristled and retaliated three-fold.

As his mind reeled with possibilities, some harmless, some infuriating, Mabel finally entered the dining room.

Dressed in a violet morning gown with gold leaves trimmed along the hem and bust, she was a vision of beauty and desirability. Short puffed sleeves were embroidered with the motif as well, and her dark hair framed her face, with most of it pinned back, and bits of curls hung around her cheeks.

Her eyes, however, appeared tired, and when her gaze met his, Derek noticed a slight jump in her.

"Derek," she said, coming forward. "I didn't know you were home."

"I slept next to you last night," he said evenly. "Did you not notice?"

"I guess I didn't," she said, noticing he didn't have a plate in front of him. "Have you already eaten?"

"I was actually waiting for you."

"Oh. That's kind of you, but you didn't have to. How long have you been here?"

"It's of no consequence."

Mabel seemed confused by the pointedly even tone of his voice, but rather than commenting on it, she nodded hesitantly as she walked to the buffet. A servant helped dish a bevy of eggs, toast, jams, and meats onto her plate, though it appeared that she didn't point at any of it.

Watching her fix her coffee, Derek wondered why she hadn't brought up her meeting with Pascal yet. Every moment she didn't mention him, his exasperation grew.

He waited as she added a spoonful of sugar and cream to her beverage. She stirred it slowly, glancing up at him occasionally, and eventually picked it up and brought it to her lips before cursing.

"Blast it, Derek, why are you staring at me like that?" she asked, putting her undrunk coffee down.

"Like what?"

"Like you're plotting my demise."

He didn't make a move.

"Tell me, wife, how was your day yesterday?"

Mabel's face became pale, and he braced himself. God help her if she lied to him.

"Why?"

"Isn't it a husband's prerogative to inquire about his wife's day to day activities?"

"From your tone, I can only assume you already know."

"Know what, my love?"

The endearment was meant to be mocking, but the moment he said it, he realized it was far too close to reality.

"That Pascal is in town," she said, the words seemingly difficult to say. "He found me in the park yesterday morning during my walk."

Derek dropped his napkin to the table.

"What have I been saying? Those bloody walks of yours—"

"Do not blame my walks for me being ambushed by that man. He would have found me somehow."

That caught his attention. Derek's gaze narrowed.

"Why are you so certain that he would have found you regardless?"

"Because if he is anything, it's persistent."

"And what did he want from you?"

Mabel opened her mouth and then shut it, instead chewing on her bottom lip as she apparently debated on what to say next. Hesitating was the wrong thing to do as Derek's fury mounted even further.

"Tell me," he demanded after a moment of unbearably strained silence. Her attention snapped to him.

"It's of no consequence. I told him no."

Derek stood up and walked toward Mabel, who was still sitting.

"What," he said slowly, "did he want?"

After a moment, she exhaled.

"Money."

"Money? For what?"

"He's convinced Charles X is poised to take over in France. Being a loyalist, he would receive state funds once he is crowned, but they need money to put him on the throne."

Derek frowned.

"And he thought you would help?"

"I don't think he has any other prospects. He kept my dowry after the divorce, but I guess he used it to repair his ruin of a castle. When he learned that I had married a wealthy man, he thought you might be the source of funds he needed."

Derek actually let out a puff of audacious laughter.

"Is he mad?"

"Yes, he is," she said, shifting in her chair to look up at Derek. "Because when I told him he wouldn't receive a penny from you, he threatened the respectability of this house."

Derek felt a cold snap course through him, as any man would whose home was threatened. It was primitive and deadly.

"And how would he do that?"

"By claiming that our divorce was improperly filed, meaning that it never went through—and that I am, therefore, a bigamist for having married you."

"And are you?"

The shocked expression she wore on her face instantly told Derek that he had gone too far, and he regretted it. But he had no chance to apologize, even if he could have found the words. After a moment, she seemed to collect herself and stood, purposely hitting his leg with her chair as she moved to leave, but Derek quickly followed her. By the time she was halfway up the stairs, he reached for her hand.

"Mabel, wait—"

But she drew it from him.

"Don't touch me."

"You cannot think that I would have been pleased with this information."

"And that gives you the right to insult me?"

"I didn't insult you. I merely asked if it were true."

"Which is insulting!" she snapped. "As if I would have married you if my divorce hadn't gone through." She paused for a moment, her gaze shifting to the ground. "Is that what you think of me?"

Regret slammed into Derek's chest as he reached for her other hand. Stepping up, he stared down at her.

"No. No it's not."

Mabel seemed at least partially pacified by his words. But before either of them could say anything more, the front door suddenly opened. They both turned to see Leona and Alfred, arguing and looking visibly worried as they hurried in.

"—means absolutely nothing—"

"—yet if it were true—"

"—but it's not!"

"Are you so certain?"

Derek came down the steps, his one hand still holding Mabel's as they both approached their siblings.

"Alfred, Leona," Derek said, halting before them as a footman hurriedly helped them out of their traveling cloaks. "I didn't expect you until this evening."

"We arrived in Watford last night, and had planned to have a peaceful enough evening, when Leona suddenly had an unsettling feeling," Alfred said, his eyes darting in between them. "She insisted that we travel through the night."

"Are you all right?" Leona asked, approaching her sister with worry written all over her face.

"Oh, Leona."

"We made it into the city just as the sun came up and I'll admit, I was rather annoyed that I had been nipped out of breakfast, so I convinced Leona to stop for something to eat."

"It's already in the paper," Leona said.

"Am I missing something?" Derek snapped, annoyed that everyone seemed informed of something other than him.

"Did you not receive the papers this morning?" Alfred asked.

"No."

"Oh no," Mabel said softly under her breath.

"Do not worry," Leona said, coming forward and gathering Mabel into her arms. "It will be proven as a lie soon enough."

Derek frowned as he saw the servants who had been in the foyer scurry away. It seemed they knew something he didn't. Something, it seemed, they were hiding from him.

"We had some trouble locating the papers this morning," Derek said, his temper rising. "Why? What has been reported."

Instead of answering, Alfred gave Mabel an apologetic look before handing over the folded newspaper he had been carrying beneath his arm.

Unfolding it, Derek read the top headline, something about the passing of the Gaol's Act, before a second large headline caught his eye from the lower right corner.

Bigamy!

The newly minted Countess Trembley, née Meadows, previously Comtesse de Retha, has been accused by her former husband, the Comte de Retha, of bigamy. The comte claims:

While my wife and I certainly partook in marital strife, I never consented to a divorce.

The words on the page seemed to shake and dissolve after that. Peering up, he saw Mabel's strained face. He handed the pages to her, feeling disconnected as she read it. Was the comte indeed that desperate? To accuse Mabel of bigamy was outrageous unless…

Unless there was a reason to.

"He's obviously lying," Mabel said.

"Even so, the damage is done," Derek said quietly. Though his anger was palpable, he wasn't sure if it was directed at her. A familiar tingling sensation began to pinprick at his fingertips, but he ignored it. "Why on earth would he publicly slander you if he didn't have just cause?"

"Because he's irate that I refused to give him any money, and he wants to punish me."

"Then maybe you should have paid him off and saved us from this embarrassment," Derek declared loudly before striding toward the front door.

"Where are you going?" Alfred called after him, but Derek didn't answer, shaking out the aggravating prickling of his hands as he left.

He wasn't sure where he was going, but he wouldn't stand another minute in this house, not when his entire family's reputation had been besmirched. Why hadn't she considered the consequences of her words, especially knowing the man she was dealing with?

Perhaps the hope Derek had felt at the beginning of their marriage had been misguided. Maybe Mabel wasn't capable of handling her new position in the ton, or maybe she just didn't care enough about it, not truly. The thought made him sick with doubt and while a part of him knew she hadn't meant to dishonor the Trembley name, he couldn't help but feel betrayed in some ways.

Mostly, however, he just felt hollow as he departed from Trembley Terrace.

Chapter Sixteen

"Why would he just leave like that?" Mabel asked, pacing the bedroom floor as she fidgeted with the Flemish playing cards Derek had given to her as a wedding present. "He's never going to forgive me for this. I know it."

"Of course, he will," Leona said, leaning against the bedpost as she watched her sister walk back and forth. "He didn't seem that mad."

"Didn't he?"

"Well, he didn't shout or yell or stomp a foot."

"No, he just left. Likely too furious to do anything else. Except hate me."

"He doesn't hate you, Mabel."

"He would have every right to, though." She shook her head. "Why would he go without telling anyone where he was going? It's not as if I contacted the papers."

"Perhaps he needed to calm down, to refrain from saying something he might regret," Leona suggested. "Or maybe he went to the papers to insist they print a retraction." Mabel sighed, shoving the cards into the pocket slit at the side of her gown.

"I'm sure he'll be home soon."

Derek had been gone for several hours, and the sun was just setting over the city. Mabel and Leona had sent Alfred out at noon to search for Derek and bring him home, but as neither had returned, Mabel could only assume that Derek was still missing. Or maybe he and his brother were at their club, privately regretting their marriages.

"I loathe Pascal," she said as she brought her thumb up to her mouth. "Why would he do this?"

"Don't bite your nails, Mabel."

"I can't help it," she said, dropping her hand. "Damn Pascal. I can't believe this is happening. What have I done to deserve this?"

"Nothing," Leona reassured her, though, in the next instance, her voice dropped. "Except…"

Mabel looked down at her sister, who sat at the foot of Mabel's bed.

"Except what?"

"Well, you cannot deny that Pascal has good reason to be angry with you. It's not a terrible surprise that he would try and ruin you—although, being a comte, you'd think he'd have more dignity."

"What did I do to him that wasn't justified, given the way he treated me?" she asked hotly, focusing on those words.

Leona tilted her head and gave her sister a nervous glance. "You've never really told me everything that he did," she said quietly. "But I know how the experience changed you. Even without knowing the details, I'm sure it must have been terrible. But to someone who doesn't know you like I do, it might seem as if the way you treated him was rather…harsh."

"The way *I* treated *him*?" Mabel repeated, incredulous.

"You did sneak away in the middle of the night, leaving him a laughingstock," Leona pointed out. "Then you told all papers what a dishonorable man he was, having lied about his fortune back in France, effectively eliminating his ability to marry anyone else of fortune in America."

"And so, because I saved other poor women the difficulties of being married to such a man, I must be eviscerated publicly?"

"No, I believe you were entirely right in what you did. Of course the other ladies in America needed to know that he was not a man who could be trusted. But I can only imagine that those who are close to Pascal have been spending this time telling him how grossly he was mistreated by you, and how justified he would be in taking his revenge. You made a significant enemy in your former husband. Not all men are sensible creatures, particularly ones who believe they have been wronged."

Mabel sighed as she walked, likely wearing a hole in the floorboards when suddenly a knock came at the door. Both sisters glanced up as Juliette entered. Mabel went to her.

"Madame," she said, curtsying, though her face was usually pale and taut. "Un visiteur est ici."

"I'm not taking guests."

"Madame… Il refuse de partir."

Mabel frowned.

"What do you mean he won't leave?"

Leona stood up.

"Who is it?" she asked, coming around her sister.

The tone of Leona's voice caught Mabel's attention. She had been too upset at first to realize that Juliette, whose usual disposition was solid if a bit cold, was shaking.

Dismay suddenly filled Mabel's heart as she took Juliette's hand.

"Who's here?" she asked quietly.

Juliette kept her head low.

"C'est le comte."

Mabel blinked once. Then again.

"Excuse me?"

When Leona's hand came up and touched her shoulder, Mabel jumped. What was Pascal thinking, coming here? Had he lost his mind?

"Do not go to meet him," Leona said, her hand gently gripping Mabel's wrist. "There is nothing good that can come from confronting him."

"But Juliette said he's refusing to leave. Derek will likely strangle him if I don't have him thrown from this house at once," she said, pulling away from her sister. "You stay here. I'll be right back."

"Oh no you don't," Leona said, quickly at her sister's heels. "I will not have you meet that man alone."

Mabel smiled at her sister as they followed Juliette out of the room and down the stairs. Juliette was obviously upset, and Mabel didn't plan to keep her in Pascal's presence for long.

"Where is he?"

"Dans le salon, madame."

Mabel hurried down the hallway, only to turn just before entering the room. "Thank you, Juliette, but you do not have to see him again."

"Mais madame—"

"No, it's quite all right," she said, straightening her back. "I don't want you to be near him, as I'm sure he only has wicked things to say." Mabel faced Leona then. "And I think you should wait here, Leona."

"Oh no, Mabel, that isn't wise—"

"I know, I know. But I've words to say to him that I don't wish you to hear."

"You'll only agitate him."

"I can't very well have him ruin my life without some critiques."

"But what if he gets angry?"

"What could he possibly do? I'm safe within my home, aren't I?"

Visibly reluctant to let her sister be left alone with such a man, Leona was still too loyal to argue for long, and gave her a nod.

Taking a deep breath, Mabel entered the room while quickly closing the doors behind her as if to protect her sister and Juliette. To her great displeasure, she saw Pascal, arms held behind his back as he peered at a painting, seemingly unimpressed. Without even glancing her way, he spoke.

"It's garish, no?" Motioning toward the painting before glancing at her. "But then, I find everything in this household rather crass."

"What the devil do you think you are doing here, Pascal?" she asked, coming forward with stomping feet. "Have you completely lost your mind? When my husband arrives—"

"But my dear, your husband is already here," he said, holding his arms out wide.

"Stop that," she hissed. "You've already made quite a large mess for me, as I'm sure was your plan. Now will you leave me alone? If you've hoped to cause me difficulty, I assure you, your revenge has been successful."

"Revenge?" he said, coming toward her. "Ma cherie, I do not care for revenge."

Mabel gave him a speculative glare.

"Then what do you want?"

"I told you. I need funds."

"But I don't have any."

"Do not lie to me, cherie. Your husband's wealth is well known and I do not doubt your father provided a small fortune for his daughter."

"I would rather die than give you anything."

"Ma cherie, do not tempt me. If we cannot force the hands of these men, we will simply have to try something else."

Mabel tilted her head.

"What do you mean 'we'? And what are you plotting?"

A chilling sneer spread over his face as the door to the parlor opened up. Mabel turned to see a man, Jean, with Leona in a brutal hold. One arm was wrapped around her waist, while the other hand had a small but vicious-looking knife clutched firmly against her throat. Leona's eyes were wide with panic, and as fear consumed Mabel, she rushed toward her sister. But she barely took two steps before Pascal grabbed her arms from behind and spoke menacingly into her ear.

"You see, your husband may not find you worthy of a ransom. But the little love affair between your sister and her spouse has been well documented. I had hoped to avoid using it to my purposes by coming to you first, but you've left me no choice."

"Let her go."

"Oh, I will. Believe me, there's nothing I like less than a Meadows woman. However, I will only release her when her ransom is paid."

"What ransom?"

"The ransom paid to a kidnapper," he said as Mabel tried to wrench out of his grasp. But he only grabbed her back and hissed into her ear. "I'm taking her back to France with me."

"Nm!" Leona tried, only to quiet herself as the blade pressed tighter against her neck.

"Pascal, please," Mabel pleaded. Terror enveloped her entire being as she faced him. "Don't do this. Take me instead. You don't need her."

"No, cherie. You've already proved worthless in this endeavor. But your sister will fetch a fair price."

"Take me as well then," she said, her fingers gripping his arm.

"So that you might help her escape? No."

"Pascal, I'll... I'll help you, I promise," Mabel said desperately, eyes darting back and forth between a frightened Leona and him. "Anything you wish I'll do, but just please, release her."

He paused and glanced at her, obviously reading the desperation on her face.

"Anything?"

"Yes, please, anything."

Mabel watched as Pascal's face contorted as if weighing his options. He was probably correct in that Mabel wouldn't fetch as high a price from her husband as Leona would from Alfred, considering how furious Derek was at her, but she could see it in his face that Pascal wanted her. Probably because he wished to harm her, but it didn't matter to Mabel. As long as Leona was safe.

She squeezed, her fingers digging in.

"Please, Pascal," she said, her tone dipping. "I'm begging

you."

That did it. Pascal's brow lifted at the mention of begging. It had been his favorite thing to make Mabel do when they were married.

"Very well, cherie," he said. "Jean?"

With the single call of his name, Jean hit Leona in the head with his closed fist, and she crumpled to the ground, unconscious.

"No!" Mabel yelled as Jean stepped over her sister and came toward her.

He grabbed her, and she tried to fight him off at first, but Pascal's voice echoed around her.

"Do not make this any more difficult. I can still change my mind and take your sister instead. Remember, you promised to be…obedient. So let's go."

The man hauled Mabel toward the door. In a desperate attempt to leave behind some sort of clue, Mabel was able to fish out a card from her dress pocket and tossed it on the ground before Jean twisted, lifting her into the hallway.

As they stalked into the hallway, Mabel saw George where a pair of maids were huddled around him as he lay bleeding from his stomach. Juliette was gone, and Mabel was grateful that she wouldn't have to see her former spouse, as well as not having to witness the attack on George. All this, because of her, she thought as she was led out of the front door and down the steps into a waiting carriage.

As the driver cracked the whip, the horses took off daringly for the darkening, crowded streets. Mabel stared daggers at Pascal as he settled into his seat.

"Do not scowl," he ordered. "You'll produce wrinkles and likely lessen your value to your husband. Or father. Whoever will want you after this."

Her frown deepened.

"You must be a desperate man if you've gone through all this trouble," Mabel spat. "Derek will be seething when he discovers what you've done."

"As long as he pays, I don't care what that little English prig thinks," he said as he called out to the driver. "Take the south road."

"South?" Mabel repeated. "Are we not going to Dover?"

"That would be the easiest, but unfortunately it is also the most likely and we don't wish to be followed. We'll be leaving out of Folkstone."

"But—"

"But will we be gone from these shores before your husband can track us down? Yes, that's the point."

Mabel glared at him.

"This is madness, Pascal. Even if you do get what you want, there will be repercussions for this. Even as a comte, you cannot just kidnap people and be forgiven."

"I'm not searching for forgiveness, cherie. I'm trying to put a king on the throne. Once that happens, I will have no more reason to fear the courts of this country," he said. "Nor will I give any thought to your pathetic husband, yet I suspect he might actually thank me once all of this is done."

Mabel shook her head.

"Why would Derek thank you for anything?"

"Because of the favor I plan on doing for him, once he pays me."

"What favor?"

"Well, as I know personally what a problem you can be, I thought I might relieve him of your miserable self." He sneered. "I think an 'accident' will occur during your return. Maybe something involving the Chanel crossing. It was water that you feared most, wasn't it?"

Mabel swallowed as she stared into his cold eyes, as a cold dread flooded her heart. He was going to kill her and by taking the south road, no one would find her in time to stop him.

Chapter Seventeen

DEREK SAT IN Gavin's billiards room, a garishly decorated space that had yet to be redone by the baroness, who was painstakingly changing each room of the London home one by one. The former baron had famously adorned his home with the most outrageous patterns, textures, and artwork. Derek had to admit that he'd always rather liked it. Not because he admired the décor in and of itself, but because most people who entered Gavin's home couldn't help but stare at the walls and ceilings, not Derek. Tonight, he sat in the corner of a burnt pink chair adorned with a tropical floral pattern, the red felted billiards table untouched as he stared blankly across the room.

Derek had gone to his solicitor's office but was informed that his solicitor's wife had just given birth and that the man would therefore be out of the office for a day or so. Derek had one of the clerks send a letter to the *Times* with threats of a libel suit before he had gone to Whites for some solace. But that had been a mistake. A number of gentlemen, some he had even considered friends, had leaped at the opportunity to mock him about the allegations of his wife's bigamy. It seemed the entire city had read the article. Derek had deserted his club and then come to Gavin's home, hoping to find a place of peace to settle his mind.

He sat in the dark room, flexing his hands to alleviate the prickling sensation that wouldn't leave. He needed to try and figure out what to do next. Derek knew that publicly, he had to deal with the comte, but every bit of him wished he could handle de Retha the same way he had Lord Nesby. A suit against the man and the paper would satisfy most of the ton, but he knew rumors would persist for some time afterward, regardless of what was decided in court. Still, he needed to take care of the legality of everything before confronting his wife.

He knew it wasn't right to sulk, but he hadn't been able to even look at Mabel before leaving that morning. Logically, he knew she wasn't a bigamist. And he was aware that her former husband was likely just trying to ruin her, but there was something deep and visceral that had bubbled up upon hearing the allegations. Mabel was *his*, and even a suggestion otherwise was a betrayal.

It was why he had come to Gavin. He knew he needed time to gather and direct his anger at the proper people to keep him from lashing out and upsetting his wife again. But when he arrived, he found only Gavin's elderly aunt in residence, as Gavin, his wife, and his wife's sister had gone out. Gavin's aunt hadn't objected to him making himself at home in the billiards room, so that was where he had gone.

Soon enough, however, his peace was disturbed when the baron returned.

Coming into the room, Gavin did not speak. He only began to set up the billiards game. Once he had, he removed one of the sticks from the wall and began to line up his shot. For nearly a half hour, he played by himself, never acknowledging Derek, who grew more and more irritated. It was a tactic Gavin had used on Derek and their friend Silas for years since they were at Eton together. He would simply ignore the others when dealing with issues until they couldn't stand it. It was annoying how well it worked.

Finally, Derek stood up.

"I suppose you'd just continue playing until the end of time, is that it?"

"Ah, Derek. I didn't see you there."

"Shut up," Derek said as Gavin sauntered around the table.

"I take it you've read the papers?" Gavin asked casually.

"The entire blasted city has read the damn papers."

His friend nodded.

"You don't believe it, of course."

"No."

"Good. Then why are you here?"

"Because I'm bloody upset and there's no other place in this city for me to find any peace."

"Why not your own home?"

"Because she's there."

"But you just said you don't believe it."

"I don't."

"Hmm," Gavin said, bending down to get a level view at the table he was playing on. "Well then, why are you here?"

Derek grumbled. He didn't want to admit his emotions, but it was Gavin, and he knew his friend wouldn't betray his confidence.

"Because I'm angry. The Trembley name has been dragged through the mud."

Gavin stood up.

"Surely you do not care more about what the ton thinks than how your wife must be feeling?"

"What do you mean?"

"I cannot imagine the countess is feeling very good at the moment. Particularly if you left her without so much as a discussion as to what's to be done about the situation."

"And why would I need to discuss it with her? I went to my solicitor and had one of his clerks post a letter to the *Times*. I also had a footman find out where the comte is staying to delivery him an ultimatum."

"And that ultimatum is…?"

"Make a public apology and leave England or stay and die."

That caused Gavin to pause.

"Die?"

"Yes," he said, standing up. "I'll be issuing a challenge for a duel at sunrise if he doesn't do as I say and if it comes down to it, I will not hesitate to shoot him dead."

"Derek, you've always been the calm sort—"

"My family honor has been insulted, Gavin, as has my wife, and I will not stand for it."

"But his claims are a lie. Maybe you could consider a countersuit? For slander. Take this frog to the courts and see what they do to him."

"It wouldn't be half as satisfying as what I wish to do with him."

"I suppose not."

"Besides, I cannot allow such slander," Derek said. "Even if it's warranted."

Gavin frowned.

"What's that supposed to mean?" he asked, but Derek ignored him. He was aggravated and didn't want to hear about how he was being unreasonable. But Gavin wouldn't let him get away with sulking. "Whatever you wish to do, do it, but don't punish your wife. She didn't have anything to do with that article."

"Except marrying him in the first place."

"You're being a right prat, you know," Gavin said, annoyed. "She's already dealt with her own fair share of gossip and snubs as a result of her divorce. I can only imagine the marriage itself was unbearable. Whatever mistakes she's made, I'd say she's more than paid for them. And now, when she finally has a husband she can rely on, you abandon her?" he shook his head. "For God's sake, Derek. You should be ashamed of yourself."

"Well, I'm not."

"Your father would be."

That was too far. Derek stormed toward the table, but his friend didn't back down.

"My father would have forbidden me to marry her in the first place."

"And you would have listened?" Gavin asked, disbelieving. "You were always so ready to push back at him when he was alive, but ever since he died you've tried to mold yourself into some person you're not."

"I should be more like him."

"But you *are* like him, in the places that count. I'll tell you what, your father wouldn't abandon his wife, regardless of what trouble she caused him and I am certain he would have some choice words for you at this moment."

Cross and ashamed, Derek left the room, ignoring his friend as he called out for him to wait. But he didn't want to listen, especially since he knew deep down that everything Gavin said was accurate. His father would have been disappointed in him for allowing such a fool to come into his marriage and try to ruin it. Derek had fallen for the comte's attempts to sow discord in his relationship with Mabel, and he knew he would have to apologize to her.

But before he could reach the front door, a man burst into Gavin's foyer. It was Silas, breathing heavily as Gavin came up from behind Derek.

"What are you doing here?" Derek asked.

"Alfred sent word to me. There's been an attack at your house."

Derek stared at his friend, unbelieving.

"Excuse me?"

"Alfred said he came home to find Leona unconscious, a footman stabbed, and the house in disarray. Mabel is missing."

Undiluted fear seemed to explode in him, but he remained perfectly still, except for the trembling in his hands.

"What the hell do you mean she's missing?"

"Just that. No one could find her and when the staff was questioned, her maid, Juliette, said that she had been taken."

"By whom?" Gavin asked.

"The Comte de Retha."

A rage unlike any he had ever experienced engulfed Derek as he pushed past his friend.

"I'm going to kill him. I'm going to fucking kill him," he bit out as he hurried down the front steps.

Without thinking, he grabbed the reins of Silas's horse and rode through the streets of London as fast as he could, nearly colliding with several people as he went. When he reached his Mayfair home, he dismounted and charged up the stairs as fast as possible.

Entering the library, he found several maids and footmen, coming in and out to tend to Leona, who was resting on the sofa, and George, who was lying flat on the ground as a doctor tended to him. Alfred was seated beside Leona while Juliette hunched over a prone lying George, wiping a wet cloth over his forehead.

"What the bloody hell happened?" Derek thundered as Alfred turned to face him.

"Pascal was here," Alfred said, his voice strained. "He tried to take Leona, but Mabel convinced him to take her instead."

"Why the hell would she do that?"

"To protect me," Leona said from the chair. "He wanted to hold me for ransom, but Mabel promised him anything if he would take her instead."

Anger, fear, and misery seemed to come in waves at Derek, hitting him one after the other. He would strangle her once he found her and made sure she was safe. Derek could understand the need to protect a sibling, but it didn't take away from the fact that he was furious that she had left willingly with a man who seemed to delight in causing her misery. It was enough to make him go mad.

"Where did they go?"

"He said he was taking her to France," Leona said.

Just then, Gavin and Silas arrived, having raced after Derek.

"They won't go to Dover then, it's too obvious," Alfred said.

"They might if they thought to throw us off, knowing we'd discount that option. We'll have to split up." He looked at his brother and friends. "Two of us will ride to Dover, the other two will ride to Folkstone."

"Alfred and I will go together," Gavin said, taking a step forward.

"Very well. You two go to Dover. Silas? We'll go to Folkstone."

"Are you sure?" the duke asked. "I should think if he was in a hurry, he'd choose the fastest route out of England."

Derek remembered what Mabel had said about Pascal. He believed himself a clever man and always preferred to make others out to be a fool.

"They might, but I doubt it." Derek swerved to see where George lay on the ground and spoke to the doctor. "Will he recover?"

"Yes, well enough," the older man said. "He's suffering a sore head more than this scratch on his abdomen. A few days rest should put him to rights." The old man jerked his head at Juliette. "Especially with this one tending to him."

"Mon pauvre," she said soothingly to the footman, who appeared rather pleased despite the cut on his head.

At least George had Juliette to fuss over him. Derek would need to provide him with some sort of gift to reward him for trying so valiantly to protect the household, even if he wasn't ultimately successful. He would think about that later.

"Very well," he said to the others. "Let's go."

But before he could leave the room, he saw on the floor a rounded card lying face up. Bending down, he picked it up and saw it was the queen of hearts. His gaze snapped to Leona.

"Why are Mabel's cards out?"

"She was fidgeting with them before Pascal came," Leona said. "She must still have them on her."

He nodded, tucking that information away. With quick orders and goodbyes, Derek, Alfred, Silas, and Gavin were out of the house and on their way to the two ports that shipped to France.

Chapter Eighteen

Mabel held on tightly to the playing cards she had in her pocket as the carriage stopped. It was dark, and while they had ridden chiefly in silence, she felt the weight of Pascal's glare on her.

"Nous sommes ici," Jean said, peering out the window.

"Oui," Pascal said, his gaze on Mabel. "Keep your head down and don't make any trouble."

As they exited the carriage, Mabel tucked her chin to her chest, but she saw out of the corner of her eye the wooden sign swinging off the post. The Black Stag Inn. Mabel had never heard of it, though that hardly mattered. She wasn't familiar with England at all and likely wouldn't have any idea where she was until they reached France.

The carriage ride had been an arduous one, as their driver had been trying to outrun the sunset and then carried on at breakneck speed well into the evening. Mabel doubted they would stay at the inn long, but the horses needed to be changed, and Pascal was too spoiled and self-indulgent to go without a meal and some rest.

Before entering the building, she plucked two cards out of her pocket and scattered them at the doorway at her side, hoping the bits of paper would not blow away. With the rounded edges, they weren't like most cards, so they would stand out if Derek were to see them—he would know they came from her. It was probably foolish, but she hadn't any other ideas. She could only hope that by leaving a trail of sorts, some sort of calling card should anyone be coming for her, she might be able to help herself be found.

How she hoped to be found...

They entered the tavern, which wasn't empty as it appeared from the outside. Some sort of merry-making was happening. A group of men and some women were carrying on, singing, and drinking from tin tankards.

"All the better," Pascal said as they pushed through the crowd. "We're likely to go unnoticed by a bunch of drunkards, and the staff will be too busy dealing with them to pay us any mind."

Mabel didn't answer, unsure what he might do if she made a scene. She had thought about it, but considering how far she assumed they were from London, she wondered if anyone would take her plight seriously. Even if they did, she doubted anyone would want to stand up to Jean, who was particularly menacing looking.

Once their rooms were paid for, Mabel was followed by Pascal as they made their way upstairs. The housemaid who showed them to their room hurriedly lit the candles and stoked the fire as another maid came in with a kettle of hot water. She poured it into a chipped blue and white ceramic bowl that sat on a small table and left, followed immediately by the other housemaid.

Mabel spun around and saw Pascal kick the door closed before glaring at her.

"Must you be in here?" she said with a sigh. She'd hoped for at least a little time to herself.

"I'm not letting you out of my sight."

Mabel thought for a minute to argue with her captor, but it would likely be in vain. He wouldn't let her go. So, she washed her face and neck in the water basin while her captor watched. He moved to sit on the bed across the tiny room as she dried her face with a towel.

"I'm sure you're distrustful, but I assure you, there's no need to watch me like a prisoner. I will not run."

"It's not only that, cherie," he said, pushing off the bed as he approached her. Mabel shivered with disgust as his index finger touched her shoulder. "You offered yourself in your sister's place, did you not? You said you would do *anything*. I intend to make good on that arrangement."

Mabel froze for a moment. Surely he didn't mean to bed her? She was married, for heaven's sake. Thinking quickly, she tried to appear nonchalant, ignoring the evil glint in his eyes.

"Very well," she said cooly. "But as I recall, the sight of blood never made you very amorous. Unless you've changed your tastes since then?"

Pascal squinted as his hand fell away.

"Oh. I see," he said with disgust. "Well, there's no need to rush, I suppose. I'll keep you alive until your ransom is paid."

"And then you'll kill me?"

"Oui. I don't see why I shouldn't."

"Because it is a sin, not to mention you'll be charged with murder."

He laughed, sending another shiver down her spine.

"My dear, the future king of France is a close, personal friend. He will not deport me to any country that calls for my hanging," he said as his cold fingers once again touched her, on the cheek this time. "Which means, I can do whatever I wish with you and no one will ever make me pay for it."

Mabel twisted her face away from his hand, but he grabbed it harshly, drawing it back so she stared directly into his angry eyes. Without hesitating, she spit in his face.

The crack across her cheek had been stiff and yet expected as she fell to the bed. Bringing her hand to her cheek, trying to soothe the tender flesh, she glared at Pascal.

"My husband will make you pay."

"Ha," he sneered, towering over her. "I'm sure your husband

will just be pleased to be rid of you once this is over with. After causing him a world of embarrassment as well as siphoning a large amount of his fortune away, I should think he'd be glad when you're dead, with all the trouble you've caused."

"I didn't cause anything—"

"Haven't you? You can't imagine any of this would have happened without you being who you are," he countered, his sneer drifting over her with repugnance. "A whore."

Mabel didn't respond but tried to push out all the genuine guilt that continually bombarded her. Derek certainly would have had a quieter life had he married someone else. But she couldn't think about that now.

She had to escape.

After Jean delivered a tray of hot stew and fresh bread, Mabel forced herself to eat while Pascal watched. After she finished, she got into bed as Pascal sat in a chair pressed against the door, unwilling to share a bed while she was, as far as he knew, on her monthly courses.

"We're leaving in two hours," he said, kicking his dirty boots off. He blew out one candle and then another. "Wouldn't want to wait around for any rescuers, would we?"

Mabel turned her back on him and stared at the small, dirty window. It was terribly small. She probably couldn't even fit through it, she thought as the candles were blown out. At least, not with her gown on. She *might* fit in just her underthings... but that would be scandalous. She couldn't sneak out the window without any clothes on. She would likely be sent to prison if she was caught. Then again, she could toss her dress out first and put it on afterwards.

Yes. That was an idea.

She tried to close her eyes and rest, but Mabel could not sleep. Minutes passed, and soon, nearly an hour had gone by since the last candle had been extinguished, and the same crazy thought hadn't left her head.

What if she *did* climb out the window?

Sure, she might get caught. Possibly even killed, but then, staying would hardly be safer. And what if she *was* able to get away? What if she could hide or run away and get back to London somehow? It was worth a try, wasn't it?

As quietly as possible, she reached behind her and searched around for the tie at the back of her gown. Once she undid it, the garment loosened, and she could shimmy around and draw her arms from her sleeves. She gently pushed it down her waist and over her hips before kicking her feet silently beneath the covers. Then she worked on the petticoat and pulled her legs out of the dress until she lay on the bed in only a shift and corset.

Taking a deep breath, she shifted one leg, then the other off the straw-stuffed mattress. With a painstaking slowness, she rolled her body off the bed as her feet touched the wood floor. Gathering her dress in her arms, she tiptoed toward the window. Wrapping her fingers beneath the pane of glass, she slowly and steadily opened it up.

When it didn't squeak or creak, Mabel was sure she was the luckiest woman to have ever lived until she glanced down. There was nothing below her except a small, thatched ledge. She would probably break a leg if she tried to jump, she thought as she stuffed her dress out the window. It dropped with a soft thud. Glancing over her shoulder, she saw Pascal sleeping as soundly as a snoring man could.

There seemed no reason not to try, as her situation was dire. Perhaps she could crawl across the ledge to a broader portion of the roof. Turning back to the window, Mabel silently sent up a prayer as she lifted her leg and began her climb out the window.

Making sure not to place too much weight on the sill, she gripped the wooden frame and, finding her footing on the roof, ducked her body beneath the open window and lifted her other leg.

The day had been warm, but the night was surprisingly cool, and it was nearly black outside, save the tiny sliver of the waning moon, partially hidden behind a large maple tree as a gentle breeze rolled through its leaves.

Mabel gripped the sill with her hands as she rotated to face outward. Realizing that she wasn't on a ledge that extended all the way across but instead was on what had to be the roof of a bay window, her heart dropped. There was nowhere to go.

"Blast," she mumbled as she eyed the stables' roof several yards away beneath her. The roof was thatched, and lord knew what lay beneath it. If she jumped, she would probably go through it.

Then again, she could crawl back through the window and attempt to overpower Pascal. Even if she succeeded, however, she was quite certain she couldn't defeat Jean.

The situation was bleak, and just as she had concluded that she would likely stay out on that ledge all night, the soft, distant pounding of horse hooves echoed. Someone was coming down the road. Worried about being seen, Mabel tried to press herself against the window as a slight creaking noise sounded behind her.

She instantly stilled as two dark-cloaked gentlemen on horseback came galloping into the stable yard. The only light came from two lanterns, one hanging off the doorway into the stables and one depending on the door to the inn and providing little illumination. However, the movements of the first man, who had come off his horse swift and eager, seemed familiar to Mabel. From two stories up, she squinted, unable to make out his face. The second gentleman took both horses to the stable while the first headed for the doorway below her. Glancing down, she watched as he came to the inn entrance, only to stop suddenly.

He seemed to bend down and pick something up.

Her breath hitched.

"Mabel," she thought she heard him say before pivoting his head over his shoulder to shout. "Silas! She's been here."

"Derek?" she shouted, just as a hand cruelly grabbed and twisted her wrist. "Ah!"

Pascal yanked her back, causing her to lose her footing as she fell. In an instant, she was being held by one hand as her body dangled from the window.

"Mabel!" Derek yelled from below.

"Merde," Pascal cursed, glancing past Mabel before refocusing on her. "Well, it seems our time has come to an end. Adieu."

Before Mabel could even consider what he was saying, she felt his grasp loosen around her wrist, and she dropped.

"AH!" she screamed as she fell from the side of the building, her body scraping against the edge of the bay window.

There wasn't enough time for her mind to reel over how painful it was going to be to slam into the earth. Before she could inhale again, she was caught by a pair of strong, almost punishing arms.

"Mabel," Derek's voice sounded through the jumble of limbs and fabric. "Mabel, are you all right?"

She flailed and swiveled as he set her feet down to the ground, but she jumped against him, arms wrapping tightly around his neck.

"Derek! Derek, thank God."

"Easy, love, easy. What the devil are you wearing?" he asked, setting her back so he could observe her attire. Fury flashed across his face, discernible even in the darkness. "What the…" His nostrils flared. "I'll kill him."

"No, no, nothing happened."

"You're practically naked!"

"Derek, listen to me."

"Hush," he said, his arms not releasing her. "You're safe. Silas!"

The duke came forward.

"Countess," he said, almost jestingly formal considering the situation.

"Take her inside. And for the love of God, get her dressed."

Mabel bristled.

"I threw my gown over there. I wouldn't have fit out of the window had I been dressed."

"Then you should have stayed put."

"And been carried away to France? I think not."

"Now, see here," Derek started as a commotion came behind them. As all three turned, two men on horseback escaped from the barn and took off down the road. "Bloody hell!"

"Derek, wait!" Mabel yelled as her husband tore away from her. "Where is he going?" she asked the duke.

"To catch them."

"He won't be able to."

"I wouldn't doubt him, my lady. Derek is an experienced horseman," Silas said as Derek stormed from the stables on the back of a horse, racing down the road. "And he has every intention on dragging that man back to London with him."

"But why?"

"Well, for the suit."

"What suit?"

"The defamation suit. He plans on suing the comte as well as the *Times* for the article declaring bigamy."

Mabel closed her eyes as shame drained through her. A lawsuit would only prolong the humiliation. They would be talked about and gossiped about for years, no doubt. Lord, how Derek would despise her at the end of it.

"What's this? What's all the noise?" a man, the innkeeper, said from the door that had opened behind Mabel's back. "Good Lord! What do you think you're doing?"

"Come," Silas said, directing her toward the door before addressing the man. "This woman is in need of a hot bath, immediately, as well as something to eat."

"I'm not hungry."

"I'm not terribly concerned about that," Silas said as he shuffled through the doorway. "But I suggest you bathe and get dressed as quickly as possible. I'd rather not have to answer to Trembley as to why you are still in your underclothes when he returns."

Mabel couldn't argue with that and was quick to make use of the tin hip bath that was carried up into the room that she had previously been in. The same two tired maids from before appeared. They hurried up and down the stairs to fill the hip bath as quickly as possible while shaking out and brushing Mabel's dress once they retrieved it from outside.

Having no qualms about modesty, Mabel was quick to undress while the maids helped with soap and towels. It was a reasonably short bath, and she was soon dressed again in her violet gown.

After her hair was braided and twisted up at the back of her head, Mabel came out of her room and headed down the stairs to meet a waiting Silas, who had a mug of some kind of steaming beverage.

"It's tea. Drink it up."

"You certainly believe that we are in some sort of hurry," Mabel said, ignoring his command.

"Because Trembley will undoubtedly be here any moment."

"Are you so sure of his abilities?"

"Are you so disbelieving in them?" he asked, which caused her to glance away. "I assure you, countess. Derek is more than capable of handling this."

A part of her wanted to argue that he couldn't possibly. Even if he did capture Pascal and drag him back to London, the fiasco that had been caused had already gotten so out of hand that he would never be able to control all of it.

But before she could decide whether or not to tell the duke her fears, they were interrupted by a terrific din coming from outside.

"Ah, that should be him," Silas said. "Best to get outside then. He'll want to leave immediately."

"Well, let's not keep him waiting," she said, her voice surprisingly sharp as her nerves displayed themselves in aggravation. She was thankful he ignored it. She knew Silas didn't deserve her hostility, and Derek certainly didn't, but she was embarrassed her issues had brought such trouble and mortification to her husband. If she could, she'd make herself disappear and take the first ship back to Philadelphia, but that wasn't an option. She was stuck here, facing Derek, who was bound to be even more furious with her than he had been that morning. He would likely never let her forget what a difficult situation she had put him in, and she loathed herself for it.

Indeed, as she followed Silas into the stable yard, she could barely look up. It was only through side glances that she saw an unconscious body, most likely Pascal, lying over the backside of a horse before she was being helped into the same carriage that Mabel had been carried off in. Silas decided to ride alongside the carriage and went to saddle his horse.

Moments later, Derek entered the carriage, and within seconds of the door closing, they were off. He hadn't even sat down yet, but Mabel was so deep in her own shame that she couldn't keep it in anymore and had to speak.

"I know you must hate me," she blurted out, her hands balled into tight fists. "I would understand if you never wanted to see me again. If you wished for a divorce, I would grant it."

The air between them became heavy and thick as the last of her words seemed to echo in the small area. But she couldn't face him. Shame consumed her until he finally spoke.

"Never."

Chapter Nineteen

DEREK STARED AT Mabel, unsure if he had heard her correctly. Surely she hadn't said divorce, not after all this. No, there wasn't any way in hell she would be rid of him so quickly.

"Never," he repeated as she finally lifted her face, her gaze catching his. "I'm never going to let you go, Mabel. Never."

"But I've made such a mess," she said, emotion making her voice crack. "The gossip, the papers... I can't bear to think of everything I've put us through."

"But bear it, you will, because there's no way on God's green earth that I'm going to let you leave me."

She looked up at him, her eyes sparkling in the dim light of the carriage lamp.

"Silas said you were going to sue. First Pascal, then the papers."

"I am."

"But you can't," she begged.

"Why not?"

"Because we will be a laughingstock. It will just drag the whole thing out. You will be humiliated and..." She stopped, shaking her head, almost unable to continue. "I don't want to bring you any more shame."

Derek tilted his head as if he couldn't understand what she was saying. It would be somewhat uncomfortable to be reported upon in the papers, yes, and there would be whispers and gossip for a time, but as the Trembleys had often been subjects in the gossip columns, he doubted it would be much different. And it certainly wouldn't be enough to convince him that divorcing her would be the best option.

He shook his head.

"So, you would be done with all of this? With us, just so that I might not know shame?"

"Yes," she said like a woman agreeing to her demise before an executioner.

"But you don't care what anyone thinks. You've said as much. Frequently."

"I don't care what they think of *me*," she clarified. "But you… I hate to think that you might… might…"

"Might what?"

"Might suffer from something I did."

Her concern was strangely moving, and Derek's chest expanded.

"But what did you do?"

Mabel sighed loudly. "I caused all of this, haven't I? The papers, Pascal. Everything is my fault. He never forgave me for humiliating him and now I've gone and done it to you and I can't bear it."

"My love," he began, shaking his head. "You did not cause Pascal to do all the things he has done."

"No, but it's because of me that he is here. If I had never come here, he wouldn't have given that story to the *Times*."

"If you hadn't come to England, he still would have wanted money, he still would have tried to extort it from your family, and he likely would have taken your sister instead. Isn't that what nearly happened anyway?" he asked, but Mabel refused to agree, the stubborn woman she was. "My love, the only thing you did was divorce a man who wasn't a good husband."

"But it's because I married him in the first place that all this happened."

"And I wouldn't have it any other way."

Mabel evidently thought she misheard him, for her countenance as she glanced up at him was one of shock.

"You... You what?"

"If marrying Pascal and divorcing him caused you to have enough concern about your sister that you sailed across an ocean to try and keep her from making a mistake, which in turn caused us to meet, then Mabel, I am glad for it." He gathered her hands into his and continued. "I loathe that he once had the right to touch you, that he was permitted at one point to kiss you. Believe me, I've been ill about it for weeks. But if marrying Pascal and then divorcing him brought you and me together, then I can only be grateful. And as for blaming yourself for all this, I will not allow it. In fact, as your husband, I forbid it. Pascal's actions are his own."

Mabel's stunned expression suddenly made Derek feel lighter. He touched her cheek, and he could see the way she fought to keep her eyes from fluttering.

"But... But what of the suit?"

"What about it?"

"The papers will report the entire trial."

"Yes and?" he asked, tilting his head. "Did you think I would allow someone to denigrate my name? Our marriage?"

"But it will cause such an embarrassment," she said, but he was shaking his head again.

"Mabel, you're the only thing I'm concerned about," he said. "Don't you understand that? The papers, the ton, the entire world could burn away and I wouldn't care if you were at least by my side."

To his surprise, tears began to roll down Mabel's cheek. It tore him apart to see her so sad. He gathered her into his arms. At first, she tried to tug away, but he wasn't having it.

"Derek—"

"Easy, my love, easy," he said soothingly into her hair as he rocked her slightly. "You are the most important thing to me,

Mabel. Not my name, or reputation. You."

"But I—"

"But nothing," he said firmly before pulling back. He framed her face with his hands. "You are my life." His gaze searched hers for a moment before words he never believed he would speak honestly bubbled from his lips. "I love you, Mabel."

A broken noise came from her throat as she leaned in to kiss him. Derek's hand drifted to her back and held her close as he kissed her deeply. Grateful to have her in his arms again, he murmured a little love between their kisses.

"I love you too, Derek. I do," she said.

A heavy sigh expelled from his chest. "My God, it is strange to hear you say that."

"Why?"

"Because I might have hoped for it, but I never believed it would happen."

That seemed to challenge Mabel, who pressed deep kiss after deep kiss across his lips, cheeks, and nose until he let out a sensual laugh.

"I do," she said earnestly. "I do love you. So very much."

"Do you also trust me?"

"Yes."

"Then understand that whatever issues might come our way, we will meet them together. I'm not going anywhere."

Mabel seemed emboldened by his words and brought her palms to his cheeks as she kissed him again. Being the gentleman he was, Derek allowed it.

"But wait," she said after a few moments, trying to put some distance between them. Derek nodded absently, waiting for her to say whatever she needed to say so they could return to kissing. "How did you reach Pascal?"

"Ah, well, it wasn't exactly a brilliant move."

"What happened?"

"I was able to ride up next to him and I grabbed his reins. He swung at me. Got me in the mouth," he said as his hand touched his bottom lip. "But he wasn't fast enough and I was able to grab his arm. I yanked him back, and his horse kept moving while he fell to the ground. I thought I had killed him but then I found him unconscious. I believe the horse's hooves knocked him out. Then I brought him back."

"What about Jean?"

"I'd guess that he continued. He cannot be unaware of what a defamation suit would mean for the comte."

"Will it be that terrible?"

"For him," Derek said, kissing the worried crease between her brow. "But you needn't worry about that."

"How can I not?" she asked stubbornly.

"Mabel, none of it matters," he said.

"But it does," she said, shaking her head. "What if he comes back? Or wishes to retaliate?"

"Will you allow me to handle it then?"

She pouted. "I hate to be such a burden."

"Would you consider me, or rather your sister a burden if she found herself in this situation?"

"Of course not—"

"Then, my love, take heed and know that it is the same for you." His thumb gently rubbed the edge of her cheekbone. "You belong here, with me." He expected her to argue more, but she bobbed her head in an agreeing sort of way. "Good."

"Derek?"

"Yes?"

"How far is London?"

"I don't expect to get there until morning."

"Will Pascal stay unconscious until then?"

"Not likely, but then Silas is set to take care of him should he wake."

"Then may I request something?"

"Of course."

"Will you hold me? Just until I fall asleep."

"Of course, my love."

And Derek did, and many hours later, he also fell asleep, at peace at last with his love back in his arms.

Epilogue

Christmas, 1828

THE FAINTEST OF thuds caused Mabel to lift her head for a moment before she rolled into Derek's shoulder. Though it was still dark and neither was genuinely awake, he lifted his arm up and drew her close to his body, their bare skin touching beneath the heavy brocade blanket and sheets.

Once again, a soft, pitter-patter noise, now accompanied by high-pitched laughter, sounded from somewhere beyond their bedroom and above their heads. Mabel's brow lifted as she fought for slumber.

"It's morning," Derek whispered, his voice thick with sleep.

"It is not," she countered, snuggling deeper into his arms. "It's still dark."

"Not for long."

Mabel lifted her head once more and peered over her shoulder. The sky visible through the large windows of Greystone Manor's guest lodgings were still an inky blue. She dropped her head once more.

"I'm not getting up," she said stubbornly.

A gentle kiss dropped to her nose, and her eyes fluttered back open. There was Derek, smiling at her with a heated gaze that she had come to know as trouble.

"My love, it's Christmas," she murmured in protest, rolling onto her back. "It's inappropriate."

"Says who?"

"The church, I believe."

"Bollocks," he said as he kissed her neck.

Mabel stretched, to give him more access as his hand came up to her breast. She purred slightly, ignoring the tenderness of her chest as Derek moved his mouth along her collarbone. She had been extra sensitive as of late, and her husband had enjoyed it immensely.

He began to kiss his way down her center, as her fingers tangled in his reddish-brown hair that had grown slightly longer in recent months.

"Derek, we cannot."

"Of course, we can," he said, as he reached for her hand. Bringing her fingers to his mouth, be began to lightly suck on the tip of her ring finger. "Besides, we've only got a few minutes before—"

A knock sounded at the door, causing them both to sit up instantly.

"Uncle Derek?" a tiny voice called out. "Aunt Mabel? It's Christmas!"

"And baby Francis is awake!" another voice called out.

"Children!" the matronly voice of the duke and duchess's nanny, Mrs. Dunlap, chided. "Come away from there at once!"

Mabel smirked and moaned as she fell back, her head hitting the soft pillow beneath. Derek snickered and bent down, nipping at the tip of her breast. She tried to swat him away, but his fingers encircled her wrist and held her hand above her head. He took her nipple into his mouth as his tongue swirled, gently pulling her out of her slumber.

"Derek," she tried to chide, but she didn't stop him. "We can't."

"What a bashful thing you are," he murmured against her skin. "Surely this isn't the woman who made love to me in the middle of the Scottish woods—"

Mabel's fingers found Derek's mouth.

"Hush. That was different," she said. "We weren't guests at our friends' home for the holidays."

"I assure you, they won't mind."

"Perhaps not, but, oh..." she said as he continued, his hand moving over her stomach and lower. "Derek. The whole house is awake."

"It's barely dawn."

"You just said it was morning."

"Easy now," he whispered, his mouth finding her. "Let me love you."

Mabel might have rolled her eyes if they were open, but as it was, she merely sighed as he shifted over her. It was indecent, to say the least, but knowing what the coming day would bring, Mabel couldn't help but indulge with her husband, as hungry for him as ever even after three years of marriage.

Mabel had been cautious in those early months of matrimony, particularly after the trial with Pascal. Her former husband had been charged not only with libel and fraud but also kidnapping. Jean had been caught and arrested, brought back to London to stand trial alongside him. To Mabel and Derek's frustration, even though they had been found guilty, their elevated connections back in France meant that neither was ordered to serve any time, and they were instead deported back to France. Of course, it hadn't much mattered a year later when it was reported that Pascal and Jean had been killed during an uprising in Marseilles.

Mabel hadn't ever wished for Pascal to meet such an end, but she couldn't deny that she had breathed easier knowing that he and Jean weren't plotting anymore. Juliette had been relieved by the news as well.

Soon after news of Pascal's death reached England, Mabel found that she was with child. Unfortunately, the happiness of that news had been short-lived as Mabel had suffered a miscarriage not a month later. Derek had been incredibly gentle with her in the aftermath, and she was sure he had been just as heartbroken as she had been.

That was why she was being meticulously careful this time, even when it came to who she told. She would not share the news with him of what she suspected until she was further along, hoping she could hide it.

"Uncle Derek!"

Mabel bit her lip to cease from laughing as Derek growled against her abdomen.

"Why did we agree to come here?" he asked, lifting up from his wife.

"Because it's what's done," she said, rolling to her side. "We will have plenty of time to lay about when we return home."

"Hmm," he said, unbelieving, as he followed her out of bed.

Mabel ignored him as she dressed before the fireplace, grateful for the warmth. English winters were freezing, and after traveling for three days and two nights to reach Lincolnshire, Mabel appreciated the heavy velvet gown Juliette had packed for her.

Her maid had stayed back in London, having been invited to George's family for the holidays. They had been engaged for several months and planned to marry in the spring.

After dressing in her gown, Mabel's hair was styled by one of the maids working for the duke and duchess while Derek pulled on his best wool coat. Soon, they were both ready and left their bedchamber arm in arm.

"Uncle Derek!" A little boy, no more than three, came forward. He was being watched by one of the nannies. "I waited for you!"

"So you did, my boy," Derek said, giving the little lad his full attention. He gave the nanny a nod, and she gratefully hurried away. "Now, do your parents know you're causing such a racket?"

The little boy frowned.

"I'm not making a racket," he said before his brow raised.

"What's a racket?"

Derek laughed as he swung the little boy into his arms as another door opened down the hall. Leona appeared, struggling to stifle a yawn as Alfred followed her out of another bedroom.

"Oh dear," she said, coming toward them, her arms outstretched for the little boy. "Marcus Anthony Christopher, you did not wake up your aunt and uncle this early, did you?"

"But it's Christmas!" the boy chirped as Derek handed him off to his mother.

"Sorry about that," Alfred said through another yawn, patting his brother on the shoulder.

"Where are the twins?" Leona asked as they all reached the top of the staircase.

"Lucus and Lucy were hungry," little Marcus said.

"Of course, they were. They're just like their father," Derek said as they descended the stairs. "Silas used to eat like that when we were in Eton."

Mabel grinned as they reached the dining room. A festive breakfast spread with the most glorious table settings practically shined before them. Gold-trimmed plates outlined with boughs of holly lined the white linen table. Gold candelabras, crystal decanters, and at least six-tiered serving trays decorated every inch of the surface as the twins tried to climb onto the table, much to the displeasure of the nannies.

Soon, their company grew as Silas and Clara appeared, followed by Fredrick and Violet, the duke's mother, and the dowager countess. Gavin, Holly, Aunt Marnie, and Holly's siblings had all come, taking seats around the massive table.

In opposition to the rules of proper dining etiquette, married couples sat next to their spouses, and the children moved freely between the adults, crawling beneath the table to play with little toys and candies they had been given the night before.

Conversation flowed easily, and the food served was delectable. Thankfully, Mabel had recently gotten her appetite back and must have appeared somewhat ravenous because halfway through the meal, she noticed Derek staring at her with a satisfied expression. She gingerly placed her roll onto her plate.

"It's just all so good," she said, speaking lowly so only Derek could hear.

He gave a slight shake of his head. "I'm just glad you're eating again."

"Oh," she said, a little surprised. "I didn't think it was noticeable."

"Of course, it was," he said, reaching for her hand beneath the table's edge. "But I guess it's to be expected. Considering..."

"Considering?" she repeated.

Derek only smiled, and Mabel's entire body warmed.

"Oh, so," she tried, her tone a little high. "You know?"

"I had an idea," he said softly, his gaze twinkling. "How do you feel?"

"A little nervous, considering the last time."

"I know." His hand tightened around her fingers slightly. "I would be lying if I said I wasn't nervous myself."

Mabel squeezed his fingers back.

"I think, perhaps, this time, all will be well."

"How do you know that?"

Her shoulder tipped up. "I have a hunch," she said, smirking, easing Derek's worry.

He lifted her hand to his mouth and kissed her knuckles.

"I love you, Mabel."

"I love you too."

Just then, Silas stood to make a toast, but Derek leaned toward her.

"Do you need anything?"

She shook her head. "No. Just you."

THE END

About the Author

Matilda Madison lives in the Pocono mountains of Pennsylvania. A history lover, she finds immense joy in knowing useless facts, exploring the woods around her home, and drinking copious amounts of tea. When she's not writing, she can be found researching obscured periods for her books, refurbishing old furniture, and baking.

Catch up with me anytime on my socials.
Website – www.matildamadison.com
Instagram – matildamadisonbooks
TikTok – @matildamadison